Praise for Bill Broder's works

Bill Broder's *The Sacred Hoop* is a special book in which the moral qualities of the human spirit, linked to a metaphysical presence moving through history and pervading life, are persuasive and affecting. —Robert Stone

The Sacred Hoop is a wise and eloquent book, outlining through story the tragedy and triumph of human evolution.
—Edward Abbey

Bill Broder . . . is a master storyteller, whose graceful prose is so engrossing that readers will find themselves instantly absorbed in what is sure to become a classic.
—Pat Holt, *The San Francisco Examiner and Chronicle*

In *Taking Care of Cleo* . . . Broder combines a storyteller's delight in complicated predicaments with a painter's eye for landscape and body language and a poet's sense of place.
—Donna Seaman, *Chicago Tribune*

[In *A Prayer for the Departed,*] Broder's careful, eloquent meditations upon family life transform this account from a mere history or memoir to a celebration of, and tribute to, family life. . . . A tender, inquisitive book that will appeal to those from old and new worlds. —*Kirkus Indy Review*

Also by Bill Broder

FICTION

The Sacred Hoop:
A Cycle of Earth Tales

Remember This Time
with Gloria Kurian Broder

Taking Care of Cleo

The Thanksgiving Trilogy:
Crimes of Innocence
Esau's Mountain
What Rough Beast?

NONFICTION
A Prayer for the Departed:
Tales of a Family Through the
Decades of the Last Century

TWO RUSSIAN BICYCLES

Wolf Keidan

Two Russian Bicycles

A Fictional Journey into
the Past on Two Novellas

*As it might have been recounted
by the author's great-uncle,
for whom he was named*

BILL BRODER

Bill Broder

THE AINSLEY STREET PROJECT

Copyright © 2014 by Bill Broder

Book design: Yvonne Tsang
Tolstoy's Wife photo: Wikipedia Commons
The Sphinx of Kiev photo: Wikipedia Commons
Photo of the author and Sophie courtesy of Gib Robinson

The Library of Congress has catalogued the
paperback edition as follows: Broder, Bill.
Two Russian Bicycles / Bill Broder
Library of Congress Control Number:
2014907977
ISBN-13: 978-1496123640
ISBN-10: 1496123646

Published by The Ainslie Street Project
First paperback edition 2014

For information regarding
special discounts for bulk purchases,
please contact: billbroder@sbcglobal.net
Manufactured in the United States of America

For my grandmother Dessie,
my great-uncle Wolf, and
their Keidan siblings who grew up
in the Kovno Gubernia of Russia

I was born about ten thousand years ago,
And there's nothing in this world that I don't know,
I saw Peter, Paul, and Moses
Playing ring around the roses,
And I'll whup the guy who says it isn't so.

—AMERICAN FOLK SONG

Fiction is a higher form of truth.

—RABBI BEN ELEAZAR TZVIE

CONTENTS

Foreword

xv

Tolstoy's Wife

1

The Sphinx of Kiev

159

Acknowledgments

297

Bibliography

299

Although the namesake of the author was indeed his maternal grandmother's brother Wolf Keidan, the character with that name in this volume is a fictional creation. The other characters and events in these two novellas are firmly based on historical research, but the scenes and dialogue are fiction.

FOREWORD

*Why do the Jews of Keidani in Lithuania have
humped backs? Because, in their vanity and pride,
they spend their lives sticking their thumbs into their
armpits and bragging about their superior learning.*

—CHAIM GRADE

Keidani, the Lithuanian native town of my grandmother's
family, with its three rabbinical courts, claimed to be
the center of Talmudic learning in all of Eastern Europe.
When the family began to move westward, they felt such
pride in their home town that they took its name as their
last name and carried it with them, along with their belief
in learning. My Grandmother née Keidan was born in the
town of Pren outside the grand city of Kovno. Her parents
ran a small shop in their house, selling fishing nets and
hooks, farming implements, and all sorts of odds and ends.
The house was built directly over the stable. The odor had
its drawbacks, but the heat of the animals helped the large

stove in the central room of the house keep the cold winters of the Polish/Russian plain at bay. Despite the modest family circumstances, Keidani pride remained burning fiercely in their veins; they looked down upon anyone who did not prize learning above all else.

My grandmother's oldest brother, Wolf Keidan, in whose honor I was mistakenly named, was somewhat of a respectable rebel. He worshipped learning, as did his parents, but rather than continue the study of the sacred texts in which he excelled as a youth, he took up secular studies, seduced by the glowing fires of the Jewish Enlightenment movement in the nineteenth century. When his education was blocked by Russian university restrictions on Jews, he departed for the United States and began acquiring his small fortune as a peddler of textiles traveling from town to town. By the force of his will, he brought the entire family to Detroit before the turn of the twentieth century. Once he had done his duty toward his family, however, my Uncle Wolf kept traveling. As he traveled, he began to write his remarkable tales and to perform them wherever he happened to spend the night.

I was mistakenly named after Uncle Wolf, because, unknown to my family, he was alive when I was born and he survived well into the 1950s. If the family had known, I would have received some other name, as Jews never name a child after a living relative. However, some years

before I was born, the family received notice that Uncle
Wolf had died in Shanghai or in Harbin or in Kowloon. He
had gone to the Far East in an attempt to find some cousins who had been marooned there after fleeing the Russian Revolution. His suitcases and a trunk of books were
returned to Detroit through the U.S. consular service.
A memorial service was immediately held, and the family carried on *yahrzeit*, the traditional annual mourning
prayers, observing the date the suitcases and trunk arrived
as the official date of death.

But Uncle Wolf had not died. As I discovered many
years later, he had entered Russia from China in his quest
for our cousins. There, he had been arrested, and ended up
in a Siberian prison camp. Somehow, he escaped the camp,
managed to survive the Second World War, and spent
his last days in Sarajevo, Yugoslavia, still studying and
writing. It was in Sarajevo that I came into possession of a
trunk of manuscripts written by my uncle late in life. He
had lived to be almost a hundred years old and, according
to the young Muslim poet whose father had acted as Uncle
Wolf's amanuensis, had been planning a radical revision of
the Koran as his next major work.

Considering my great-uncle's omnivorous appetite
for knowledge, it was fitting that he ended his days being
cared for by a family as dedicated to learning as he had
been. Uncle Wolf, whose joyous pose with straw hat
and cane introduces this volume, was a rather dramatic

personality. He loved reading his work aloud. He even apportioned out parts to his audience and sometimes the readings turned into dramatic presentations. I think that he was a frustrated playwright whose peripatetic life precluded theatrical productions. He was a confirmed bachelor, although he loved women dearly and received a great deal of love, it seems, in return. Even in his old age, my Muslim friend assured me, the young women of Sarajevo found him irresistible. It appears that he truly savored women's souls and appreciated women for their strength and moral courage—for everything, in fact, that women admire in themselves.

I have chosen two of my uncle's works that share a seriousness in their commitment to history and the moral ambiguities forced upon humans once they leave the cradle. Through his later years, Uncle Wolf kept working over the dilemma he felt at being alive in the twentieth century—a century bedeviled by a brutal destiny. I present these two works together, because they seem curiously related and prophetic of the future course of Russian and world history. After much research, I've determined that Uncle Wolf's writing is historically accurate. I'm sure that he drank tea with Lenin and Krupskaya and visited the Tolstoy family on their estate at Yasnaya Polyana with the purpose of teaching Count Leo Tolstoy how to ride a bicycle.

Wolf Keidan lived a truly representative eclectic

twentieth-century life. I only regret that he did not live to rewrite the Koran. His version might have changed the history of the twenty-first century.

— Bill Broder

(William Keidan Broder,
named after his great-uncle)

Sophia Tolstaya

Tolstoy's Wife

INTRODUCTION

Upon my return to Russia from the New World at the
beginning of the new century, I was sought out, wined,
and dined. I paid for my supper with hard facts, information, and amusing anecdotes of life in a material wilder-
ness unfettered by thousands of years of culture, morality,
or the rusted manacles of feudal and monastic rule.
Europeans considered the United States new, brash, and
barbarous —a frontier experiment in pure capitalism.
I had survived the ordeal, had thrived, and I could speak
of my adventure in a language my hosts understood. They
looked upon me as a worthy representative of commerce
and material progress, an explorer with an exciting tale to
tell. Engineers and industrialists questioned me closely.
Even revolutionaries, like Lenin, who hoped to replace
the old habits by an entirely new order, found my reports
enlightening.

The pattern of my life in the Old World in many ways mimicked my habits in America. I peddled, as it were, but I was not peddling goods. I gathered ideas and cultures, not money. At one of those vast Moscow banquets dedicated to progress, I happened to sit at a table with the president of the Velocipede Lovers of Moscow, who assumed that, because of my years in America, I was an expert in the art of driving myself forward on two thin wheels mounted in a straight line. The more I demurred, the greater was his insistence upon my expertise. As we were both drunk on the excellent and progressive vodka served at the banquet, I finally admitted that I had ridden a velocipede once or twice in the New World and had even discussed the art of cycling with an obscure revolutionary in Geneva who was a dedicated cyclist.

The next morning, when I descended from my hotel room with my luggage, prepared to depart for the province of Tula, I discovered that an elaborately constructed crate had been delivered to my hotel along with a note from the secretary of the Velocipede Lovers of Moscow. She thanked me for agreeing to deliver an honorary velocipede to Leo Nikolayevich Tolstoy at his estate, Yasnaya Polyana, located near my destination. In the note, I discovered also that, in my convivial, drunken state the night before, I had promised to instruct Count Tolstoy on the arcane art of maneuvering the devilish machine.

It was in this bizarre role as a professor of velocipedia,

that I came to know the Count and Countess Tolstoy, their daughter Alexandra, or Sasha as she was known, Tolstoy's strange disciple, Doctor Vladimir Petrovich Kholkov, and another guest, the court pianist, Ablumov.

To most people, Count Tolstoy is known only through his writing, the great novels—*War and Peace* and *Anna Karenina*, and the novella *The Death of Ivan Ilyich* among others—, the short stories, and his teachings on simple Christianity. But, of course, Count Tolstoy was a man also: a husband, a father, the head of a vast household that included not only his wife and children, but relatives, servants, guests, an entire village, hectares of valuable farmland and forest, and a host of disciples. It was the charming, intelligent Countess Tolstaya who ran this household. The countess lived in the brightness of her husband's genius, a task I came to believe as heroic as anything the count accomplished. Gorki, who admired Tolstoy immensely, in his *Reminiscences* spoke eloquently on the dimensions of the heroism that, daily, Countess Tolstaya had to call up within her bosom:

> Personally, I should find it impossible to live in the same house with him [Tolstoy], not to mention in the same room. His surroundings become like a desert where everything is scorched by the sun and the sun itself is smoldering away, threatening a black and eternal light.

I had no idea that my innocent mission, conveying a trivial toy to the count, would carry me into the midst of so intense a family battle. When I was a student in our Lithuanian town, my friends and I all read Tolstoy's *Anna Karenina*, and we knew the magnificent first sentence of that work by heart: "Happy families are all alike; every unhappy family is unhappy in its own way." Indeed, during that summer day I spent at Yasnaya Polyana, I was certain I had stepped into the midst of an extraordinarily happy and gifted family. The boisterous behavior of the family seemed so joyous that I questioned the wisdom of that first sentence: this family was unlike any other "happy family" I had ever experienced. Although I did not remain long at Tolstoy's estate, I was sufficiently intrigued to continue communication with members of the household for years, a correspondence that informed me of the intimate details I am about to recount.

Yasnaya Polyana, Summer

A fortnight's visit of the Countess Tolstaya's sister had left the countess in a rare happy mood. This noon, the countess carried on a mock battle with the master of the house, impertinently questioning his doleful habit of beginning each day by noting in his diary that he might not live another twenty-four hours. At one point, she declared by ukase that she, for one, would never die. She said this with gaiety, her eyes flashing, her skin glowing, her magnificent vitality breathing such life into the room that for a moment everyone at dinner believed her. Death itself seemed to die. The count himself was so invigorated by this improvement in his wife's spirits that he commenced a series of wild pranks designed to defeat his charming opponent—pranks which sent the family and guests into gales of laughter. The venerable white-haired, white-bearded patriarch, the idol of millions throughout the world, galloped around the table in imitation of his favorite filly, nuzzling his wife and demanding to be fed sugarplums from her hand, because he was the reincarnation of Pushkin. At table were the count and countess; their youngest daughter Alexandra, known affectionately by all as Sasha; the distinguished court pianist and composer Ablumov; Doctor Kholkov, one of Tolstoy's principal religious disciples, who lived on the estate; and several guests from the neighborhood.

As the company sipped Cognac and coffee, the countess burst into song. Ablumov sat down to the piano in the adjacent drawing room, accompanying her in a tune by Balakirev, and soon the whole company joined in:

> When I hear thy voice
> Ringing so tenderly,
> Like a bird in a cage,
> My heart leaps joyfully.
> When I meet thine eyes
> Deep and blue as the sky
> My soul pleads to leave my breast
> Flying to meet their gaze.
> Merry and bright I feel,
> And yet I wish to weep.
> Ah, if only I could
> 'Round thee throw my arms.

Countess Tolstaya was so delighted with this festive lunch and her husband's gaiety that she burst into laughter and leaped up from the table. Holding her skirt daintily with one hand, she began to dance an old-fashioned polka in time to the music. She danced out into the drawing room and did some graceful turns about the piano. As she danced, she gazed at the pianist with an approval that she had, until then, withheld, because he had been invited without her permission to visit the estate. The pianist Ablumov's mission, which she resented, was to alleviate her habitual depression and to make her more malleable to her husband's demands. Ablumov responded to the countess's change of heart with some dazzling glissandos, a brief interjection of a Bach-like fugue, a Mozart march, and a Schubert song, registering through his music an appreciation for her grace. She matched her steps to his music and twirled back into the dining room. Ablumov returned to the polka while she continued her dance up and down: one-two forward, one-two back the countess went, circle, circle, stop, and then one-two forward, and so on. Finally, the countess gasped that she could not breathe indoors, and she danced right out the door onto the verandah. Laughing at her mother's excess, the nearsighted Sasha, wearing her thick glasses, followed her out the door, clapping her hands and stamping her feet to the tune. The two made a strange couple. The delicate, plump countess, elegant in very high heels, wore a fashionable black mourning costume—a style she had adopted ever since little Vanichka, the favorite of the family, had died. Sasha, broad-shouldered and sturdy, imitated her father's custom of dressing like his villagers in a simple peasant smock, vest, skirt, and boots. The guests, watching through the open French windows and doors, applauded as they marveled to see mother and daughter, so unlike and often at odds with one another, united joyfully by the relentless rhythms of the music.

While the court musician continued to accompany the luncheon guests, responding to their shouted requests, the graceful countess descended the verandah steps toward Yasnaya Polyana's extensive garden, urged on by her plodding daughter. Below, paths wound their way through pleasant groves of trees, lawns, flowerbeds, and ornamental bushes. At intervals, rustic benches, fashioned from birch limbs, invited a stroller to sit and rest. In the midst of the garden, a pond, shaded with two grand old willows, reflected the showering leaves of the graceful trees and the broad, pale provincial sky. At the foot of the garden, where the estate's great forest began, lay the family cemetery. Among the venerable monuments, four small headstones indicated the graves of the Tolstoy children who had not survived childhood. The most recent stone bore the name *VANICHKA* in large rough letters, carved by the inexperienced hand of the great author himself; a smaller, more professional legend below read *Ivan Lvovich Tolstoy (1888–1895)*.

Countess Sonya danced her way along the main path of the garden and fell onto a bench, spreading her dress as if she were a young girl. Sasha sat down next to her mother and took hold of her hand with both of hers.

"Oh, Maman, everything's so pleasant for a while after one of Auntie's visits."

"Your auntie, she can't stand disagreements. Quarrels make her indignant—they spoil her enjoyment of life."

"She always charms you and Papa out of your morbid moods. For a while, anyway. I wish it would last. I loved it when Papa warned you that you too would die sometime and you shouted, 'Nonsense, never!' right in his face."

"He laughed so hard that tears flowed down his cheeks."

"And Doctor Kholkov was scandalized." Sasha paused, gazing earnestly into her mother's face. "Or do you think the doctor pretended to be scandalized?"

The countess failed to notice the intensity with which her daughter posed this question. "Oh, I wish your auntie would come more often. Only she can make us feel that we can do away with death by proclamation. She's the model of your father's greatest heroine."

"I know, Maman. And you are, too."

Indeed, the countess took great pride in the fact that both she and her sister had been models for Natasha Rostova, heroine of Tolstoy's greatest novel, *War and Peace*. The countess boasted to the most casual visitor that she had copied and recopied and recopied again and edited and proofed every page of her husband's greatest works, late into the night—even when she was pregnant or nursing or rocking feverish infants. She explained at length that her husband had drawn the Rostov family from her own family. How he had questioned her! she declared. How he had pursued every twist of feeling and emotion that she and her sisters had confided in one another! When she spoke about her husband's great novels, her voice took on a breathless, exultant tone, color flooded her cheeks, and visitors felt that, indeed, they were in the presence of a mature, commanding Natasha Rostova Bezukhova, one of the most vivid heroines in all modern literature. Countess Sonya Tolstaya was not shy about her contribution to her husband's works. In recent years, she had personally taken over the job as his publisher.

In the garden, while the pianist continued to entertain the count and his other guests, the countess lifted her daughter's hands to her lips and said, "Your father was up to his old pranks. I thought I'd split my sides when he galloped around the table. Poor Doctor Kholkov was beside himself."

At the thought of her husband's pranks, Countess Sonya could not contain herself; her entire body shook with silent laughter. Embarrassed, she covered her mouth with her hand. "Oh, oh, it hurts." She had recently undergone a serious operation—a large benign tumor had been removed from her lower intestine—and now her insides had begun to ache.

Her daughter, large, awkward, and young, hovered

over her, shaking her head affectionately, "Maman, you shouldn't exert yourself so much. Vladya said you must rest."

"Who?"

"The doctor. Vladimir Petrovich."

The countess's laughter ceased, leaving a sly smile on her lips. Her eyes narrowed. "Vladya, eh?"

Sasha blushed. "It's none of your business."

"You're my daughter, aren't you?"

Sasha drew back and muttered. "That's not something you notice very often."

The countess shivered. At one moment, everything was warm and happy, and suddenly, without notice, a chill wind seemed to cut through the landscape and land on her shoulders. The countess later identified this moment as crucial in the downward spiral that seized the family that summer and fall. In actuality, the weather had not changed a bit; the leaves hung motionless and the still water of the pond reflected them, along with the expansive, light blue sky of Tula Province, and the brilliant sun. Unfortunately, the countess did not immediately understand the full import of her daughter's inadvertent reference to the doctor as "Vladya"—but then, neither did Sasha, nor, it turned out, Doctor Kholkov. All were soon to be caught up in a confusing web of romantic folly, shrewd manipulation, and mistaken idolatry.

Idly, the countess looked down at her graceful little shoes next to the large, clumsy boots of her daughter. She tried to speak in a soothing voice, but the contrast of the shoes and the boots irritated her. The words came out rather sharply, "Stop feeling sorry for yourself, Sasha."

Sasha, too, looked down at her mother's feet and her own. "That's all right. I've made my own life. There are people who appreciate me." She wiggled her feet, knowing the boots disturbed her mother.

"Vladya, for example?" Sonya forced a laugh. She could never find the right note with this, her most difficult child. "Pretty familiar with old Sobersides, aren't you?"

Sasha turned and looked directly at her mother. She too wanted desperately for this conversation to proceed naturally, affectionately. The countess understood this. It was becoming obvious to her that the subject was important to her daughter. "At the clinic, he's not so formal. In fact, he's a different man altogether."

Suddenly, from the house, a burst of music and song reached them.

> Quickly, oh, quickly
> Kiss me!
> I'm burning with passion,
> Kiss me!

The two women looked toward the verandah and saw Doctor Kholkov, dressed immaculately in an English tweed cap, a Norfolk jacket, and knickerbockers, step out

of the house. He stopped, shook his head mournfully, took
a notebook from his pocket, and began to write.

Sonya called out, "Doctor Kholkov! Come join us!"

Sasha, her face reddening once again, murmured,
"Maman!"

Sonya, her eyes bright, her own cheeks showing a
touch of red, as if she were feverish, waved imperiously
toward the doctor. "Vladimir Petrovich! We're lonely out
here."

"Oh, Maman, how could you?" Sasha wrapped her
arms around her breasts and pulled her feet back under
the bench, folding herself up into a tight knot as if she
were a turtle hiding in its shell.

Doctor Kholkov tucked the notebook in his jacket and
made his way carefully down the steps. He was a tall, slim
man in his early thirties who held himself in a military
manner. Before he took up medicine, he had been an officer in the tsar's Horse Guards. Today, as usual, he affected
the dress of an English gentleman. At the bench, he bowed
to the ladies and addressed the countess. He had a handsome face, thought the countess, perhaps too handsome,
with fine features that tended to compose themselves in
what seemed like a series of self-conscious masks.

"An excellent lunch, Sonya Andreyevna."

Sonya grinned. "A bit too boisterous for your taste,
I'd guess."

"Laughter helps the digestion, I'm told." He allowed
his displeasure to display itself through the nasal tone and

drawl of his comment. He turned to Sasha and, in a more gentle voice, said, "Let me say, Alexandra Lvovna, I have never seen you look so beautiful, the perfect picture of natural simplicity."

Sasha groaned. "Oh, stuff and nonsense!" Her face fiery, she leaped up and strode down the path.

The countess called after her. "Sasha! That's no way to acknowledge a compliment."

Kholkov raised a hand as if to quiet his hostess. "Please, Sonya Andreyevna, you'll just embarrass her more."

The countess shrugged. "Twenty years old, and she has the manners of a muzhik."

"She's doing excellent work at the clinic."

"Look at the way she dresses for guests. And her language! Doctor Kholkov, if you could only encourage her to act more like a lady . . ."

Kholkov shook his head mildly. "What could be more desirable than honesty?"

Suddenly, a strange-sounding bell sounded somewhere behind the house. Doctor Kholkov and the countess turned. The voice of Count Tolstoy boomed out: "Clear the way! Clear the way!"

What a sight! The greatest writer in Russia, the venerable master of Yasnaya Polyana, the Christian conscience of the world, in the peasant garb of a smock, breeches, and large boots, wobbled into the garden, perched high on a large-wheeled velocipede.

"Clear the way!" shouted the count, his gray-white beard flying over his shoulder.

Doctor Kholkov leaped off the path moments before being run down by the count, who waved gaily as he careened past his wife. The countess nodded in acknowledgment and waved gracefully, a small gesture accompanied by a demure smile, as if a suitor had ridden by on horseback and tipped his hat.

Sasha, alerted by the bell and the shouts, ran back from the forest where she had taken refuge. "Papa, Papa, let me try. Let me. Let me." She followed him as he negotiated his way around the maze of paths on the bicycle.

"No, no, Sashenka," he shouted breathlessly, "it's too dangerous."

Dr. Kholkov sputtered, "What on earth—" he gasped. "Who—what—I've never —It's not dignified." His face had turned ashen.

"It's simply a velocipede," said the countess, contentedly. "That Jew brought it down last week and gave him a lesson, and now he thinks he's an expert. What a show-off!" Her eyes fastened now upon the graveyard and the four small stones of her lost children. She clasped her hand to her breast and sighed. "Oh Vanichka, how you would have loved to see your father cavorting . . ." Her voice faded as that bright, ghostly child, her constant companion, rose up in her imagination. She closed her eyes so that no other shape could blot out that memory.

Doctor Kholkov, standing well off the path, bent over the countess. "Now, now, Sonya Andreyevna, you mustn't let yourself brood. Leo Nikolayevich bends his will to the Lord's will, while you—"

The countess opened her eyes and frowned at the courtier. "My husband's Lord and mine are quite different." She rose. "Your arm, Vladimir Petrovich."

Dr. Kholkov offered his arm and the two made their way through the garden, careful to avoid the count on his two-wheeled vehicle. Sasha continued to follow her father like a child, demanding her turn. At the cemetery, the countess let go of the doctor's arm and stood before the small grave marked *VANICHKA*.

At the top of the garden, the count failed to negotiate a sharp turn and fell to the lawn, laughing. Sasha caught up with him. She grabbed hold of the velocipede, pleading. "Please, Papa, please, please."

The count rose and clasped his daughter fondly. "What would the Velocipede Lovers of Moscow say if we ruined their gift on the very first week?" He picked up the machine, inspected it, and then jumped on once more and went pedaling away.

"You tricked me, Papa! You tricked me!" Sasha ran after him.

Tolstoy looked back as if to argue with his daughter and in a moment went down once more. He remained on his back, arms and legs spread, laughing boisterously. Sasha ran up to him and stood looking down at him, laughing too, chiding him. "I wouldn't fall as much as you, Papa! I can ride any horse in the stable."

"True. You're a damned fine rider. But this is a machine—and besides, it's your papa's toy—"

"That's not fair, Papa. Please, Papa, please. You should share."

"Your mother'd never forgive me if you had an accident."

Sasha pointed across the garden at her mother. "Maman wouldn't notice—she's too busy with Vanichka's grave."

"Don't be unkind, Sasha."

"Its the truth: she doesn't notice me."

The count rose and talked gravely to his daughter. "She just doesn't understand you, Sashenka. Your mother's been ill and, until your auntie came, morose. You should go to her—"

"I will, I will, but first I want to see you ride again."

"We all should help her," said the count. "Come, Sasha, let's go to her. Give her a hug and a kiss. We don't want her to fall into one of her mourning moods again, now that your aunt and the court pianist have cheered her up, do we?"

Sasha, intent upon her quest, ignored the question. Instead, she challenged him. "I'll bet you can't do five rounds without falling."

Tolstoy stared at his daughter. "You think I can't master this paltry toy?"

"You already fell twice."

"It's a bet, Sashenka. If you win, I'll let you sit up on the seat."

Sasha stared into her father's eyes, her hands on her hips. She stamped her boot. "No, no, if I win I get to ride it." She put out her hand.

The count clasped his daughter's hand. "Done! Five rounds!" He picked up the velocipede and began to mount it once more. "Now, I mount the demonic machine . . ." Sasha put out her hands to help, but her father waved her off. "No, no, I must do it all alone—no help, no help."

He took a running start down the path and vaulted once more onto the seat. He wobbled his way down and around one turn, gaining confidence as he rode. Sasha clapped. After the third turn, she called out, "Wonderful, Papa, excellent. I hope I lose, I hope I lose."

The count threw a kiss to his daughter as he passed. "What a good-hearted child!"

"You'll go on forever now."

"I think I'm getting the hang of it."

"Tomorrow, it'll be all the way to Tula."

"And then Moscow! Onward, Hussars!" He waved his arm as if he were clasping a broad sword. "Onward to Moscow!"

At that moment, Doctor Kholkov took his leave of the countess and began up the path toward the house. Count Tolstoy took a sharp turn and came up behind the doctor, snatching his cap off his head as he passed him.

"My cap!" shouted Doctor Kholkov indignantly.

The countess turned, aroused from her reverie. She stood, nodded a goodbye to the grave of her beloved son, and walked slowly up the path, watching her husband's antics with amusement.

Tolstoy rode ahead, waving the cap. "The spoils of war! The enemy's flag!" The count, riding one-handed, wobbled along, at every moment about to fall. In spite of his precarious position, he continued to wave the cap.

"My cap!" shouted the doctor, running after Tolstoy.

"Down with the English, the French, the Swedish! Down with the Turks!"

Sasha ran along behind, shouting, "Only one more, Papa, and you've won."

Tolstoy slowed, dangling the cap just beyond Kholkov's grasp.

Kholkov reached in vain. "My cap!"

"Onward, Russians!"

Sasha darted across the lawn and tried to block the doctor, who was threatening to overturn the velocipede. Adroitly, the doctor dodged around her. "Out of my way, damn it!" This latest indignity infuriated him. "My cap!"

Laughing and waving the cap, Tolstoy attempted to make a one-handed turn. The back wheel brushed Kholkov's side, and Tolstoy fell in a heap.

Sasha ran up, her face white with anger. She stood, confronting the doctor and stamping her boots. "Just look what you've done, Vladimir Petrovich! You're clumsy, clumsy!"

Kholkov, his face white, his lips curled, his nostrils distended, turned, his hand raised to strike her. She stiffened, prepared to receive the blow. The countess, who had come up to them, crouched to launch herself in defense of her daughter. But the doctor's arm froze in the air. In an instant, his furious face composed itself into an expression of humble apology. He bowed, bent down, took up his cap, and began to brush it off, murmuring, "Such foolishness!"

The countess, alarmed now by her husband's awkward posture on the ground, approached. "Lev, are you all right? Have you broken something?"

The count waved her off and rose. Laughing good-naturedly, he clapped the doctor on the back. "Sorry, old man."

The doctor bent over his hat, concerned with a grass stain on the fabric. His face was stern. "Hijinks! Frivolity!"

"Now, now," began the count, but a mosquito, buzzing in the air over the doctor's bent head, distracted him. He followed its movements like a hunter, his hands out, poised to capture it.

"What a child!" the countess later wrote her sister. "This man who hunted bear and deer and had fought the enemies of Russia on horseback, stood ready that day, with the same intense concentration, to destroy the enemy insect."

The mosquito circled the doctor's head and then landed upon the bald crown.

"Death to the invaders!" exclaimed the count, squashing the mosquito firmly, smearing blood across the doctor's head.

Kholkov straightened, a look of horror on his face. The countess burst into hysterical laughter, igniting the laughter of Sasha. The count immediately raised both of his hands in apology. "Sorry, old man. Here, I'll clean it up." He whipped out a large red work kerchief, grasped the back of the doctor's neck, bent his head down forcibly, and attempted to wipe off the blood and the remains of the mosquito. Surprised, the doctor yielded for a moment, but when the count then took the kerchief in both hands and began to polish the crown of the doctor's head as if it were a shoe, the doctor recoiled, pushing the count away.

The countess sank laughing onto a nearby bench. Sasha pointed at the doctor and then the count and joined her mother's merriment.

Kholkov straightened and glowered at Sasha, his body rigid with solemn, angry pride.

Feeling guilty, Sasha took the offensive, appealing to her father. "Look what he's done, Papa, made you lose your bet—all because of his stupid English cap."

The count shook his head and waved his finger at his daughter. "Enough, enough. It was my fault, Sashenka."

Kholkov spoke crisply, his tone belying his words, "No harm done." He pulled out his notebook and began to

write, murmuring at the same time, "Dear Leo Nikolayevich, how can I describe such carrying on?"

"What carrying on?" called out the countess from the
bench.

Kholkov ignored her, continuing to write. "Such
pranks!" He looked up and stared solemnly at the count.
"And you force me to go along with you."

Tolstoy shrugged. "Come now, Vladimir Petrovich,
youre smarting from my small joke."

"A little, I suppose. I'm embarrassed by such events—
but not for myself."

Sasha spoke up. "You're not his custodian, Vladimir
Petrovich." The countess could see that her daughter was
confused by the doctor's reaction. "And you don't have to
note everything that occurs. You should just join in. We're
all in a gay mood today."

The doctor, his face doleful now, appealed to Sasha.
"But I do join in—even when I become the—target."

The count nodded and placed a hand on his daughter's
shoulder. "Vladimir Petrovich is a conscientious man,
Sashenka."

"Too conscientious," said Sasha.

The countess clapped. "Bravo, Sasha." She could not
bear to see her daughter confounded by the doctor's many
masks.

Tolstoy gazed reprovingly at his wife. "Consider what
this man has given up—the court, the tsar's favor, the
Horse Guards—to follow my teachings."

Kholkov put out a hand toward Sasha, "Don't you understand, Alexandra Lvovna, when the world reads that Leo Nikolayevich rides about like a—and humiliates his—"

Tolstoy put out his arms as if to embrace his disciple, "I apologize, *mille fois*, for making you the butt of a joke."

The countess snorted, "It's only his pride that suffered."

Kholkov clasped his hands humbly. "Perhaps I am too sensitive, Leo Nikolayevich, but I couldn't help feeling there was a touch of un-Christian malice in your prank."

Tolstoy hung his head. "I was wrong."

"No, no," said Kholkov, "perhaps I am too diligent."

All trace of joy had disappeared from the count's face. "I'm guilty on all counts. Childish."

Sasha stamped her boots on the ground and waved her finger at the doctor. "Look! Look what you've done to Papa—see how he hangs his head."

"Sasha is right, perfectly right." The countess rose. "Let's put an end to this farce!"

Tolstoy spoke sharply now, his lips set, his eyes hardened. "Enough bickering!" The countess went to her husband, taking his arm and caressing his cheek as if to calm him. Tolstoy shrugged her off impatiently. "Enough nonsense! Do you hear?" He addressed her as if the entire event had been her fault.

"So cold?" said the countess, embarrassed at this public rebuke. She attempted to get hold of her emotions and to answer with dignity, but she had no defense against her husband's unjust attack. She looked to her daughter and then to Doctor Kholkov, as if they would spring to her aid, but both greeted her appeal with frowns. Stifling tears, she stumbled back toward the cemetery, moaning, "Oh my Vanichka, see how he treats me. He blames me whenever life became the least bit difficult for him. In his diary, he calls me his jailer, his torturer, his executioner. Oh, Vanichka!"

Tolstoy, shamefaced, pushed Sasha along the path. "Go to your mother, Sashenka. I shouldn't have spoken so harshly to her."

Sasha balked. "I can't stand it. She's forever talking to Vanichka."

"Go! Vladimir Petrovich and I have things to discuss." Sasha looked at her father, at Kholkov, and then at the bike. Reluctantly, she moved toward her mother, her face glum. The count called after her, "With a hug and a kiss, like I said. I haven't forgotten the bet. Later, you can try the velocipede."

Sasha turned. "I didn't win."

Kholkov continued to write in his notebook. "It's without dignity."

Tolstoy, feeling he had been too short with his daughter. too, shouted, "Later, Sasha, I promise."

"Doctor Kholkov interfered," she replied without turning. "I didn't win."

Once everyone was out of earshot, Kholkov continued his complaint. "This gamboling about on a velocipede will not do!" he said, pointing disdainfully at the offending vehicle.

Tolstoy did not answer immediately. He kept his eyes upon his daughter until he was certain she had obeyed his command to comfort her mother. Sasha embraced her mother ostentatiously and kissed her on each cheek. The countess, deep in a dialogue with her dead son, received her daughter's embrace absentmindedly, smoothing Sasha's hair and straightening her clothes without looking at her. The two sat on the bench before the grave of Vanichka.

Now, Tolstoy turned to his disciple, took his arm, and began to walk him along the path. In his diary, the count later detailed this interview precisely. Tolstoy's account, however, revealed that the doctor was not the only one intent upon manipulating the inhabitants of the household. It was obvious from his account that Tolstoy himself was shrewdly playing upon the emotions of his family and of his disciple for his own ends. The count understood, better than anyone, the complex emotions and motives of Doctor Kholkov and of the countess.

"I apologize, Vladimir Petrovich," said the count, humbly. "My dignity is my affair, but I shouldn't play fast and loose with yours."

Kholkov spoke with great reserve, as if it cost him dearly to speak at all. "Your dignity is of great concern to others."

"What's wrong about enjoying myself, simply, like a

boy?" Tolstoy stood over the velocipede and regarded it with affection.

Kholkov sniffed, "A horse has dignity."

"Look at this wonderful human invention!" Tolstoy proudly lifted up the velocipede and held it toward his companion.

Kholkov refused to look at it. Instead, he gazed out over the pond. "A man on a horse has dignity."

Tolstoy twirled the pedals. "Levers! With so little power, to create such great force."

"Leo Nikolayevich Tolstoy upon a contraption—"

"Every man's entitled to a share of natural lightheartedness—even you."

"Such activities are not consistent with Christian ideals."

Tolstoy regarded him with affectionate disbelief. "What a funny thing to say. Riding a velocipede, 'not consistent'—oh come now, my friend, you can't say such a thing without laughing."

"It's more than a question of the velocipede—it's the contradiction between—"

"Now you'll succeed in making me gloomy, dear friend."

"When I compare your spiritual message with—"

Tolstoy placed a hand upon the doctor's arm to forestall his words. "I can't bear your reproaches. You and I are amazingly as one, Vladimir Petrovich—separated by so many years, and yet in our youths we passed through the very same cauldron of lust and violence. How we rioted, brother! How we served the sword and the cock!"

Kholkov looked deeply into Tolstoy's eyes. "I left all that behind. You showed me the true path. That's why I dare to offer my—suggestions."

At Kholkov's reproof, Tolstoy sighed and turned away. "At moments like this, I sense that you feel hardly any love for me—for me, the human being who loves you."

"Certainly I've proved my love for you, Leo Nikolay-evich. I turned my back on the tsar's own Horse Guards—a promising career."

Tolstoy, his voice low, breaking slightly as he spoke, "Respect, perhaps, but not simple love, ordinary human feeling."

Kholkov squared his shoulders and thrust his long chin forward as if he were being inspected. "To be honest, I find it hard to love—individuals."

Tolstoy bent over the velocipede to hide his unhappiness.

Kholkov continued in a clipped voice. "I'm not a warm person—my worst failing, maybe—"

"Love is at the heart of —" began Tolstoy.

"Love, of course," responded Kholkov. "But love of God—love of humanity—not some—ordinary love."

Tolstoy continued speaking to the velocipede, afraid that he would become too emotional were he to look at his disciple. "I was speaking of a simple feeling between two ordinary men."

It was difficult to believe that the doctor would reject this appeal. But he did. "To be honest," he replied, "the life here at Yasnaya Polyana, the ordinary life, like today, is not conducive—"

Tolstoy looked up. "I am trying to extricate myself. I am. I need your help, Vladimir Petrovich."

"Your wife—"

Tolstoy stared across the garden at his wife and daughter sitting on the bench before the little grave. "I tell you, Vladimir Petrovich, her love for Vanichka elevated her, softened and purified her."

"Ah, she has relented, then?"

Tolstoy sighed. "In time, perhaps, in time."

"She'll give up this frivolous life? She'll join you in sharing your wealth with the world?"

"I had hoped she would come to that—I still hope—"

"Tolstoy will live as Tolstoy preaches?"

"I can't press her quite yet—for some reason, after all these years she has begun to mourn Vanichka once again."

"A remarkable youth. Still, fifteen years have passed since his death."

"He understood everything—intuitively—a mere boy. He should have carried on God's work for me."

"A terrible tragedy."

"Tragedy? No. A great spiritual event." The count threw back his head and gazed into the sky. "Vanichka's death was God's gift to me—revealing the lie of life. It brought me closer to God."

"And your wife—"

"The pain of her grief obscures all spiritual values— but not her gentle feminine instinct."

Kholkov coughed and began to pace back and forth on the path. "Leo Nikolayevich, certain correspondence has left this house." He had tried to speak of this matter at lunch, but the subject had been sidetracked by the countess's declaration of immortality.

Tolstoy pulled out his great kerchief and dabbed his eyes. "Yes, he was a delightful, a wonderful boy."

"—a significant article submitted without having been logged—"

"Death has no compunction."

"It is your duty to God and your followers that our efforts be coordinated." Kholkov could hardly contain his frustration at the count's unwillingness to address the question of correspondence. The problem was one of control.

"Vanichka was too good to remain among us."

Kholkov sniffed and threw up his hands. "Any hint of private gain, for yourself or your family, must be eradicated. You must make a will concerning your works— all your works. The early copyrights—"

This was a matter Kholkov had broached many times before. Instead of replying, Tolstoy knelt on the grass. "But what does it mean to say he is dead?"

Kholkov stood over him, his voice raised now. "The chaos of this situation cannot—" Suddenly, Tolstoy leaped up, seized the handlebars of the velocipede, took a running start. and mounted. The doctor slid behind the bench to protect himself.

The shrewd count had seized upon this distraction to escape a confrontation with his disciple, but as he continued, he found himself plunged into renewed grief for his dead son. He pedaled in precise circles around the bench, chanting slowly, obsessively, "There is no death! There is no death! There is no death!"

Sasha, seeing her father successfully mastering the vehicle, pulled her mother up and away from the grave, hurrying her toward the count. As they approached, Kholkov bowed and withdrew down the path in the direction of his cottage.

"Four, five, six, seven," shouted Sasha, counting her father's turns, "all the way to Tula!"

Tolstoy continued to chant, "There is no death! There is no death!"

"What are you saying, Papa?"

The countess raised her hands beseechingly toward her husband, "Lyovchka! Be careful!"

Now, the count began to circle his wife, his chant turning from one of desperation to one of triumph. "There is no death! There is no death!"

The countess called out to her daughter, "Quick dear, run back to the house and get your father's pills—on my dressing table—and the Cognac. Quick, quick! He's getting overexcited. He'll have one of his fits."

Sasha dashed toward the house.

"Do you hear, my Sonyusha? There is no death!"
Tolstoy pulled to a stop in front of his wife, dismounted
gracefully, and knelt before her.

The countess regarded him affectionately. "Hurrah for
my brave warrior!"

"For my lady, I defy even death."

The countess laid her hand on each of her husband's
shoulders and then on his forehead. "I dub thee my Knight
of Imagination, of Family, of Love."

"Since your recovery, my dear Sonyusha, you've
become so gentle and understanding."

"My brave cavalier!"

"How easy it'd be for you to turn to God, especially
because you love me. How easy!" The wily count had
heard his disciple's plea and was intent upon using all his
genuine grief, his vulnerability, and his duplicitous charm
to win over his wife.

"Yes, I have always loved you." The countess shook
her head.

She knew very well what her husband's God would
demand of her, but she was tired of arguing. She wanted
simply to love and to be loved by this tortured, joyous soul
who had knelt so humbly before her.

That afternoon marked the ending of an unusual
period of peace and happiness in the family. These respites
from family tension occurred infrequently, but when they
came, they reminded the countess of the beauty and con-

tentment life could contain. She talked and wrote a great deal about beauty. "Our family happiness," she later wrote to her sister, "is like the eye of a great storm—a false, but joyous calm. When we finally reach these oases, I employ all the necromancy in my power to immobilize the storm, to create an enchanted, timeless island of Yasnaya Polyana, a perfect noble household, filled with the finest moral and sensitive intentions." She went on to describe how, lying in her bed, she would dream of a gallery of such calm and manageable still-lifes in the midst of which she could placidly exist. But she well knew that Yasnaya Polyana seethed with plots and counterplots. Cabals arose and dissolved away; motives warred with motives; and the paint of those placid domestic still-lifes ran, dissolving everything—love and candor and beauty—in a fearsome cauldron.

When her sister wrote back to protest, she had replied, "All this is not simply in my head, and you know it." She had gone on to repeat the complaint her sister had heard countless times without the variation of a single word.

My husband chronicles the violent storms of this household daily in his diaries. You know very well that the great Tolstoy has kept a meticulous record of the horrors of his life since before our marriage. My first duty during our engagement was to catch up on his disgraceful exploits and worse thoughts as a bachelor. He deflowered my imagination before he deflowered my body. And since our marriage, every day I have been privileged, sentenced rather, to read his loathsome, complex, instantaneous confessional. My husband, the resident genius of this estate, thinks it necessary to share with me his every thought, resentment, anger, love, suspicion, fear, and lustful fancy.

That night, the countess was so pleased with her husband's repentant attitude that she agreed to trim his hair and beard. This operation took place in the countess's sitting-room, strategically placed between the count's study and the Remington Room, where the typewriter sat along with all the count's manuscripts, letters, and files. The countess, who had managed her husband's affairs and acted as his principal secretary since early in their marriage, presided in this wing of the house, a guardian of the great author's sacred precincts and of all the estate matters.

By accident, the court musician chose that same empty hour to practice the piano. Again and again, he worked over the brilliant, wild passages of that irritable genius Beethoven, lured on by the sense that with just a few more repetitions, he could achieve a more complete understanding of these complex compositions.

As the music echoed through the house, the count sat upon a straight chair in the middle of the sitting room while the countess moved around him, lovingly snipping away, shaping the beard and the hair as if she were an artist. It was almost like old times, she thought, the courtier and his mistress—all smiles and soft words.

With a hand mirror, the count followed the operation with intense concentration and pleasure. His happy mood of the early afternoon of pranks and his usual horseback ride through the estate had conquered his annoyance at the contretemps with Kholkov.

"Brambles!" exclaimed the countess, holding up a knotted piece of hair she had just cut off.

"Silk."

"The hedge is easier to trim."

"D'ye hear?" asked the count, a broad smile on his face as the sound of the piano penetrated the sitting room where his wife was cutting his hair.

"Practicing already." Such sounds echoing through her house filled the countess with contentment. She clipped away at the white hairs of her husband.

"Cheers the place up, doesn't it?"

"I know you invited the pianist to distract and amuse me. I'm grateful."

"What I'd really wish is for—" the count began, reaching around his wife's waist.

Like a wizard gazing into her dusky ball, she knew exactly where the cunning count was headed. "What you'd really wish is for me to rejoice in Vanichka's death as you do?"

Tolstoy released his wife. "God called him, not I. If you

believed truly, you wouldn't suffer so. Death has taken so many of ours—and it will soon have us."

For a moment, the countess managed to restrain herself, but she was no match for the furious grief that possessed her at the thought of that small grave in the garden. "Praised be to heaven for the emptiness . . ." Her shrill voice resounded through the room. She snapped the shears wildly in the air close to Tolstoy's face and then close to his heart and to her heart. ". . . here, and here, and here."

Tolstoy, remaining very still, murmured, "We shouldn't talk about this while you're—"

She snapped the shears over his head. "For once, I have you at my mercy."

"For once?"

"Poor chap! A slave in your own house, eh? Come now."

Tolstoy sighed. "And the music doesn't please you?"

"I'm not made of stone. He plays with great elegance and feeling."

"Darling Sonyusha," the count pleaded seductively, "if you could open your heart to God's wonder."

"I don't understand Tolstoy's God, who condemns the world into which I was born."

"You distort my teachings."

"It's all there in the diaries—your contempt for me and this life we lead."

"The diaries are private—for our eyes only."

"Private or not, those pages will be read long after we're gone. What a terrible wife Tolstoy had! That's what the world will say."

"I'll lock them up from now on."

"Now, perhaps. But later? A frivolous, ill-tempered shrew, they'll call me, who denied the great genius salvation because of her luxurious ways."

"I . . . I . . . I must write in my diary—it's my life's blood."

"Don't move, or I'll cut off your ugly ear."

Tolstoy groaned. "But how can we live this way when there's such suffering in the world?"

"Now, stand up so that I can measure the new blouse. Even your poor peasants sew new clothes."

Obediently, Tolstoy stood while the countess draped on the panels of a blouse, pinning it so that she could sew it later. As he stood there, patiently, his arms out, he spoke of the suffering in the world. "I walk to Baburino and whom do I meet—eighty-year-old Akim, still plowing, and Yaremich's old woman, who owns only one caftan and no winter coat, and then Marya whose husband died of the cold, whose child is dying of hunger, and who has nobody to cart away the rye."

"You think I don't pity those poor creatures?"

"Pity is one thing, responsibility another."

"And their drunkenness, their diseases, their gambling and whoring are our fault too? You leave the management to me and expect me to reward them?"

"On the way back, I stumble over the crouched bodies

of Trofim and Khalyavka, a husband and wife who are dying of hunger along with their children."

"The husband wastes their substance on drink and the wife plays the strumpet."

"And you want masked balls and a discussion of 'higher things.'" Tolstoy clasped his hands together until the knuckles turned white.

"Out, out, keep your arms out—like this—"

Once more, the count stretched out his arms while his wife pinned the material for the sleeves.

"Sonyusha, I pray every night that the Lord release me from this frivolous life."

"Behold, the crucified count!" Deliberately, she jabbed a pin into Tolstoy's arm.

"Ouch, damn it." The count flinched as the pin penetrated his skin, but he did not lower his arms. "You're worse than the Romans."

"Gently, gently." The countess had crooned in the count's ear. "One more seam."

"Am I allowed to smoke?"

"If you behave and stop whining about your soul." Expertly, she rolled a cigarette and placed it in his mouth. From time to time, she removed it and tapped the ashes into an ashtray. "And what do you offer in return for our child's death?"

"The gospels—"

"Your version of God without the Church has infinitely less substance for me than your novels—"

"Blasphemy."

"Your books, which were based upon everything I know and love."

"I'm done with art."

"You're not a saint, never will be, no matter how you try. You don't know how to stifle the joy in your heart. Look at you this afternoon, *méchant!* A child! A delightful, bad, small boy."

"I can no longer tear myself away from the living in order to describe imaginary people."

"The characters of your novels are not imaginary— they endow our lives with reality." The countess looked up at the bookshelf, her eyes caressing the handsome bound volumes of her husband's work. "You're a first-rate artist, Lyovchka, a second-rate prophet. Speak in fiction and stop all these boring sermons."

"For God's sake, Sonyusha, help me give up everything."

"Renunciation is an act of arrogance, dear Lyovchka, not humility."

"The copyright, please."

"I've lost Vanichka. I can only clasp onto the dear remains of my life—your works—like a drowning woman."

"Give my best works to the people. Just my best works—you can keep all the rest. Then we all will live simply, like Christians."

"They are my works too, Lyovchka."

"I admit I could never have written them without your superhuman help, Sonyusha. Every night, you copied—"

"Copied? Those novels came out of my flesh itself, out of the life of my family—Papa and Maman, sister, our joyous house, the games and pleasures and balls. You clasped us to your heart, you transformed us with your imagination and your sensibility, and now you ask me to give up those glorious creations?"

"We can be happy again, dearest Sonyusha, if you would only join me in God's work."

"If I give away our fortune, will the suffering of the world cease? With nine living children, do you expect me to follow you out to the monasteries, to beg at the crossroads, to take in washing?"

"Simply try to worship with me—the rest will come."

Now the countess's thoughts veered back to the subject of the diaries. "Why do you write so badly of me in the diaries? Every morning when I read them, your complaints burn deep within my soul."

"Don't take what I say in the heat of the moment as the final word."

"For that, I have to wait, eh?"

"Sonyusha, I've never felt such a need to love you—"

"A need is not love."

"—and such a hatred of everything that separates us—this frivolous life we lead."

Sonya sank down in an armchair. She seemed to have

lost all her strength. "But do you never feel—good—about me? I have—have done so much."

Tolstoy stood before her, like a boy before his mother —a boy with a full white beard and white halo of hair. "You were the very wife I needed—"

Sonya waved his words away. *"Need again."*

"An ideal—"

"Ah." She looked up at him with hope.

"Ideal in the heathen sense of loyalty, devotion to family life, self-sacrifice, family affection."

"A heathen! How dare you, with your smelly feet, your garlic breath, your toothless mug—call me, daughter to the tsar's physician, a heathen?"

"Deep within," the count continued, crooning, "you have the possibilities of being the wife I need now—a Christian friend."

"And when have I ceased being your friend?"

"Sonyusha—" Tolstoy rolled his eyes toward the ceiling.

Sonya clasped her hands. "Oh Lyovchka, sometimes I am so afraid for us."

The slow movement of a Beethoven sonata echoed through the house, swelling with feeling. Tolstoy put his finger over his lips. "Listen, listen." He walked to the window. He gazed out and tears cascaded down his cheeks. To cool his emotions, he leaned his forehead against the pane.

Sonya rose and approached him. She dried his cheek with her handkerchief.

"Here is the Tolstoy I know."

"Beethoven. Such a great soul!" He turned and with his rough hands began gently to caress her. She gave herself to him, her hands clasping the back of his neck. However, as he became more purposive, digging beneath her clothing with his rough hands, she gently restrained him.

"Please, Lyovchka. My illness, my grief."

"Please, Sonyusha. Please, please. It's so long between—"

"Tonight, perhaps."

"Now, in the warmth of our love for one another?"

She yielded. "For that love, then."

They moved in time with the music toward the study. Overcome with excitement, the count tried to wrestle his wife down on the chaise longue. "Quick, quick. Here. Now."

"My God, the guests! In the study, at least."

"Here."

Sonya ducked under his arms and escaped into the study. Tolstoy pursued her. They fell upon the leather couch, clasping one another. Sonya found herself amazed at the passion that coursed through her body at her husband's touch. All through her youth, even through her child-bearing days, her body and her husband's had terrified her: the moment he bared himself, she felt a cold chill sweep up her legs. Now, in middle age, her body felt like a cauldron, her skin sensitive. Waves of heat coursed through her veins and arteries. When her husband entered her, she screamed in pleasure, even though she knew the house was full of family and guests. Her scream thrilled the count into great effort—he was like a youth again. From a distance, the powerful beauty of Beethoven's imagination caressed their minds, surrounding their love-making with a halo.

But then, then, too soon for the countess, the passion was over. As strong as the count was in his old age, he was overcome with excitement and the climax came very quickly. Almost immediately, he began to pull away.

"Lyovchka," she pleaded. "Stay a moment. Hold me now. Talk to me."

"No, no." He leaped off the couch, pulling up his breeches. "What filth I am!"

The countess flinched as if she had been struck. "I want your affection, Lyovchka," she panted.

Tolstoy stared down at her disheveled form, her naked-ness still uncovered. "A sound, healthy woman is a wild beast," he snarled and ran out into the sitting room.

The countess pulled her clothes together and slipped off the couch. When she got to the door of the sitting room, she saw her husband before the mirror, staring at himself. Leaning against the door jamb, her hands out in supplication, she pleaded with him. "Why can't you come to me as a friend, Lyovchka."

He did not turn. "The standards you live by have driven me nearly to suicide."

"I didn't drag you into the study."

"I renounced my property, renounced my ambition—
and you grasped—"

"You renounce with one hand and you grasp with the
other—fame, comfort, vanity, power, even my body."

Now, he turned, his face distorted in furious anger. "A
struggle to the death is going on between us. Either God's
works or not God's works." He charged out the door onto
the verandah.

Sonya spoke aloud to the empty room. "He is mad and
so am I." In a daze, she moved to the mirror on the wall
and began brushing her hair. From the drawing room
came the sound of the slow movement of one of Mendels-
sohn's "Songs Without Words." She ceased brushing her
hair and listened. Like a sleepwalker, she walked through
the house to the drawing room and stood at the entrance
listening to the music. Expressions of satiety and frustration flitted over the surface of her face. Suddenly, she
started and stared, her eyes dilated. There before her, on
the lap of the musician, sat her dear dead son.

"Vanichka!" she moaned. "My little lost boy! Why
are you sitting there on the pianist's lap, beckoning,
beckoning to me, with one hand cupped to your ear? Such
heavenly music! How joyous you two look, bathed by the
lamplight!"

She glided to the piano bench and sank down at the
musician's side. The apparition of her son disappeared.
She sighed.

"A friend, Ablumov, that's all I wish for," she put out

her hands in supplication toward his hands on the piano keys, "an affectionate friend with whom I can talk about— lofty subjects."

The pianist raised his hands from the keyboard, but she gently pressed them down. As he played on, she saw her husband peering in through the windows from the verandah, an odd look in his moonlit face. Was it jealousy, she wondered, satisfaction, prurience, or the pure curiosity of a storyteller, plunged into the midst of a new tale: *The Countess and the Court Musician?*

Full of malice, the countess took hold of the hands of the pianist and clasped them in hers, drawing them toward her bosom. "We shall be friends."

The pianist stared at the countess, paralyzed. The countess, glancing for a moment at the window to make certain her husband still watched, pressed the musician's hands to her lips. The count disappeared from the window. The countess rose, smiled charmingly, and in a tone of cordial authority commanded her guest: "Come to me tomorrow afternoon. We shall have tea and talk—as friends."

The next morning, the countess had recovered from her passionate encounter with her husband the night before. Once more, she was the purposive director of a vast household and estate. Before church, feeling quite calm and reasonable, she wrote to her sister about the dilemma she now faced:

> You know I've been battling Doctor Kholkov's influence over my husband for some time. It's a question of the copyright to the great novels. I will battle him to the end, of course. But now, I fear the doctor may be interested in poor Sasha. I just wonder whether you noticed anything between them on your visit. Sasha refers to him as "Vladya" when she speaks about her work at the clinic. He flirts with her, and now and then she becomes inordinately angry at him—a true mark of affection in my experience. I wouldn't want to do anything to injure Sasha's chances—at marriage. I'm just afraid the doctor might simply be using her. Doctor Kholkov's a strange creature. I wish I could decide what to do. It wouldn't be a bad match, y'know. His mother is very close to the Tsarina. And poor Sasha has had few suitors. And then, there is the possibility that such an alliance might relax the doctor a bit on all matters, even the copyright question.

The countess paused for a moment and then laughed to herself, before finishing off the letter. "There's no predicting how our noble peasant Lyovchka would react.

Joy? I don't think so. Indignation would be more likely. He'd be furious that his beloved disciple could be lured away—even by his own daughter." She smiled maliciously as she thought what a blow such a match might be to her husband's vanity. "In either case, it might not be a terrible development." She signed and sealed the letter and set it with the other letters for the post.

That afternoon, Sasha, wearing a velvet dress with a sash and ribbons, stood before the mirror in her mother's sitting room. She was not at all happy with her image. Behind her, in the middle of the room stood the dressmaker's dummy, draped with the count's half-sewn peasant blouse, a knitted cap on its head. Doctor Kholkov stepped into the sitting room from the verandah and stopped. Sasha, who caught sight of him in the mirror, wheeled around, looking for a place to hide.

Kholkov bowed. "You look charming. A perfect young lady."

Sasha blushed. "My stupid church dress. We went this morning and Maman insists that I wear it all day. Papa says that people shouldn't dress up to worship."

"There's nothing immoral about dressing well." The doctor straightened his jacket as if to indicate his immaculate taste.

"I hate this dress, hate it, hate it."

Kholkov advanced slowly until he stood directly before her. "And how are your excellent horses?"

Sasha blinked, surprised by the question. "My horses?"

Kholkov nodded solemnly. "Dushka and Blackie . . . and that magnificent bay."

"Strider. They're healthy enough." The young woman regarded the doctor suspiciously. She didn't trust him when he came to the house; he had so many faces and moods here—unlike at the clinic.

Kholkov turned aside and pretended to examine a framed cameo on the wall. He spoke casually, "The other day I noticed Strider limping on his left foreleg."

"A small matter—a stone lodged in his hoof." To her surprise, his observation made her happy. "You have sharp eyes, Vladimir Petrovich."

"It's no great matter. After all, I was in the tsar's own Horse Guards."

"I keep forgetting that—it's hard to believe."

"I've always had a weakness for horses—since my childhood."

"I pried it out. The bruise is healing."

"A veterinarian, I see, as well as a superb rider. I'm impressed."

Sasha whirled around and strode to the window, looking toward the stables. "Ahh, if I were a man—that is what I would most like to be—a member of the Horse Guards, or the cavalry."

"But instead you are a beautiful young woman."

"You speak such stuff and nonsense, Vladimir Petrovich. I feel like a hypocrite when I appear before Papa all dressed up like this, going against his teachings—"

"Don't be so harsh on yourself. Come closer, Alexandra Lvovna, there's something I'd like to confide."

Sasha blushed. "To me?"

Kholkov lowered his voice and murmured. "You were kind enough to speak frankly to me, and so I thought—"

Sasha grinned broadly. "Oh yes, I'd like that." Frankness, that's what she craved, rather than all these court affectations the doctor put on when they met outside the clinic.

Kholkov stared directly into the young woman's eyes. "Alexandra Lvovna, I admire you more than I have any other woman."

Sasha fell back a step. "Please, Vladimir Petrovich, you know I—"

"Your work down at the clinic has been excellent. Your energy and intelligence—"

Sasha turned away and spoke out the window. "Am I performing my duties well?"

"I've made no secret of my feelings. I can't understand why you haven't married yet—a beautiful, energetic, well organized—"

Sasha clasped her hands before her and writhed in agony. "Please, Vladimir Petrovich, I—I can't stand to hear such things."

Kholkov placed a hand on Sasha's upper arm as if to comfort her. "I don't wish to make you suffer. But I have to tell you how I feel. You see—"

Sasha gently drew away from the doctor's touch. "Another time, perhaps. Mother will be here in a moment."

"After clinic tomorrow?"

Sasha sighed in despair. "Yes, if it must be."

"It must be. I can't go on without knowing—you see we share so much. Our feeling for horses, for the poor, for your father."

Sasha turned, her eyes shining. "Yes, yes—working with you—working for Papa—"

"Your father is a very important man, not just to us, but to the whole world. You understand?"

Sasha stepped toward the doctor. This talk about her father gave her courage. "Oh, I know."

"Unfortunately, some who are closest to him are not completely sympathetic—"

Sasha nodded violently. "My sister Masha says that Maman tortures him."

Kholkov gestured gracefully in the air as if he were amazed and exasperated. "I am sorry to say that our common effort hasn't had a great deal of support here in his household, where it counts."

Sasha's enthusiasm waned. "Are you talking about those letters again?"

"I shouldn't have brought that up at lunch today again—but without an orderly process, your father's teaching will be weakened."

"Papa is very particular."

Kholkov sought a new tack. "I've noticed that you perform certain tasks for your father."

Sasha smiled in satisfaction. "It's true. I've learned to prepare his manuscript paper and now and then take dictation and even type correspondence."

"I think that he will come to depend upon you more and more as time goes on."

Sasha gazed with interest at the doctor. "Do you really think so? He gets so furious when things aren't done just right."

Kholkov smacked his fist into his palm. "I predict that before long the success of his entire grand enterprise will come to rest upon your young shoulders."

Sasha regarded the doctor with surprise. "My shoulders? You're making fun of me, Vladimir Petrovich."

"I am completely sincere. Your father needs your help."

Sasha stumbled, unsteady. "Such an idea makes me dizzy."

Doctor Kholkov rose and assisted her to a seat on the couch. He sat and leaned toward her, his hand still on her arm. "My dear Alexandra Lvovna, I need you." Sasha turned away and gazed toward the window. Kholkov took her hand up gently. "I'm sorry for burdening you—"

A paralysis gripped Sasha's limbs. Her hand and her arm where the doctor's hands pressed her burned. She didn't know whether she wanted to draw away from him or to throw herself into his arms. "Oh, my. Oh, my." Her voice quavered. "I wish I were in the stables. Everything's clearer out there."

Kholkov pressed her arm and her hand. "Leaving childhood is very difficult."

Sasha felt dizzy. "I don't understand."

"I want you for my ally—more than an ally."

"More than an ally?" Her voice wavered.

"Why not? I'm not so old, am I, or unattractive?"

"Oh no, Vladimir Petrovich, Vladya, that is, I— I— I don't know what—"

The countess glided into the sitting room through the French doors. Sasha pulled away from the doctor and stood.

"Well, well," said the countess, contemplating the pair. "What are you two up to?"

Sasha cried out. "Why do we have to be up to any-thing?"

Tolstoy marched into the room from the verandah, whistling. He held a bouquet of flowers in his hand which he presented to his wife with a bow. "Forget-me-nots, wild morning glories, violets, lilies of the valley scarcely open. Smell them, and just look at the colors!"

The countess clasped the flowers to her breast. "Thank you, dear Lyovchka." She was amused and delighted. His "Christian" disgust for their lovemaking had passed, and as usual, he strutted around quite contented and proud of his manliness. "I'll put them in a bowl." She kissed her husband's brow and danced back through the French doors.

Tolstoy turned to his disciple. "A beautiful day, Vladimir Petrovich. A prance in the forest and now to work. Come, my dear fellow, we'll knock off a chapter before dark." He marched into the study. Doctor Kholkov began to follow, but then turned and spoke in a whisper to Sasha. "After clinic tomorrow?"

Sasha could barely force her reply. "Yes."

The countess returned with the flowers arranged in a bowl. She placed the bowl upon her desk and stood back, her hands on her hips, admiring them.

Sasha approached her mother. "Papa's certainly very happy today. I thought he'd mope around now that Auntie's left us."

The countess turned, smiling smugly. "You're almost old enough for me to tell you the secret of your father's joy and his gloom, too—but not quite. Men, ahh, men."

Sasha began to pace back and forth in the sitting room. She shook her head as she attempted to sort out her recent interview with the doctor.

The countess regarded her daughter's vigorous figure with some suspicion. "Why are you hiking about the room like that, dear?"

Sasha snorted. "Sometimes, I feel that Vladimir Petrovich is inhabited by two entirely different souls. At one moment it's sermons, pedantry, lectures— and then he's all kindness, consideration, and, and— whatever."

From the other room came the sound of the pianist

practicing; he had begun work on Beethoven's "Apassionata," a favorite of the countess. Sonya tilted her head, immediately distracted. Instead of pursuing her daughter's comment, she performed a coquettish, gliding circle around the dummy, caressing it. She rearranged the hat and repinned the cloth in an intimate way. The Tolstoys' impetuous coupling the evening before had invigorated her, too. "The moods of men are like the weather—don't ever depend upon them."

"And your moods?"

"Today, I feel such a mixture of joy and sadness, hope for the future, and foreboding."

Sasha became alarmed. "Now, Maman—"

Sonya put her fingers to her ear. "Listen! That music. As if we were nearer to heaven."

Sasha sighed. "What a passion you have for music."

"In my remaining years, if I can be allowed your father's affection, how grateful I'll be to God."

"Approach life more calmly, Maman, and try to please Papa. It will be like old times."

Sonya launched into a vigorous waltz about the room, a joyous, dreamy look on her face. She stumbled and almost fell. Righting herself, she stood, breathing heavily and clutching her side. Sasha rushed to her and helped her into the chaise longue. "You should be more careful. The doctor—"

Sonya lay back. "How loving you are today! As if you had begun to understand my nature, my longings—"

Sasha stood up straight. "Now, Mother, none of that nonsense."

Sonya put her hands behind her head and gazed up at the ceiling. "For all his faults, that Doctor Kholkov is not a bad-looking fellow. Quite idealistic, too." After her letter to her sister that morning, she had decided to bring this matter of her daughter and the doctor out into the open.

Sasha put her fingers to her ears. "Please, Maman, I asked you not to—"

"Well, he keeps mooning around here—and when I came in earlier, you and he—"

"When he's away from Papa, Vlad . . . Doctor Kholkov's a different man."

"That may be, but yesterday and today at lunch—such storm clouds. How he raved about some article and correspondence that left the house without his knowledge!"

"He knew he was in the wrong."

"I can't imagine that man ever laughing."

"Well, he does laugh. He can be very gentle, too."

"Oh ho, gentle? I know he can be very polite."

Sasha shook her head and began to pace once more. "I don't know. When he's here, with all of you, it's as if he puts on masks."

Sonya stretched and sighed. "Too bad we can't remake the personalities of those we love."

Sasha stopped in front of her mother, anger rising suddenly. "Love? Who's talking of love?"

Sonya shut her eyes. "Just before our marriage—ugh—your father confessed his—he made me read the exploits—ugh—of his youth, all written out in his diary. What a libertine he was, your father!"

Sonya once more stuffed her ears with her fingers. "Maman, I don't want to hear such tales."

"There were times early in our marriage—I was younger than you are now—when I wished I could—kill your father." Suddenly, the countess leaped up, seized a pair of scissors off her desk, and plunged them into the dummy's breast. She stood back and contemplated the upright figure with the scissors protruding. "Ahh, to be free," she exclaimed, "of all that cold meanness, and preaching, and cant, and the constant fear of death!"

Sasha stared in horror at the dummy and then at her mother.

Slowly, the countess stepped forward and withdrew the scissors from the dresser's dummy. "And then to re-create him into the same man, only pure and unmarked by folly." With a needle and thread, she proceeded to mend the tear in the fabric of the dummy, rearranging the half-finished clothing as if to make everything all right again. She gazed with adoration at the dummy that now represented Count Leo Nikolayevich Tolstoy, the great novelist, the gentle, sensitive husband and lover, the wit and genius of his age.

Sasha cried out. "Maman! You're always so . . . excessive."

The countess turned to her daughter. "I'm terrified,

dear Sasha, that this renewed affection of your father's won't last very long."

"Only because you refuse to submit to his wishes."

"I do my duty toward my husband, and there's some satisfaction in that, even a little pleasure, I'll admit . . ." The sounds of the piano resounded plaintively through the house, the themes twining about one another, rising from crescendo to crescendo. The countess turned to the dummy and began again to arrange the material of the blouse. "But I'm often very sad, and then I have other desires, platonic—and sometimes such a loathing for the physical act of love—he does, too—"

Sasha gently seized her mother by the shoulders and shook her, as if to bring her back to reality. Confused, the countess gazed at her daughter, hardly recognizing her. "Since your illness, Maman, your mind wanders so."

"Nonsense. I've just become more introspective. What were we talking about?"

"Husbands—a subject that bores me. Besides, look what love did to Masha and Tanya. One dead child after another!"

"Until little Tanya came along, like a miracle."

Sasha shuddered. "How they suffered! Dreading for months that the child would be lost, then terrified that they themselves would die in childbirth. And all fruitless!"

"Don't despise your sisters for their needs. We women are slaves to our bodies and to our duties—we all want children, and a husband as well." The countess could not forget the moment her husband had entered her the night before—like a glorious, fiery eclipse of all except their shuddering union.

Sasha sighed. "Every time I think of pregnancy, I feel sharp pains all through my body."

"Hasn't little Tanyusha given us great joy!"

"She's a darling."

Now, the countess seized her daughter by the shoulders and shook her. "And you don't want a child of your own?"

"I didn't say that."

The countess threw her hands up in the air and turned away, a small grin on her mouth. "I'm sorry that you despise Doctor Kholkov and dislike your work at the clinic."

"Why put words in my mouth? I do enjoy working with him—and when we are alone together, he's modest and gentle and never arrogant."

Sonya clasped her hands. "Now you're speaking from your heart."

Sasha fell back into an armchair, her legs splayed out before her. "Oh, what's the use of it all? According to Father, marriage is the most agonizing and complicated suffering of all."

Sonya hissed. "How can you listen to such a man?"

"I'll make up my own mind."

A surge of hope sent Countess Sonya to her knees in front of her daughter. "Then Kholkov's asked you?"

Sasha shrunk away from her mother. "Not exactly. Mother, I won't be—"

Doctor Kholkov came out of the study with a pile of correspondence in his hand. "Sonya Andreyevna, let me apologize for my outburst at lunch."

The countess rose and straightened her dress with dignity. "You are an enigma, Vladimir Petrovich. An hour ago, you were utterly rude, and now you are the mirror of courtliness. Even Sasha remarked upon your moods."

Sasha leaped up and went to the window. "Don't bring me into this."

Kholkov bowed. "There is so much to do, my dear countess, and so much—chaos—I get carried away."

"If you weren't so zealous, Doctor Kholkov—"

Sasha turned, her hands behind her back. "You make Papa feel so bad, Vladimir Petrovich."

Kholkov turned, his voice softening. "Don't be cross with me, Alexandra Lvovna. Someone has to keep track. Although I was ill-mannered to have brought it up at lunch, nonetheless, significant letters have been leaving this house without having been properly logged, copied, catalogued—" He seemed unable to contain these thoughts, even as he apologized for them.

The countess finished his sentence for him: "—and censored!"

"— and an article—an important article sent off who knows where without my being informed—"

Sasha pursed her lips. "Father can write whomever and whatever he pleases. As for articles—"

"You twist my meaning, Alexandra Lvovna. No one censors your father's writing—"

The countess interjected, "It was I, Vladimir Petrovich, who accused you of censoring."

The doctor, ignoring the countess, continued to appeal to Sasha. "We are simply keeping track for posterity."

"I don't care. It's not right of you to shame Father."

The doctor approached the young woman. He spoke in a low tone. "Calm down, dear girl. Don't let this household infect you."

The countess, who heard this remark, laughed. "She's infected by a plague of independence!"

"Mother! Stop interfering!" Sasha pushed her mother over to the chaise longue and turned to renew her attack upon the doctor. "I speak for myself, Vladimir Petrovich."

The countess clapped. "Bravo!"

Doctor Kholkov suddenly screwed up his face in a comic grimace. He bowed to the dummy and addressed it in exaggerated tones. "Do you hear, Leo Nikolayevich? My years of toil reviled, spit at, held as worthless by the very family who should bless my labors and thank me for my love of their patriarch! Oh my, what is a true believer to do?"

Sasha stamped her foot. "Stop that stupid comedy!"

Kholkov grinned at her and waved his finger playfully. "Only if you apologize for your unjust accusations."

The countess called out from the chaise longue. "Children, children, don't carry on so. It was I who sent out my husband's articles, Vladimir Petrovich, without informing you. And the letters, too."

Kholkov turned, his back stiff once more. "Then you're the culprit."

"Maman! How could you?"

The countess was unfazed. "I was Tolstoy's secretary long before either of you learned how to talk. My husband needs no permission to communicate with the world."

Kholkov's lips pressed together until they were white. He could barely speak. "He and I have an agreement."

"At his convenience only, Vladimir Petrovich. You are his servant, and you should remember that."

Sasha looked back and forth between the two. "She's right, you know, Vladimir Petrovich. Father is the master in this house. There's no reason why we have to ask your permission."

Kholkov took a deep breath and then assumed the pose of a court dandy. He drew the words out into an affected drawl as he spoke. "Sabotage! After all the sacrifices I've made for your father's sake."

"Go tell your tale to Father if you like."

Kholkov reached out toward the young woman's face, grazing the skin with his fingertips. "Your impertinence, dear Alexandra Lvovna, brings a charming color to your cheeks!"

Sasha slapped his hand away. "Tell Father that I refuse to see him shamed for feeling joyful."

Not to be outdone by her daughter, the countess rose. "Nor will I allow him to be abashed for sending his own writing where he pleases."

Kholkov saluted. "Indeed, Leo Nikolayevich will be my judge." He skipped to the door, where he turned and blew a kiss at Sasha and went into the study.

The countess embraced her daughter. "You're growing up, Sasha."

Sasha threw off her mother's arms and paced about the room. "Damn, damn, damn. I lost my temper like a child."

"It was my fault, dear," said the countess. "I shouldn't have taunted him. Especially now that you've told me—"

"He was making fun of me."

"He was flirting. His mother attends upon the empress herself—there's that to consider." The countess took her daughter's arm and paraded up and down the room with her. "Tell me, dear: are you in love?"

For a moment, Sasha yielded. She leaned on her mother and shook her head gently back and forth. "'It's hard to know how I really feel."

"He's of very good blood."

"I thought you and he were enemies, Maman."

The countess laughed. "Wars end, you know, and enemies become allies in new wars."

"Then you think you could—get along with him?"

"If your happiness is at stake—I could do anything."

"Oh, Mother, sometimes you can be so generous."

"I'll talk to your father about the matter."

Sasha stopped and clasped her hands. "No, no, please, Mother. Papa would feel that I betrayed him."

"Then you must talk to him."

"I will. At the proper time. After all, nothing's really happened yet."

"If you don't, I'll have it out with him. It's a parent's duty."

When Sasha took her leave, the countess, quite contented, kissed her on the brow. A marriage to such a man, she thought, would mature her daughter. No matter how much the doctor revered the count, he would not stand for Sasha's odd manner of dressing and talking. With joy, she contemplated her daughter's development into a true lady. And, considering Sasha's sturdy physique, there would be children, many children. The countess's greatest pleasure, though, was to imagine her husband's reaction when she told him that his beloved disciple wished to marry their daughter. She murmured to herself: "That will send the old codger reeling!"

The next evening, the light hung suspended in the sky as if the gods were reluctant to allow the sun and its warmth to depart. Frogs croaked from the pond and stream, cattle lowed as they prepared to bed down in the fresh warm grass, insects droned, and from the village in the glen, laughter and singing and the sweet chords of an accordion echoed up through the great forest.

Sasha and Doctor Kholkov, side by side, came up from the hospital in the village where they had worked all afternoon. They laughed together at the quaint reticence of the villagers, who found medical treatment of any kind strange and threatening. The two walked close to one another, but they were careful not to touch. At last, Sasha allowed herself to bring up a personal matter that had been bothering her since the day before.

"It was childish of me to lose my temper at you yesterday, Vladimir Petrovich."

"I don't blame you in the least, Alexandra Lvovna. I acted like a boor at lunch and later like a fool, scolding your father. I get immersed in your father's work—"

"When you're with Papa, everything's so—so serious."

"I don't mean to spoil his fun, but the entire world watches him. As for your mother . . ."

The doctor, seeing the young woman flinch, did not finish his sentence. Instead, he gently grasped her arm and seated her, politely, on one of the rustic benches, just above the pond. He sat down next to her, his thigh touching hers.

Sasha trembled to be in such intimate contact with this man, whom she feared and whom she hoped was about to ask for her hand in marriage. The water of the pond reflected the bright sky and the dark trees. The croak of the frogs sounded particularly deep here, like a chorus of bass fiddles. She waited. When he did not speak, she forced herself to break the silence. "I wish you and Maman would get along better."

"You yourself accused her of tormenting him."

"My sister said that." Sasha would have liked to hit herself in the head for distracting the doctor with this talk about her mother. "I feel so guilty when I talk about Mother. It's just that I always get so angry when she—and I have no one to talk to."

"You can talk to me."

"It's really a family affair."

"The dissemination of your father's thought is my life's work."

"You and Maman fight over him like jackals over a piece of raw meat." Sasha wanted to howl at the turn the conversation had taken.

Kholkov leaned forward suddenly and rested his elbows on his knees and his head in his hands. "Ahh, me, I suppose you're right to blame me. I don't act well toward your mother these days."

Sasha regarded him sympathetically. "On the other hand, she's beginning to look upon you with—favor."

Kholkov remained motionless, speaking through his fingers. "Because of my family, no doubt. There's a maddening conventionality to her outlook that drives me crazy. She has no understanding or sympathy for your father's spiritual genius. When she starts carrying on about music, art, culture—"

"All the same—"

"Please forgive me, Alexandra Lvovna." The doctor seized the young woman's hand and leaned toward her. "I am arrogant—that's the way I'm made. But I will try. And whatever you say, I am essential to your father's well-being. If I ever left him—"

"I don't dispute father's affection for you." Sasha gently feigned an attempt to remove her hand from Kholkov's. He grasped the other hand and squeezed them both. The girl's heart beat so fast that she feared he could hear it.

"I need your help, dear Sasha."

His use of her familiar name left her breathless. "I'll do anything in the world for . . . for Father."

"What a beautiful young lady you've grown to be!"

"Nonsense. I'm not at all pretty."

"Not pretty at all!" Kholkov leaped up and pulled Sasha to her feet. He let go of one hand and led her around him as if they were dancing a gavotte. Sasha joined in the game, playfully. She reached out and took the doctor's other hand. Hands clasped, they began to twirl, first in one direction, then in the other. The tempo of their dance increased. They laughed, twirling vigorously. Sasha hurled herself around in abandon, never missing a step. The doctor could hardly keep from falling.

When they finally stopped, he was breathless, but she was ready for another round. "More? More?" she laughed.

"Oh no, I'm too old," he said, a little embarrassed at his weakness.

Sasha thrust her face in his. "So, I'm not pretty at all, is that it?"

Kholkov threw his hands up in mock terror. "Not pretty at all! You're beautiful! A rare combination of soul and laughter."

Sasha dropped down on the bench. "Next, you'll say that I'm kind—that's what they say about plain girls."

"Kind? I suppose you are—the peasants certainly think so—you're very gentle with them at the clinic. But more than kind—you're a vital, attractive young woman. How the young men must court you!"

Sasha, feeling she might explode with joy, exclaimed, "Dolts."

The doctor sat down, his knees touching hers. "How many proposals?"

"A few—dolts and fools and wastrels. They court the daughter of a count—not me."

"It seems like just yesterday you were a child, and now—"

"You've been patient with me at the clinic. I'm not used to the blood and filth, the sores—"

"After all your time in the stables?"

"My horses are healthy creatures."

"I dare say. And well fed."

"At the clinic, I was terribly frightened at first."

"We all are—it would take a monster to get used to the

suffering of our people. Oh, what the lack of nourishment does to their bodies! And the way they treat each other in their misery! They beat their wives, their children, each other."

"I'm still terrified of the syphilis—"

"It's most important to disinfect yourself when—"

Sasha waved impatiently. "Yes, yes, I always do."

"Let's not talk about such things on a summer's evening like this, with the frogs croaking away as if they could burst—"

"—the crickets tuning up and the nightingales singing their hearts out—"

"—to us. Just smell the jasmine. Ahhh. Hear the accordion and the laughter down in the village?"

"From this distance, the village seems like a happy refuge. Even the cows sound content."

"*Mooooooo.* You know, the peasants are not sorry for themselves—they don't complain."

"To be accustomed to such lives—it makes me angry!"

"Alexandra Lvovna—"

"Yes."

"—I want to continue yesterday's conversation."

"I'm not sure—" Terror and joy warred within the young woman's breast.

"You promised."

"Not . . . not . . . exactly." *Please, please go on* she entreated silently.

"As I said, I admire you more than I have any other

woman. I've made no secret of my feelings. Your energy and intelligence—"

"Virtues wasted on women, according to Papa."

"Why haven't you married?"

"Maman wants me to marry every prince who sticks his nose in the door— whatever his beliefs. And Papa— who knows what he wants? He doesn't think I'm . . ." Sasha fell silent, kicked the sand of the path, and damned herself for her absurd awkwardness. Why on earth should she be talking about her father's criticism now? To this man?

"Your father doesn't think what?"

"Nothing. Nothing. Why haven't *you* married?"

Sasha's question startled the doctor. Somehow, he had strayed from his original purpose. And yet, perhaps he hadn't. From his earliest childhood, he had lived by careful calculation. But this Tolstoy household threw all reasoning into chaos. "Pardon me, dear girl, what did you say?"

"Why haven't you married?"

"Ahh, well. What with your father, and the clinic—and my beliefs, which few women would . . ."

The doctor's confusion emboldened Sasha. "Vladimir Petrovich, I've never heard you so tongue-tied."

Panicked at the young woman's coquettish, almost demanding tone, the doctor, who was an excellent duelist, felt he had lost the advantage of his age and experience. His blood up, he knew he must act boldly. He stood and bowed. "May I have this next dance, Alexandra Lvovna?"

"With pleasure, sir."

This time, the two engaged in a more sedate waltz, their arms entwined intimately with one another. After a few rounds, they slowed, and then stopped, still holding on to one another. Slowly, they dropped their arms, embarrassed. Soberly, they sat once again upon the garden bench.

Kholkov, lost now in his turbulent emotions, found himself pursuing his adversary in a contest, the issue of which remained hazy in his mind. As in a duel, though, or a battle, it was of prime importance to remain on the attack. "And you've never been in love?"

"Such a silly topic, Vladimir Petrovich." Sasha's voice wavered. "Let's just remain quiet for a moment and breathe in the evening. Look how the light lingers on the water."

"You call me Vladya down at the clinic."

"It's different down there—as if we're all workers together."

"But we're alone here, Sasha—no one will hear."

"Vladya, then. Oh Vladya, what am I to do? The smell of the hay, the heavy evening air, the crickets."

"And you—vital, attractive, surrounded by courtiers—"

"I didn't say that. Several proposals—that's all. Few and far between. Even Papa says I'm not pretty." Sasha could not believe she had revealed this.

"You keep using that terrible word. Children are

pretty, little animals, sometimes. You, Sasha, are devilishly attractive, honest, strong."

She felt as if her father were gazing down upon her, appalled at her desire to believe the doctor. Her father was correct, though. Such praise was absurd and high-flown. She was a perfectly plain and awkward child with little to recommend her except an ability to handle horses. To think otherwise would be to expose herself to terrible mockery. Her heartbeat slowed, her voice flattened out. "To be perfectly honest, so far young men have resisted the attraction."

"That's been your choice, not theirs." The doctor, sensing a withdrawal that would take his opponent out of range, impulsively grasped one of Sasha's hands. He leaned forward, one leg bent at the knee, the other out, almost as if he were kneeling before her, but not quite. "I want to propose—"

Sasha pulled violently away, tearing her hand free and almost overturning Kholkov. "Doctor Kholkov!"

"Then I've offended you?"

"I ask you, please think what you are saying." She had no idea what she herself was saying. Her head was in a whirl. She thought she might faint to the ground or leap up into the sky. Never before had she been in such a state.

Kholkov drew himself up. "Is it so bad that I—after all, I too am from an old family."

Sasha stood up, trembling. Kholkov stood.

"It isn't your family." Poor Sasha had no idea how to respond correctly. The words tumbled out, helter-skelter. "I just don't think that it's—appropriate that we should be—"

"Not appropriate? Oh, I see. Hmmmn." The doctor sat down, leaving poor Sasha standing, uncertain about what to do.

She wanted him to continue, but had no idea of how to encourage him. She sat on the bench next to him. *"Appropriate,"* she stuttered, "isn't the right word. I'm not very good with words."

"You've made yourself understood." Kholkov leaped up and began to stride away down the path. Suddenly, he stopped and spoke to himself, his words not audible to Sasha, who remained, devastated, upon the bench. "A refusal," he muttered, "inappropriate!" He was not even certain what he had intended to propose. It was enough that his intention had been balked. His pride, the vital center of his belief in his superiority, had been wounded. The épée of his adversary had reached its mark, and he would surely leave the field of battle in defeat unless he parried immediately. He wheeled around in a military fashion and returned. He sat down upon the bench in an attitude of courtly attention, half-turned toward Sasha, one leg bent, the other out as if he were wearing a sword.

"Thank God, you've come back. I didn't mean—"

Sasha smiled encouragingly, hoping for him to continue his courtship.

"I see nothing wrong with proposing—that you join me in protecting your father's legacy to the poor starved souls of the world."

Sasha, taken aback by this ending to Kholkov's proposal, slumped down on the bench. She muttered, "My sole aim in life is to be of use to Father."

"Your father must be protected at all costs. You will be my eyes and ears here in this house. I must know everything, all the obstacles that stand in the way of your father's generous nature. Report, especially, on what happens between your mother and your father."

Sasha was stunned at this request. "Spy on them? On my own parents?"

"No, nothing like that. It's simply that you and I, together, must try to protect your father from anything or anyone who does not share his beliefs."

"Together." Sasha's voice was small.

"You'll keep your eyes open, and then we'll meet—"

"I'm not sure I—"

"And tell no one I've spoken to you like this."

"Maman would be furious."

"Not even your father."

"Not even Papa."

"Allies then?"

"What exactly—?"

"Your father is depending upon you."

"I wouldn't fail Papa, you know that."

Kholkov, still angry and hurt at what he took to be the young woman's rejection, took up her limp hands, roughly pressing them between his.

"Together, then, let us swear to help your father accomplish his goals."

Sasha tried to remove her hands, but Kholkov held on, pulling her close to him. She stared into his eyes, which were fixed angrily upon hers. She could barely make them out in the fading light.

"Please, Vladimir Petrovich—it makes me uncomfortable—like a blasphemy or something."

"Sasha, let us swear together. I—"

"I—"

"—swear!"

"—swear!"

"Once more!"

Together, they repeated the words. "I swear!"

That evening Sasha did not appear for supper. She remained in her room, pacing back and forth, talking to herself and pulling at her hair as if she would tear it out. She looked like a wraith—pale and distraught, her hair flying in all directions. Again and again, she went over the disastrous encounter with Kholkov in the garden. She could not believe it possible that the handsome doctor— her father's faithful disciple, a former officer in the tsar's own Horse Guards, a man over thirty who had grown up in the court and whose mother was an intimate of the tsarina—could possibly consider proposing to her. And yet . . . and yet . . . he had bent his knee and almost made her an offer. If she hadn't been so damnable awkward and unsure of herself. She wrung her hands and moaned, "Oh I don't know what to do. I don't know who to ask. If he thinks that I . . ."

And then she remembered the oath he had made her swear. She clutched her throat and collapsed on the bed. She went over the conversation again. "He thought I rejected him. But I hadn't. I was just terrified, scared, frightened. What a proud man! And then he made me . . . swear to spy on my own parents."

Oh, if one of her sisters were here, she thought—but they would just laugh at her. They detested the doctor for his grip on their father. She couldn't possibly ask her father—he was much too involved in important matters to care about a silly romance. And her mother—sometimes she suspected that her mother was mad, even though she knew she cared for her, or thought she knew it. Oh, how she wished her parents did not fight so much. As for Vladya, he was always so furious at her mother's interference in her father's affairs.

Sasha clasped her hands and tried to get control of herself. Why wasn't it possible for two adults to have a difference of opinion about proper procedures without erupting? And Vladya kept claiming that her mother was intent upon undermining all of her father's beliefs, when it was just a matter of jealousy and love and a difference of opinion. One thing she knew for sure. Her father and the doctor and even the tsar himself could never convince her mother to let go of her father's great books. And so the battle of Yasnaya Polyana would continue, with Vladya intent upon getting her father to make a will leaving everything to the people.

Sasha sat up in the bed, startled by the sudden suspicion that the doctor's interest in her had more to do with the will and his battle with her mother than with any attraction she might have for him. She leaped up and began to stride around the room, groaning and tearing at her hair again.

She stopped in front of the dressing table and stared at herself in the mirror. "No, no, no. It has to be more than that. I work so hard at the clinic. He genuinely admires my feeling for the peasants. We both love horses. I'm young and strong. He said I was beautiful. He danced with me. If I weren't so stupidly awkward, he might actually have declared himself."

By the early hours of the morning, Sasha had convinced herself that there was still the possibility that her Vladya would renew his entreaties.

The next dawn, Count Tolstoy lay asleep on his leather couch, which served as his bed at night. A gentle knock

sounded upon the shutters. Tolstoy started up, his
arms held in front of him to ward off an attack. "Who?
What?"

"It's Vladimir Petrovich. An emergency. Open the
shutters."

Tolstoy rose and unlatched the shutters. Doctor
Kholkov stepped over the windowsill into the room.
His face was haggard, unshaven, his clothes muddy and
unkempt. "Please forgive me, Leo Nikolaevich, but I've
been marching about all night, tortured."

"Poor boy, you look a mess."

"I must leave you, master."

"What?"

"The situation here is insupportable. I'm off to my family's estate today."

"But, but, this is absurd." The count sputtered the
words. He sat down upon the bed as if he had been struck.
"You can't go away. I need you."

"My behavior here is considered—by certain people—
inappropriate."

"I wasn't aware that so much has—"

"Inappropriate!" Sasha's word had lodged deep in the
doctor's heart and had been tormenting him since their
aborted meeting. Her rejection of him, however, was not
the object of this visit.

"How so?"

Kholkov strode back and forth in the room, apparently

distraught. "The specifics are unimportant. The climate has become increasingly hostile to our collaboration. And so, before—"

Tolstoy raised his hand with a commanding gesture. "Stop! Stop before you say something neither of us wants to hear."

"'Here at Yasnaya Polyana there is only confusion, frivolity. I can't carry on our work. And then there's the matter of the police."

Tolstoy stood. "The police?"

Kholkov turned and looked at the count. "Look at you, master. Barefooted, uncovered, in your nightshirt. Quick, back into bed! You'll get pneumonia." Gently, the doctor helped the count back into bed, covered him, and propped him up with extra pillows.

"What about the police?" demanded the count.

The doctor went to the window and peered out. "Agents of the tsar! They follow me, watch my every movement. They're just waiting to pounce, confiscate my papers, and embarrass you." Kholkov had rehearsed his approach carefully.

Tolstoy clapped. "At last, the battle begins!" He leaped out of bed and rushed to his desk where he rummaged in a drawer. He pulled out a pistol and some cartridges, which he proceeded to load.

"Calm down, master! Calm, calm!" Doctor Kholkov hurried across the room and wrested the pistol from the count. He had planned to arouse the count, but not to this degree. Kholkov tried to hustle the count back to the couch, but the count struggled with him.

"Damn it! What d'you think you're doing?"

"Your battle began long ago, with the pen—and will continue, God willing. Please, get back to bed."

"Give me my pistol, you rascal. Let 'em try to take my papers!"

"Calm, for the sake of God." The doctor spoke harshly, exasperated by the count's mad theatrics. He often wished he had picked a less volatile master to follow. "They don't dare attack Tolstoy."

"Then I'll attack them."

"With words, master, with your inspired words."

"The pistol!" The count put out his hand, commandingly. "The pistol, damn it!"

"Only if you promise to be reasonable. The police are not coming here, I can assure you."

The count placed his hand over his heart and spoke in the voice of a small child. "I'll put it back in the drawer."

Kholkov handed the pistol to Tolstoy, who immediately ran to the window and brandished it to the right and the left, endeavoring to see the intruders. When Kholkov lunged toward him, he hopped away, quite agile, laughing. "Thought I was going to shoot the bastards, didn't you?" With a comic gesture, he replaced the pistol in the drawer and slammed the drawer shut.

Beside himself, Kholkov could hardly keep from striking the count for his mockery. Instead, he put out his hands, pleading. "Please, master, get back in bed—I don't want you coming down with the flu."

"Nonsense. The day's begun." Somewhat refreshed by his little joke, Tolstoy spoke casually. "Just tell me what's happened to cause you such distress."

While Tolstoy dressed, his disciple sank into an armchair, his head down. One could only deal with the count, he decided, by feigning extreme weakness. "Last night, someone broke into my study, ransacked my papers." This was not exactly the truth. There had been a break-in some months ago, but he had not mentioned it for fear of alarming the count. Since the revolution of 1905, the tsar's people had been monitoring the Tolstoyan movement closely; the count's ideas provided volatile fuel to the enemies of the state. Tonight, Kholkov decided to play upon Tolstoy's fear of the tsar's secret police to gain certain strategic objectives. "Tore my room apart!"

"Damn it! Let them harass Tolstoy, not his followers."

"It's better if I put some distance between us—to save you embarrassment."

"I'm prepared to go to prison." Tolstoy stood at attention as if he were being sentenced in court. "I'd be proud to go to prison."

"They're smart enough to leave you alone. As for the rest of us—let them do their damnedest. I'll keep in close touch, master, I promise. But I must go away now."

Kholkov rose and went to Tolstoy, his hand out as if to say goodbye. Tolstoy, terrified, grasped his arm and his shoulder. "No, no, I can't live without you, Vladimir Petrovich. You're my only protection against—"

"They won't touch you."

"I'm not afraid of them."

"Of what, then?"

Tolstoy hung his head. "To remain here alone, with my soul eternally exposed to damnation." He thought of his wife and his desire for her flesh.

"Goodbye, master."

"If you leave, I'll go to the commissioner and confess a conspiracy against the state."

"No such thing. You will remain here and carry on our battle."

Tolstoy, half-dressed, stumbled around the room, muttering. "I cannot carry on alone. I cannot. I cannot."

"You are stronger than all of them."

"I'm not afraid of the tsar, his ministers, his police. It's myself I'm afraid of, my own horrible imaginings."

"What imaginings?"

Tolstoy put his hands up to his forehead, his fingers grasping his skull as if it would burst. "Imaginings, imaginings."

Exultant, the doctor felt on the verge of the great discovery he had been seeking for years: the innermost workings of his master's soul. He took out his notebook and pencil. "It's time, dear master, that you let me into your heart."

Tolstoy stared at his disciple in dismayed surprise. "But you fill my heart. I've told you that."

"There are still secrets which you haven't shared."

"But you withhold your love, Vladimir Petrovich. I'm a man of pride, too."

"On the morning of my departure, perhaps both of us could overcome our pride."

Tolstoy began to pace again, wringing his hands. "I can't talk about it."

Kholkov turned away. "Then you don't love me at all. It's just as well I know that before I leave. It's obvious that I am an intruder in this household—"

Tolstoy approached his cherished disciple. "Never. No one alive—no one in the world is closer to me than you are. No friend. Not even one of my children."

"I speak of this household—not your friendship."

"We agree about the household, dear boy. And I have attempted to tear myself away—you know that."

"I know your good intentions—as for results . . ." The doctor refused to turn and face the count, who remained at his side, his hands clasped in anguish.

"Come now, my friend. I cannot bear your anger."

"I am not angry—that would be arrogant, to be angry at Leo Nikolayevich Tolstoy—but I am disappointed. My life has been devoted to you, all my efforts are on your behalf, and yet at every turn I am blocked, undercut, reprimanded. There are intrigues, cabals—and all accompanied by, by, hijinks. Just now, you brandished the pistol out the window, mocking me."

Tolstoy took hold of the doctor's arm. He patted his back as if he were an angry child. "Come now, Vladimir Petrovich—it's not as bad as all that."

"My pride. Damn it all, I am arrogant. A member of the tsar's own Horse Guards, a family as old as any in the realm—and all that to be called 'inappropriate.' " Kholkov could not escape that word.

"Inappropriate?" Tolstoy shook his head, puzzled. "I don't understand you, Vladimir Petrovich. I just know that I will be lost without your support, your daily support. Lost, lost, lost."

"When letters and even important articles leave this house without being recorded—"

Tolstoy could not believe that the doctor had reverted to this complaint. "For God's sake, man, in all enterprises there must be some room for error."

Indeed, the doctor still stalked his main target. He had been approaching craftily, pretending false turns. "It's more serious than mere error. I've been told that this slippage occurred deliberately—"

Tolstoy stamped his foot. "Who told you this?"

"Your wife freely admitted it—in order to undermine my efforts. She's jealous of my power—she sees me as an interloper."

Tolstoy sighed and turned away, now that they had returned to this familiar argument. "Sonya Andreyevna simply wants to protect me."

"And your daughter supports her in her subversion."

"I'll talk with the girl."

"You know that I have never, in any way, attempted—"

"Please, Vladimir Petrovich, calm yourself. Sit down. No one in this house desires to undermine you."

"Why pretend? Sonya Andreyevna does not care for me—she never has."

"My wife is a sick woman."

"She has recovered from her operation."

"Sick in the head—in the soul. But since her illness there have been signs—she has become much more gentle, meek, Christian."

"That's how she keeps you chained to this intolerable situation."

Tolstoy sank onto the couch. "I beg of you, Vladimir Petrovich, don't press this matter. We will both be sorry—"

Kholkov glanced sharply at the count and quickly retreated. "All right, I'll restrain myself. Not another word about Sonya Andreyevna. However—" The Doctor marched over to the desk and perched upon it. "However—" He paused dramatically and leaned toward the count, "I must insist upon access to your private diary."

Tolstoy threw his hands up. "No, no, no, no. Not that again."

Kholkov continued relentlessly. "If the record of your

torture in this household is not preserved, your teaching will be seen as a great hypocrisy by future ages."

Tolstoy's voice wavered. "It is not fair to Sonya Andreyevna that you see my momentary cries of outrage—"

"And if there is no copy of your true words—what will happen when she gets hold of those diaries, deletes, revises. What a saint she will appear!"

"No, no, no."

"And what a devil Leo Nikolayevich Tolstoy will appear! No one will understand the gentle, true Christian, who merely attempts to greet his death in spiritual peace."

"I cannot write freely of my torments if anyone reads—"

"You will never see me open those pages. I will come when you are away. I will never refer to them. I will be an impartial machine. But those words—your most private hell—must be recorded."

"It's impossible. The diaries are locked away in my bottom drawer. Only one key."

"I'll have another made. The key, please, Leo Nikolayevich."

Tolstoy wound his arms about his half-buttoned tunic. "No, no, no, and again, no."

Kholkov rose and stood over the old man. "For the sake of your teachings."

"I must write my complaint in private. I cannot betray my wife."

"Then you betray your followers."

"You try my patience, Vladimir Petrovich." The count

attempted to maintain a reasonable tone, but his voice trembled. He had been awakened too early, and under the doctor's hectoring, he felt weak. "I'll talk to my wife, and to Sasha. No letters or articles will leave this house without passing through your hands. Let the key rest in my pocket."

"It's your wife, then, over God."

"I won't have you—"

"Until you leave that frivolous woman, every word you preach to the world will be a falsehood."

Tolstoy pleaded. "I fear for Sonya Andreyevna's sanity."

Kholkov sneered. "A convenient excuse."

The count straightened. His eyes fastened piercingly upon his disciple. His voice took on a tone of command. "I warn you, Doctor Kholkov, you are a guest on my estate."

Kholkov shouted. "Leave your wife! She corrupts you!"

Tolstoy leaped up. "How dare you!" The count seized a riding crop from his desk and moved toward Kholkov, the crop raised to be brought down upon the head of this insolent intruder. Kholkov, who regretted his momentary loss of control, stood his ground, staring Tolstoy in the eye. Tolstoy hesitated and then crumbled to his knees. "Oh, my God! Such violence." He slipped the crop into his left hand and whipped his right hand as if to punish it for its trespass against the most fundamental of his Christian teachings. Kholkov fell to his knees and grabbed the riding crop.

"Master, master, I'm sorry. Hit me, not yourself! I'm an

arrogant bastard! I lose my head. Punish me!" He bowed his head. "Hit me, please, hit me and I will be yours forever."

"Hit no one! That is our creed. And we sin, sin, sin. Please forgive me, Vladimir Petrovich!" The count raised the doctor's head, caressing it tenderly.

"Forgive me, master."

"My brother!"

"I overstepped all bounds."

The two men embraced, sighing with pleasurable relief at the climax they had experienced together.

Tolstoy dug into his pocket and pulled out a large key. "Here, here, take the key." He pressed the key into Kholkov's hand.

Kholkov slipped the key into his pocket, and the two men embraced again. "Thank you, master, I'll never betray—"

The door flew open, slamming against the wall. Sasha and the countess burst into the room.

"My God!" exclaimed the countess. "What's going on in here?"

"It sounded like a murder!" Sasha bent over her father. "Papa, are you hurt?"

The two men rose, smiling at one another, and then, composing themselves, turned to the women with dignity.

Tolstoy waved his hand through the air, dismissively. "Nothing, nothing. A small misunderstanding."

"Hijinks!" said the doctor, winking at the count.

"Hijinks?" asked the count and then understood the reference. "Ho, ho, hijinks! Ha, ha! Nothing but hijinks!"

The countess regarded the two men suspiciously. "Embracing?" It was as if all her fears had coalesced into that single image of her husband and the doctor, kneeling, their arms about one another.

"A joke, my dear Sonya Andreyevna," said the count, stroking his wife's back. "Please, dear, don't be alarmed. A bit too much wine at supper. Sasha, dear, I would like to speak to you for a moment—alone. Vladimir Petrovich, would you please take this article into the Remington Room and find the proper references. And you, dear Sonya Andreyevna, you should get a full night's sleep. You don't want to open the wound again."

The doctor bent solicitously over the countess. "Yes, yes, Sonya Andreyevna, too much excitement will undermine your recovery. Eight hours of sleep is a necessity; ten hours is even better." He took hold of the countess's arm.

The count took the countess's other arm, and the two men led her gently to the door. Sasha folded the bedding and placed it in an armoire.

"Embracing?" murmured the countess. She looked dazed, as if she had been caught out in the midst of a nightmare. "Embracing?"

"Hijinks," said the count, looking at the doctor over his wife's head.

"The battle of the Persians, the Turks, the Numidians," pronounced the doctor, and the two men laughed.

At the door to the study, the count embraced his wife gently and kissed her on both cheeks. She smiled up at him gratefully, but as she left the room, she turned back again once more and stared at the two men, a puzzled frown returning to her face. "Embracing?"

Kholkov clasped Tolstoy's hand and then his shoulders, and he too left the study, shutting the door behind him. Sasha beckoned her father to sit down on the leather couch she had cleared. She sat next to him.

Father and daughter were silent for some time, each attempting to frame this interview so that it would gracefully approach subtle and complicated matters. Tolstoy sighed.

Sasha sighed. "You shouldn't be up so early, Papa. All this excitement is bad for your heart."

"Nonsense. An old rooster like me must crow in the day." He pounded his chest and let out a cock's crow. "Cock-a-doodle-doo!" He shrugged diffidently and turned to his daughter, his expression serious, concerned. "I know it's not been easy for you with Doctor Kholkov so active in my affairs."

Sasha looked alarmed. "Why do you say such a thing, Papa?"

"You've seemed—out of sorts, lately. Nervous."

"Not a bit, Papa. I'm just as I've always been."

"A trifle touchy, perhaps? Just a trifle?" The count tickled Sasha, who laughed.

"Well, perhaps. There is something—"

"Having to do with the doctor?"

Sasha stared at her father. "Papa, you are amazing. In fact, Maman has urged me . . ."

"Let's not involve your mother."

"My feelings exactly. Doctor Kholkov—"

"I know, I know, he tends to be possessive of my work. A regular bureaucrat."

"I wasn't—"

"There's no need for jealousy between you."

"But, Papa—"

Tolstoy placed a finger on his daughter's lips to forestall an argument. He rose and began to walk about the room, his hands behind his back. He paused at the window and stared out at the garden, which was slowly becoming distinct in the light of the dawn: the full-leafed trees, the moist paths and garden benches, the mist-shrouded pond. The roosters began to crow, waking the dogs, who took up the dawn's song with their barking. "There, there, darling Sashenka, the day begins. The creatures welcome the sun." The count breathed in deeply.

"I love the dawn too, Papa. Do you remember how you always used to come to my room and hold me to the window so I could see the sun rise?"

"Yes, yes, you were a strange little girl. It took so little to please you."

"Now Papa, what were you saying about—the doctor?"

Once more, the count paced. "I would like your mother to apologize to Vladimir Petrovich for sending out letters and articles without first submitting them to him."

Sasha stared at her father in surprise. "Oh Papa, you know that she will never apologize, never in a million years, not even if the tsar commanded it."

Tolstoy coughed. His eyes narrowed, slyly. "Then perhaps if you apologized—for us all. He's done so much."

Sasha thought for a moment and then blushed. "All right, I will do my best, Papa. I will talk to the doctor—try to make him understand. He and I—"

"Now, that's a good daughter." Tolstoy sighed and sank down into the armchair. He felt exhausted, but pleased that his strategy had worked so easily. His daughter's apology would satisfy his disciple's sensitive feelings, and there would be no reason to disturb his wife.

Sasha rose and knelt next to her father. She took up his hands and kissed them. "Oh, Papa, I would do whatever you ask."

Tolstoy kissed his daughter's hands in return and then began to examine them carefully. "Look how rough and dirty your hands are!" he said.

"It isn't dirt, Papa. My work at the stable hardens the hands—calluses, you know—whatever I handle gets ingrained." He noticed that the middle finger of her right hand curled unnaturally. He tried to straighten it, but could not. "What are you doing with my finger?"

"It isn't straight."

"Strider meant no harm. I was careless scraping his hoofs. He felt terrible."

Tolstoy frowned. "How unattractive! You know, a person's hands tell a lot about her personality. Look at your nails!"

Sasha tried to pull back, but her father held onto her hands. "Please, Papa. Stop joking."

"Not joking at all. Here, I'll show you what you must do when you wash your hands." He leaped up and went to the corner where he dipped a towel into a bowl of water. He returned, seized Sasha's right hand, and began to push at the cuticles with the wet towel. "Push the skin in this manner each time you wash so that it does not grow over the nails." Sasha laughed, her cheeks blazing with color. "It isn't funny. People look at your hands. If they're unattractive, why—"

"Oh, Papa, you have such theories sometimes."

"Well, you are important to me. I want you to be happy. You go about as if you didn't care how you looked. Those glasses, for example—take them off." The count snatched the glasses off the face of his protesting daughter. He held her shoulders and stared at her. "Now, that's a lot better."

"But I can't see. I'll bump into things."

"That's all right, you'll get used to it. Even blind people learn how to sense objects—and your eyesight isn't that bad. Now, stand up and walk to the door and back—try to walk straight, move only your legs, not your upper body."

Sasha did not move. "Papa—"

Tolstoy pulled her to her feet. "Just once to the door and back, as I asked."

Sasha, walking artificially, made her way to the door and back. Just before she reached her father, she knocked over an end table piled with magazines. She fell to her knees to gather them up and set them back on the table. "There now, I told you. I can't see. Give me back my glasses."

The count returned the glasses to his daughter, who put them on and finished her task. She then stood and stared at her father, who looked at her and sighed. "How large you are, and homely. Poor thing."

Sasha flinched. She shut her eyes, took a breath, and then shrugged and laughed. "I'm Sasha, as I've always been."

"Don't worry, good looks aren't everything. The best young men look deeper. Those who marry good looks— I can tell you—are often deceived."

"Sometimes, Papa, I feel that I wasn't intended to marry."

"Nonsense. Every young woman—"

"Nevertheless."

Tolstoy now busied himself with his clothes, completing his toilet in front of the mirror in the corner. Sasha went to stand at the window, watching the day grow brighter. This morning, her father's judgment of her looks had cut even more deeply than it usually did.

In the mirror, the count noticed his daughter standing at the window. Something in her pose caught his eye: a young woman watching the dawn approach through a great provincial landscape, as if she were looking toward some distant promise. "You say 'sometimes,' daughter. What does that mean?"

Sasha spoke bitterly, without turning. "Men have noticed me now and then, in spite of my—my size."

Tolstoy darted to the window and stared at his daughter. "Look at you, Sasha. You're blushing. My dear Sashenka, are you being courted?"

Sasha clutched her arms. "I—I don't know. I think that I shall refuse him—if he asks."

The count was struck with amazement. He had never expected such a reply. "But that's a ridiculous thing to say. Why should you refuse whomever this is?"

Sasha stared out of the window and remained silent for some time. The count did not move. Finally, Sasha spoke. "But if I should fall in love with a good man, and if you approve, and if we were able to stay here, close to you—"

"If, if, if—enough philosophy this morning."

"Well, it's a little more than an *if*—I think."

The count began to pace nervously about the room. "Ah ha. I suspected there was something more—the way you stand there, gazing out with your 'sometimes.'"

"It's premature, I think—"

Tolstoy came to his daughter's side. He stood straight, like a general inspecting his troops. "Who is it?"

"—and yet he declares that he respects me more than any other woman he has ever met, and—"

"And? And? And he's declared his love for you?"

"In a way."

"Who?"

"Vladimir Petrovich."

Tolstoy's eyes opened wide in astonishment. "Doctor Kholkov?"

Sasha turned and smiled shyly at her father. "Yes. Doctor Kholkov."

The count fell back upon the windowsill. "Disaster!"

"I love him, Papa—I guess."

Tolstoy moaned. Sasha stared at him and then stumbled across the room to sink onto the couch. She was in a daze.

The count did not move. "And did you declare yourself?"

Sasha replied hesitantly, stammering breathlessly, watching her father to try to gauge his reaction. "Not really. It happened on the way home from the clinic. We had worked hard all day together. A warm summer breeze filled with the smell of hay and earth, the frogs croaking, birds singing, crickets, women laughing down in the village, the sound of an accordion. It all filled me with strange feeling for that good doctor who follows your teachings and can still praise me with gentle words so that I believe he is sincere." Her voice filled the room with its full warm tones.

Tolstoy walked back to the corner and stared at himself in the mirror. "Madness."

Sasha, sobbing, leaped up and ran back to the window as if, only there, could she hold onto her dream of happiness. The count began to pace once again, this time conversing with himself, striking himself upon the forehead and the chest. Once more, he stopped by the mirror, lowered his head, and composed himself. He then approached his daughter at the window and began to speak, quietly, firmly. "Of course, I should have realized how much romance you had saved up over all these years, how many dreams of happiness, how many illusions."

"Illusions?"

"And then this handsome, polite gentleman, older, serious, my disciple who has suffered on my behalf appears again and is kind—polite and kind to you—and naturally it would seem to a girl who has been languishing here in the country all these years—"

"Do you mean—" Sasha could feel hope ebb from the tropical splendor of her imagination.

"—an inexperienced girl who knows nothing of the forms of courtliness, of polite conversation—a sincere, authentic girl."

"Then you think I was mistaken?" The words emerged clearly now, almost a statement.

"Not mistaken, exactly. Vladimir Petrovich cares for you a great deal—just as he cares for me."

"Affection, then? Admiration?" Her tongue curled around the words spitefully.

"You are a—sister to his spirit—a wonderful colleague."

Sasha's voice, which had sung out in full chords when she announced her love, now became dull, flat, grating. "A colleague."

"I'm sure he admires you as much as he says. But as for the other—"

"He was simply being kind."

"I can't say that for certain—it's simply that there is something so . . . so . . ." he searched for a word, and suddenly one came to mind, "inappropriate . . . your characters . . . your activities . . . your ages . . ."

Sasha pursed her lips. "Inappropriate? How strange that you should use that word. Inappropriate. You were much older than Maman—"

"And that wasn't a mistake? It was a great, great mistake!"

"Unlike you and Maman, Vladimir Petrovich and I share many . . . views."

"I can say nothing for certain. I will talk to the doctor, immediately."

"My God, I would die of embarrassment. It is for me to talk to him."

"You don't want me to question him?"

"It was most probably nothing, as you say, and nothing more will come of it."

The count allowed the statement to stand there

between them while they contemplated it. He nodded and waited a minute longer, his mind working over the strategy he must use. When he spoke, his voice was gentle, tentative at first, but as the sentence grew, so did the conviction of his tone. "Maybe . . . you should . . . give up your work at the clinic for a while."

"And if he does declare himself, if he is serious, I shall tell him that it's impossible—inappropriate. I will never marry." She declared her fate.

Tolstoy's gaze softened. "I thought you said that you—"

"No, no, Papa, it was just as you said—illusion, a yearning for romance—all those novels."

"But, dear Sashenka, but, I did not mean to—" The count smiled fondly at his daughter, his eyes moistening.

"Shhshhh, Papa." Sasha put her fingers to her father's lips. "Come sit with me for a moment on the sofa. I could never leave you, Papa—you are my whole life." Sasha led her father to the couch. They sat, holding one another's hands.

"If you stopped working at the clinic and had more time to devote to my work—"

"Exactly what I've been thinking. I can take over all your secretarial duties."

"Of the entire family, I can trust only you these days, Sashenka. But still, should someone suitable, appropriate—"

"Who could possibly replace you in my heart, Papa?"

"Another Strider, perhaps." The count laughed.

"Not even my horses or my dogs."

The count turned away smiling contentedly. Sasha kissed him on the cheek. They gazed at one another and embraced.

Tolstoy, ashamed that he had given Kholkov the key to his desk, began early the next morning to write two diaries: one, which he would show his wife, omitting crucial details that might upset her, and another relating the true events of his life as he saw them. When the countess woke, she confided to her servant that she had experienced a nightmare the night before: a horrible dream that she could not quite remember. As she dressed, though, she began to recall bits and snatches of the events in her husband's study; immediately, she dismissed them as too absurd to have really happened. Instead, she lapsed happily into a romantic fantasy of her daughter's wedding and her future in the court of the tsar.

Before her illness, the countess had taken up amateur photography. She had made great strides, hiring a local photographer to instruct her and to set up a darkroom in a curtained alcove between her husband's study and the Remington Room. During her operation and recovery, she had been forced to put the hobby aside and had not thought about resuming it until this morning, when she heard the pianist begin his practicing. "There is within everyone," she said to herself, "an impulse toward art." With that thought, she resolved to work at her photography the way the pianist practiced—every day. Indeed, she would photograph her daughter's wedding and her husband's old age. Somehow, she felt that the perfection of her art would hasten the day of Sasha's marriage and would lengthen her husband's days on earth.

Every morning, the countess took photographs in the house, the stables, the garden, the fields, and even in the great forest; every afternoon she closed the drapes in her sitting room, while she developed and printed the pictures in her improvised darkroom. As she worked, the sitting room remained quite dark except for a dim red light that escaped under the curtain of the darkroom alcove. A large, square camera on a tripod stood in the center of the sitting room. In the main part of the house, the court musician practiced Beethoven sonatas, the sound of which sent waves of pleasure through the countess as she brought the images to completion.

Five days after the fateful events in the count's sitting room, as the countess worked and listened to Beethoven, she sighed. "How slowly the image appears—like the themes of a sonata." She waited for both to emerge with the clarity of a new view of life. Lately, her sleep had been troubled by that same recurrent vague and frightening nightmare, which had now become clearer: the vision of her husband and her enemy, on their knees, embracing.

The door to Tolstoy's study opened, emitting a wedge of light into the sitting room. Sasha entered, closing the door carefully behind her. From behind the study door, a hammer began to tap away, intermittently, with pauses marked by explosions of muffled wrath from the count. Tolstoy, irked by his wife's artistic pretensions, had decided to make himself a new pair of boots. He had learned boot making years ago but only applied himself to it when he wanted to irritate his wife.

"Listen to him," said the countess to herself, "Tap, tap, tap! Lord spare us the bumbling boot maker!".

Sasha stumbled over the tripod, upsetting it. "God damn!" she shouted, just managing to catch the apparatus before the camera smashed to the floor. "God damn!"

"Alexandra!" called the countess from her alcove. "You mustn't use such language."

With vigorous, heavy movements, Sasha sprang to the windows, opening the drapes, only to see that the shutters had been closed too and latched from the outside. "Bear turds and chicken vomit!"

"Alexandra! You swear like a muzhik! Like your bumbling father!"

Sasha threw herself out the door onto the verandah, where she unlatched the shutters and banged them open. Returning, she slammed the door. As usual, she wore a simple peasant dress, vest, and boots. The countess emerged from behind the black curtain, her sleeves rolled up, a wilted rose pinned to her bosom. She held two dripping photographic prints by her fingertips. From the house came the sound of the slow movement of Beethoven's "Moonlight Sonata." Now and then, the music stopped and phrases were repeated.

The countess confronted her daughter. "Sasha, darling, must you clump around like a lame horse?"

"What's a person to do, with the house shut up and dark and stupid objects cluttering the rooms?"

"A camera is not a stupid object." Carefully, the countess laid the prints upon the sunny windowsill.

"I was simply trying to walk from Papa's study to the Remington Room."

Sonya stood over the photographs, admiring them. "Come here, dear, and see how it's proceeding."

"But Maman, you're not a photographer. Papa says—"

"Is he a boot maker?"

"At least he took lessons—for years."

"The cobbler couldn't understand why this awkward count should want so passionately to make bad boots. Listen to that tap, tap, tap. Instead of writing his wonderful novels . . ." The countess went to the corner and snatched up an ill-made peasant boot, holding it up in the air. ". . . he makes this. Behold, Volume 12 1/2 of the works of Leo Nikolayevich Tolstoy."

"He thinks people should do for themselves."

"Poor man, he doesn't know what to do with himself since your brother died."

"Do you?"

The countess turned suddenly and gazed at her daughter. "Why were you in your father's study at this time of day?"

"I was taking Papa's dictation as he worked on the boots." Sasha held up the dictation pad proudly.

"Dictation? When did you learn?"

"Masha and Tanya taught me."

"Let me see."

The countess reached for the pad. Sasha hid the pad behind her back. "You'll smear it all with your chemicals." In dismay, the countess looked down at her hands, which had become discolored by the photographic chemicals. "Papa wants more manuscript paper, and afterward I'm to transcribe this." Sasha darted into the Remington Room and emerged with five large sheets of paper and a knife.

The countess walked into the darkroom, where she scrubbed her hands in a bowl of water. She emerged to see her daughter fold the paper to copybook size, cut it, and crease the side to leave a margin. Sasha worked with a flourish, showing off. "So, you take dictation and prepare your father's paper and everything."

"Who else is there? Now that Masha and Tanya are married, and you're so busy with all of your business affairs, and mourning, and now becoming a great photographer and musician and special friend to our visiting pianist."

"Why are you so angry with me this morning?"

"I have to take Papa his paper, and then I have to type up this morning's work."

"And your studies? Your horses? The clinic?"

"Everything will get done. Papa is the most important. He needs me."

"He needs you?" The countess cocked her head and pointed toward the drawing room. "The 'Moonlight Sonata'—do you hear, Sasha? He plays for the tsar himself."

"I can't believe that you've taken so to that . . . ordinary man. Doctor Kholkov says he's probably sneering at all of us behind his jolly smiles."

The countess listened to the music, distracted. She clasped her heart. "That adagio—like silk. I'm so pleased your father pressed him to stay. He knows how to talk to a woman."

"Really, Mother, you must stop mooning about like a lovesick girl. With such a man—it isn't proper."

"We talk as friends, not lovers. You know so little about love. Your father and I were so happy—and then so miserable—and now, perhaps, happy again."

"It's all such an illusion."

"Love, an illusion? But you yourself, Sasha—why have you been avoiding me this week?"

"I haven't—"

"What did your father say about you and the doctor?"

Sasha held out her hands in front of her. "Maman, do you think my hands ugly?"

"Your hands? Well, no. You have strong hands. Good hands." The countess examined her daughter's hands. "Look here, I forgot about that middle finger. It never did heal straight, did it? Why on earth do you ask about your hands?"

"Papa objects to my hands."

The countess laughed. "Oh, pay no attention to that madman. While we were engaged, he thought my hands remarkable, but then, somehow, he changed his mind."

Sasha hid her hands. "You're right—it's unimportant."

"But we've forgotten about the doctor. You promised you'd ask your father about him. That's important."

Sasha paced about the room and paused at the window, gazing out. "I told Father everything, and he understood everything—sentimental dreams right out of novels—and so there it is."

"That's all? Sentimental dreams? And you're going to refuse—"

"It hasn't come to that, but if it does, I shall refuse."

The countess picked up the badly sewn boot and stared at it. "Another victory for your father."

"Don't talk that way about Papa. He wants very much for me to marry—the right person for the right reasons."

"Which have nothing to do with love."

"All this talk of love, such a waste of time."

"I cannot live without love. Nor can you."

Sasha approached her mother. "If you're feeling so loving, why don't you bend your will to father's, lead a simpler life here, and give up the copyright to Papa's novels?"

The countess shuddered and let out a sharp sigh. "Your father and I made a contract with one another years ago. I took over all the practical matters of his life so that he could pretend to live as a saint."

Sasha put her fingers to her ears. "That wasn't the bargain."

The countess reached out to embrace her daughter. "Oh, Sasha, giving up those novels would be like giving up one of my children, like giving up music."

Sasha pulled back from her mother's embrace. "This over-emotional craving for music is unbecoming."

"You think your saintly father is indifferent to music?"

"He bears all this racket for your sake."

"Music awakens my soul; it ignites his lust."

"You always speak of Father's lust." Sasha paused, drew in her breath, and stared impudently at her mother. "Do you never feel desire?"

Flustered, the countess stared back at her daughter. She remained silent for a moment and then began to speak hesitantly.

"There is an important—difference between men's passion—and women's."

"I didn't ask that." Sasha thrust her face into her mother's face.

"Of course, I am dominated by his passion—" The countess turned away and retreated.

Sasha followed, grasping her arm, and turning her. "Have you ever felt desire?"

The countess stared into her daughter's eyes. When she spoke, she did so forcefully and a little too loud, as if she were trying to convince herself, as well as her daughter. "It's very strange, even in the midst of carnal pleasure I feel as pure in soul and thought and body as a newborn child—"

Sasha turned away. "What nonsense."

"My conscience is clear before God, my husband, and my children—after all, we must have husbands and children, and so the rest follows, doesn't it? If one's body didn't—then the world would stop, wouldn't it?"

Sasha turned back. "Rationalizing. Do you ever feel desire?"

"In my heart of hearts, that is not what I want or ever have wanted. I've always dreamed of a platonic relationship, a perfect spiritual communion like you and Doctor Kholkov in the infirmary, perhaps."

"Don't drag me into your sordid tale."

"You can't deny your needs, my dear."

"Perhaps you and I have different needs."

"And your love for the doctor? The life you could have together? The children?"

"But it wasn't real, just summertime and childish romantic yearning."

"Of course you'll never know, will you?"

"Besides, the doctor and I have more important things

to do." Sasha retreated across the room. The countess followed. Sasha turned, her arms crossed over her breast, and declared, "I'm content!"

The countess grasped her daughter's arms and turned her. "I wasn't truthful before. I have felt desire, lust even—and I still do, more than ever." The words thrilled her as she spoke them.

Sasha tried to turn away, but her mother held her tight. "What does that have to do with me?"

"You asked me."

"Well, I'm no longer interested."

"I'm telling you that all through my life, and even now, I want to feel the flesh of a man . . ."

"This is insupportable, Maman—inappropriate." The young woman tried to go back to the study, but her mother blocked her way.

"No, dear, you must listen. I can't let you go off without telling you—there are certain needs—certain pleasures that all women share. There are moments of passion."

Sasha tore herself away from her mother. The countess pursued her. "When your father and I—for many years during our marriage—to be with a man in a bed, to feel—you mustn't deny your flesh—"

"No, no, no. I can't stand it."

"To conceive a child with a man, to bear the child, to give suck to that child who bears the stamp of your husband and—"

Now Sasha turned on her mother and screamed. "And to abort that child?"

The countess fell back. "What are you saying?" She could not catch her breath.

"You didn't want me."

"Who told you that?"

"You favored Vanichka from the beginning."

"You loved him as much as we all did. Don't be a monster."

"There, you see? You've always thought I was a monster."

"That's not true."

"You tried to get rid of me. You tied your legs together and jumped from the dresser."

Sonya shrieked. "My God!" Her cursed husband's God had suddenly appeared to punish her now, twenty years later.

Sasha continued, unrelenting. "You went to the Tula midwife."

The countess sank on the chaise longue. "Where did you hear all this nonsense? Where?" How could she deny it? she wondered. Especially now, when she had spoken the truth to her daughter about her desires.

"I don't know. I've always known it. You would have been happy if I had died instead of Vanichka—and so would I."

"Oh you foolish, unhappy child. How hard you make it for one to love you—why do you hate me so?"

"I don't hate you; I just hate all your sentimental lies. You did try to abort me, didn't you?"

The countess cradled her cheeks in her hands. She wanted to lie, but she could not. "You think that I abandoned you—and perhaps, in a way I did, at first. I was driven crazy by the situation and I acted badly, perhaps, but only in a half-hearted fashion—certainly if I had really wanted to—"

"Ah. There!" Even though she had known about her mother's dereliction, she was appalled to hear it spoken aloud. "You admit it. You admit it."

"But—but you couldn't begin to understand. Before you were ever conceived, your father began to go away from me and almost everything else in his life—his children, his art, his responsibility as a landowner—at one point, he even contemplated suicide." There, she thought, the truth is complicated; Sasha must be made to understand it all.

"That's not true. Papa wouldn't ever—"

"He's terrified that he's lost his eternal soul—that terror has been pursuing him for years."

"Papa would be happy in his beliefs if he were allowed to practice them."

"Oh, he has every opportunity, because I do everything he ought to be doing: manage his estate, publish his novels, educate his children—"

"Don't start that old song again. You're very happy with your power."

"There I was, pregnant for the twelfth time, and your father, moody, angry, contemptuous of his family and his art. What does a woman do?"

"Not what you did."

"How could I know that you—merry, energetic Sasha—were in my womb?"

"What difference does it make who was in there?"

"You were simply a nameless, growing burden then, adding to my other burdens. If it was my fault, it was your father's, too—the fault of our battle. I wanted nothing but your father's love and sympathy."

"How can you, of all people, urge me to seek a husband and children?"

"You must let me explain."

"I've heard enough—too much. I'm sorry I ever brought it up." Sasha put her hand on the door handle to the study, but she did not leave.

The countess pleaded. "When you were born, we all loved you and were happy to have a girl about the house again after so many boys."

"Sentimental drivel again." Sasha stalked over to the window and peered out.

Sonya followed her, beseeching. "Please, Sasha, don't be so—hard, so cynical. You have a good nature full of love and merriment and laughter, and I love you."

Sasha looked down and picked up one of the photos her mother had just printed. The door to the study swung open, and the count entered with a boot held proudly in front of him. He looked quite pleased with himself.

The countess rushed toward him. "Stop! Not another step in those muddy boots, scoundrel!" The count looked down and saw that the boots on his feet were, indeed, still full of caked mud from his morning hike in the forest. The countess pushed him across the room and out the door to the verandah. "Out! Out! Out!"

Sasha cried out. "Maman! What's gotten into you?"

"I won't have my house turned into a pigpen." The count, in his socks, reappeared from the verandah. "That's better. And now I want an explanation of why you're determined to ruin your daughter's marriage opportunity."

The count regarded his wife fearfully. "What daughter?"

"This daughter." The countess pointed to Sasha. "Alexandra Lvovna!"

"Mother, I won't have you—"

Tolstoy thrust out his chest. "There have been no proposals."

"Because you're determined to keep your daughter in bondage for life."

"The old madness again," said the count to Sasha.

"Don't talk to us about madness. It is you who has been stalked by death for twenty years, preparing yourself for the grave. And now you want to drag your youngest daughter down with you."

Tolstoy moved warily toward Sasha, who turned away

from him and sat upon the chaise longue, burying her head in her hands. Tolstoy approached his wife with resolution. "Stop this nonsense, Sonya Andreyevna. No one has proposed to Sasha. You keep trying to fill this house with romantic nonsense, and instead, you make us all desperately unhappy. Please go to your room and rest before you do yourself damage."

"I insist that you allow Vladimir Petrovich to declare his intentions to our daughter."

"Vladimir Petrovich's eyes are upon God, not upon the miseries of domestic life. He is twice Sasha's age. And neither are fit for such an infernal pact."

"You were twice my age when—"

"And look at the disaster that ensued!"

"You call our love, our children, your great novels a disaster?"

"Your mad refusal to abandon the decadent life of the flesh and turn to God is sinful." The count marched to the study door.

"When Count Tolstoy gives up his arrogance and his title," declared Countess Sonya, "I will reject my birth, family, and the culture that has nourished my life."

Tolstoy entered the study and slammed the door.

"Sasha," said the countess, turning to her daughter. "I want you to run away with the doctor."

"Calm yourself, Mother. Neither Doctor Kholkov nor I intend to run away from the one person who gives our lives meaning."

"That man, that egotist you adore, ruined your sisters' chances at a good marriage, and now he's ruining yours." The countess sank down upon the chaise longue next to Sasha and tried to take her in her arms. "Poor, unloved child."

Sasha stood abruptly. "I'm not unloved. I lead a perfectly useful life. Now then, Mother, not another word about Doctor Kholkov."

"But you've chosen such a narrow life, dear Sasha. It makes me shiver."

"I don't want to hear of marriage and children, the life of the spirit embodied in music or platonic relationships—such nonsense doesn't exist for me."

"Then you're not quite human."

"Thank you for the compliment, Maman." Sasha curtseyed.

"Have you never been humbled by life?"

"I was born humbled, and you know it. You're a hypocrite: virginal when it suits you and full of lust the next moment. Don't talk to me of love."

"Oh, I can talk of love and of respect. Before your father went mad, our marriage was built on both and upon desire too. Don't let him deny life—"

From the study came the voice of the count, bellowing, "Sashenka!" Sasha ran into the study, shutting the door behind her.

PART TWO

Autumn

As autumn progressed, the count withdrew from the countess more and more each day. She became increasingly frantic, blaming Doctor Kholkov, who, she declared, had been poisoning the atmosphere of the estate. She became particularly incensed when the count replaced her photograph on his study wall with photographs of the doctor and of Sasha. She made a scene, forcing the count to return her photograph to its proper place. He accused her of suffering some sort of breakdown and sent for mental doctors to examine her. She found no one to comfort her. Every night before falling asleep, the countess was assailed by the memory of her husband and Kholkov kneeling on the floor of the study in one another's arms. She had wrung from the count an admission that it hadn't been a dream. Indeed, something like that had occurred, he said, simply the results of "hijinks." She could not understand how he could admit such carrying-on and yet treat her as if she were going mad. Finally, and most disturbing of all, rumors had been appearing in the press, hinting at marital problems between the Tolstoys. She was certain that Doctor Kholkov had planted these stories. Determined to prove them false, she decided to take a loving photographic portrait of her and her husband on the day of their anniversary. She would send it to all the newspapers, along with a statement about the happy, fruitful years they had spent together.

On a dull, gray, chilly afternoon in autumn, the Tolstoy family gathered in the garden just below the verandah for the photograph. The brilliant fall color of the trees had fled the coming winter, leaving behind only the brown, dead remains of autumn's glory, which the wind pulled and tugged at this afternoon, disrobing the branches one by one. The smell of snow was in the air. It had been years since snow had come this late.

The countess, in a white silk dress resembling a wedding gown, stood behind her large box camera mounted on a tripod, with a black drape hanging behind. "Attention! Everyone, attention!" she called out and ducked her head under the drape, attempting to focus and frame the shot she had planned. Count Tolstoy stood dejectedly before the camera, staring at the ground. "A step to the left, Lyovchka," came the muffled voice of the countess. The count did not move. "Come now, please be cooperative."

"A pointless exercise," he muttered, shuffling slightly to the left.

To one side, Sasha stood, holding her father's cap and his sweater. Doctor Kholkov peered down on the scene from the verandah.

The countess pleaded for her husband's cooperation. "One photo of the two of us—that's all I ask."

"Even our children refuse—"

"Sasha!" ordered the countess. "Give your father his cap and sweater."

"No!" said the count.

"Don't be an ancient old fool! The wind is cold."

"It's enough that I stand here—"

"One step forward, Leo Nikolayevich—Sasha, go stand with your father—to the right of him, where I will stand."

Sasha joined her father. She attempted to hand him the cap and sweater, but he pushed them aside. "Please, Papa, Maman is right. The wind is cold."

"I won't humor her."

"Sasha! Stand still. Now one step forward and one half step to the left."

Reluctantly, Sasha and Tolstoy complied.

"Ahh, perfect!"

"Well, take a picture of me and my daughter," declared the count, smiling as if for a photo.

The countess ducked out from under the black drape. "Only one picture today—as I promised." She beckoned to Sasha, taking the cap and sweater from her and handing her the trigger mechanism and the flash palette. "Set them off simultaneously when I tell you, Sashenka darling. And you, Lyovchka! Stand still! Right on that spot."

She carried the cap and sweater to her husband, who thrust them away again, snarling, "Put them on yourself. They'll go with your costume."

"You think I'm crazy, don't you?"

"Death will be a welcome release from this torture."

The countess threw the cap and sweater up on the verandah and linked her arm through Tolstoy's, turning toward the camera. Tolstoy removed his arm and turned away from his wife.

"Hold my arm, Leo Nikolayevich! Turn toward me! This is our anniversary photograph."

"Hypocrisy! A travesty! Better to show how we really are."

"Wife and husband, that is how we really are."

"Forget the photo, Mother," Sasha pleaded. "It will flatter neither of you."

"They printed in the newspaper that Tolstoy has divorced his wife. Let them see it isn't true. Photographs do not lie." The countess jerked the count's arm, forcing him to turn toward her. She smirked at the camera. "Are you ready, Sashenka?" Sasha nodded. "Smile, Lyovchka!" she commanded, but at that moment, in the distance, down the side drive, the countess spotted some peasant lads in an argument with the estate gardener. Distracted, she shouted out, "Hey! Hey! Off the drive, fools. You're to carry the bricks around the back of the house. And you, shoo those chickens back to the side yard. The count and his family are not to be disturbed." Suddenly, she darted toward the disturbance, waving her fist. "Cigarettes and trash all over—no respect! Slovenly idiots, revolutionaries—even the policemen are not neat—serfs still, in spite of emancipation."

Sasha cried out. "Mother! Mother! Please stop that racket!" She lay the photographic equipment down and started after her mother. "The photograph! The photograph!"

The countess disappeared around the side of the house, shouting, "Disobedient, churlish fools!"

Sasha called after her. "Come back this instant. Mother!"

"Let her go, Sashenka," said the count, "and let's be done with this business."

Sasha returned to her father's side. "No, no, Papa. Don't move. If we don't do this now, she'll be at us until doomsday. Don't move!"

Kholkov, seeing his opportunity, came rushing down the steps, waving some papers in the air. "Leo Nikolayevich! The will is complete now and ready for you to copy."

Tolstoy squinted up his eyes in displeasure. "Yet another will?"

"This one is legally correct, at last—we've had a lawyer—"

"All this secrecy, all this manipulation."

Kholkov stepped back. "Accusations? Just because I am trying to carry out your wishes?"

"Now, now, Vladimir Petrovich. I simply would prefer to call my entire family together and explain openly to them what I have in mind."

"Then you don't really want to leave your work to 'the people.'"

"Vladimir Petrovich!" exclaimed Sasha, frowning in annoyance. "Papa hates all this underhanded skulking around, secret wills, copying out his diaries behind Maman's back—"

"—before she alters them," interrupted Kholkov. "In her right mind, she'd wish us to do it. The diaries will clear your father's name of her mad, fantastic lies."

Tolstoy pleaded with his disciple. "Please. It's not Sonya Andreyevna's fault. The doctor's examined her this week—"

Kholkov was adamant. "Made a scene, didn't she, threw the distinguished doctors out?"

Sasha scowled at the doctor. "You know so much about us, Vladimir Petrovich—more than the tsar's own secret police."

Kholkov held out the papers toward the young woman. "In this will, your father grants you the great honor of being the guardian of his word."

"You're using me."

"But you were involved from the very beginning. You assented."

Tolstoy shivered. "I want to inform my wife and my other children of my wishes—"

Kholkov stiffened. "Leo Nikolayevich! If you wish to turn over your affairs to your wife—then do it. I shall pack tonight and be gone in the morning."

Tolstoy sighed. "Not again, dear friend! You keep threatening to leave."

From the other side of the house, the countess's shriek came through the air. "Guard! Stop them! Stop them!"

Tolstoy ignored the ruckus. "I merely wish to declare myself openly to my family. For that you scold an old man?"

"And I simply want to spare you a wounding open struggle with your loved ones who share none of your thoughts or beliefs. Once it's all in writing—" The doctor waved the papers.

"Christ did not trouble himself in such a way."

Kholkov shrugged. "Christ wasn't an author. If you don't secure the public use of your writings by leaving them to—"

"I want to leave everything to 'the people.' "

"Then you must cease this vacillation. The will names Alexandra Lvovna, the one member of your family you can trust."

Tolstoy wrung his hands. "I'm sorry, dear Vladimir Petrovich, for causing you such pain. You see, I gave Sonya Andreyevna my word, and—"

Kholkov thrust the will at the count. "Here is the will.

Do with it what you like. When you have read it you can inform me of your decision."

Two loud shots sounded out, followed by a chorus of shouts. The countess's voice rose above all others. "Guard! Guard! Arrest those boys. They've shot the gardener. Arrest them! And put out that cigarette. You're not to smoke while you're on duty! Do you hear?"

Kholkov darted around the corner of the building and then returned. "My God, what a fiasco! The guards have arrested the peasants. The countess is coming."

Sasha threw up her hands. "Disaster! Arresting our own people right in front of Father! He'll have a fit."

"Master, put the will away before she sees it!"

As the countess appeared, she saw Kholkov helping the count thrust the will into a pouch around his neck.

"What sort of treachery is this? What is that paper?"

Kholkov stood in front of the count. "Just some details—figures from the Christian publishing venture. Good day, Sonya Andreyevna." The doctor bowed and climbed the steps of the verandah and disappeared into the house.

The count spoke to his wife sharply. "You make a spectacle of yourself, Sonya, shouting so at one and all. And the guards! How could you?"

"It's impossible to live in peace with these people. They lie and steal and destroy property—"

"It's all your own fault, wife—the way you mismanage the estate. If our people were more prosperous, they wouldn't have to steal."

The countess looked at her husband, amazed. "Just now they shot at the gardener, and you blame me?"

"They are only lads trying to find something to eat, and you call the guards, arrest people, throw them in jail."

Sasha shook her head. "All this at the home of a man who preaches nonviolence! It's intolerable."

The countess could not believe these words. "Tomorrow, they will shoot at us, and then they will carry off everything."

Tolstoy waved a finger at his wife. "Under your rule, the bitterness between the estate and the peasants grows and grows. What can I say when these poor people who have been part of our family for years come up and ask me to intercede?"

Countess Sonya threw her hands in the air. "You wave off all responsibility, put everything on my shoulders, and now you ask me to stand aside while your precious peasants rob our family and shoot at our faithful servants."

"Maman, Father cannot live with this intolerable hatred growing daily around him. Seven armed men on the estate! No wonder he wants to run away."

"He ran away long ago and left it all upon me."

"Enough, enough. Wife, daughter, let us go inside."

The countess put out her hands pleadingly. "You all attack me because the serfs rise up? They rise up all over

Russia, they burn estates and crops, they revolt against the tsar, and it's my fault."

Tolstoy started up the verandah steps. "I'll listen no more."

The countess grabbed at his arm. "The photograph! Come back for the photograph."

Tolstoy pulled away. "No more, no more."

"If you don't come back, Leo Nikolayevich, I'll throw myself into the pond."

Stubbornly, Tolstoy began to mount the verandah stairs. Sonya ran toward the pond, shouting, "I'll kill myself."

The count hurried to the door of the house. In despair, the countess threw herself into the pond. The water came up only to her knees. Determined, she pitched forward onto her face, burying her head in the cold muck. Sasha leaped into the water and pulled her mother back to the bank. She held her mother's head in her lap and, with her skirt, wiped her mother's face. Then she supported the countess into the house and up to her bedroom, where she bathed her, got her into dry clothes, and insisted that she rest.

Sonya lay on the bed for an hour. Then she rose and sat, pale and listless, staring out the window. Her old servant brought a light supper, which she nibbled at. The servant offered to prepare her for bed, but she refused, sending the servant away. She remained sitting by the window and soon fell asleep in the chair. After midnight, her old servant arrived with the message that the count was in pain and needed her in his study. She jumped up and declared triumphantly: "You see, he calls out to his wife when he suffers."

"You must remain calm," cautioned the servant.

"I know, I know," she replied. "I shouldn't have gone into hysterics this afternoon. Made a fool of myself, didn't I? Tonight, I'll be the perfect wife—calm and loving." She threw a shawl over her shoulders and rushed from the bedroom.

In the study, Tolstoy lay on his leather couch. The countess sat next to the count, massaging his body. High on the wall, a photograph of the countess gazed down on the room. Next to her photograph, two bare hooks remained as evidence of the removal of the photographs of Sasha and Doctor Kholkov. Every now and then, the countess sprinkled oil on the skin and worked it in. From time to time, the count sighed.

"To the left, now, Sonyusha, just under the rib. Ahh, now higher, higher."

"Your scrawny old man's legs are pitiful to behold." She spoke affectionately. Although the countess still felt the effects of her plunge into the pond, she had recovered enough to minister vigorously to her husband's needs.

"The other side. No, no. Not there. That hurts. The other side."

"Ah, how you accept all my care without notice, as if I were your servant."

"You demand these duties and then complain."

"Just as I predicted: the passionate husband is practically gone. The friendly husband never existed—how could loving kindness be reborn now, in old age?"

"Friendly? When you throw yourself into ponds?"

"You're right," she replied, pinching his thigh.

"Ouch!"

"My plunge was excessive, theatrical. But it did catch your attention."

"The world is laughing at us."

His reply annoyed her; it seemed unnecessarily combative in the face of her generous and lighthearted acceptance of blame. "Why is it, dear husband, that after all the long years of toil at your side, I am left without affection or comfort to face my own later years. You refuse even a simple photograph together to prove to the world that we are married."

"Leave off then if it gives you no joy to take care of an old man."

"Such a mean tone of voice? Such a nasty response?" She waved her finger provocatively, attempting to keep a teasing lilt to her voice. "During the day, you revile me and prepare secret documents, and at night you call me to your room to massage your stomach. And now you shout at me?"

"Sasha! Sasha!"

Sasha appeared immediately at the door. She had been waiting. "Papa?"

"Where has Vladimir Petrovich gone off to?"

"He and I are working in the Remington Room."

"What? He's back again—in the middle of the night?" The countess's determined goodwill fled. She had not forgotten the guilty look on her husband's face that afternoon when she caught his disciple stuffing papers into his wallet. "What sort of mischief are you two up to?"

"I wish to speak with Vladimir Petrovich. Leave off, Sonya Andreyevna. You can go to bed now."

The countess rose. "Dismissed? Like a servant."

Doctor Kholkov appeared in the door.

The countess confronted her enemy, poking her finger toward his face accusingly. "Corrupter! Defiler! Decadent bugger!"

All blood fled from the doctor's face. He stepped backward and fell against the door frame as if he had been mortally wounded.

"What's she saying, Sasha?" cried out the count, his voice hoarse and weak. "What's she saying?"

"Vile, vile things," said Sasha, her face flaming. "Oh Maman, you're delirious."

The countess thrust her face up toward Kholkov's. "You made love to my husband in order to steal my novels," she said in a low, determined voice.

To ward off the countess's attack, Kholkov raised several black notebooks that he had been holding discreetly at his side. He grasped the notebooks in both hands before his chest and slowly pushed the countess away.

"What do you have there?" She pointed at the notebooks.

"They belong to your husband."

The countess put out her hand. "Give them to me!" Her voice quavered.

Kholkov, recovering his strength, straightened and spoke in an authoritative, calm voice. "Count Tolstoy asked me to return them to him personally."

"Am I not his wife? The mistress of this house?"

Tolstoy called out. "Sonya! Let me work in peace."

"Then I don't exist any more, Lyovchka?"

Now, deliberately, Kholkov waved the black notebooks in front of the countess's face. He tapped at them casually with his other hand and fanned the pages, displaying their contents.

"Lyovchka, he's stealing the diaries."

"Of course," said the doctor, grinning maliciously, "Leo Nikolayevich asked me to catalogue their contents."

Tolstoy groaned.

"Those are my husband's private thoughts," said the countess, reaching for them. "He keeps them locked."

"So he does." Kholkov waved the key to Tolstoy's desk through the air in front of the countess.

"You have no right to touch the diaries."

Tolstoy called out, "For the Lord's sake, Sonya, leave us in peace."

"Lyovchka, you promised to keep the diaries locked."

"They have been locked. It's just—Sonyusha—I don't mean—"

"Husband, you are not a man of honor. You favor this man over your family? You love him and let him make love—"

"Please, wife—"

"He's stealing the diaries."

Kholkov bowed. "I steal nothing, madam."

"I appeal to your honor as a gentleman, an officer of the tsar, to turn over my husband's private thoughts this instant."

"My dear Sonya Andreyevna," a look of mock innocent bewilderment came over the doctor's face, "first you accuse me of being a common thief, a decadent bugger, and then you appeal to my honor. Either you are confused, or I haven't heard correctly."

"You are worse than a thief."

"You're terrified, Countess Tolstaya, aren't you, that I'll release your husband's words of agony to the world and expose you for what you are."

The countess clutched her head. "You aim at nothing less than my complete moral destruction—simply in order to get control of all my husband's work." She threw herself down upon her knees at her husband's side. "Lyovchka, my darling!"

As she begged her husband, Kholkov leaned toward her, grimaced and stuck out his tongue, mocking her. Horrified, Sasha ran over and stood between him and her mother as if to protect her mother. "Vladimir Petrovich, stop your taunting. You've both gone mad!"

The countess wept to her husband. "Unless you order your disciple to turn over all your private papers to me for safekeeping, I shall kill myself."

Sasha moved to her mother's side. "Enough of the comedy, Mother! You won't kill yourself; you'll just expose us all to ridicule like you did this afternoon. Another swim in the pond and Father will surely leave."

The countess drew herself up. "I'm ill. The doctors declared it. I'm trying very hard to keep control of my feelings. But this beast who calls himself a doctor—"

"You're determined to make Father's last days miserable."

"He has made me ill with all this secrecy. I saw the document Kholkov was pressing on him this afternoon. And now the diaries."

"Papa, please, order him to give the diaries to Maman."

Tolstoy put out his arms toward his daughter. "Sasha, dear. I have no strength left. You deal with them." He turned toward the wall.

Sasha approached Kholkov. She whispered. "Give the diaries to Maman this instant, Vladimir Petrovich, or I shall revoke my consent to the will."

Kholkov spoke aloud. "As you wish, Alexandra Lvovna. We've copied all the pertinent passages, haven't we?"

"Damn you!" Sasha hissed. "The diaries! Or no will."

Languidly, Kholkov strolled to the kneeling Sonya and placed the diaries in front of her as if on an altar.

He bowed, several times, backing away from Sonya. He picked the will up from Tolstoy's desk, waved it at her, and then took a post at the head of Tolstoy's couch as if he were the old man's guard. Sasha bent over her mother and helped her to rise. Sasha knelt, picked up the diaries, and placed them in her mother's hands. "Now, you alone have possession of the diaries to do as you like. Will you please leave Father in peace?"

The countess muttered. "Tomorrow, they shall be placed in the bank at Tula." She knew very well that the doctor had copied the diaries, and that the document Vladimir Petrovich brandished was most likely the will she feared, but her strength had left her. Her body was wracked with a succession of chills and fever. She wanted only to go to her bed, where she could try to think more clearly. She leaned over her husband's back and kissed him on the top of the head. Then, holding the diaries possessively to her bosom, she left the room, closing the door behind her. Sasha leaned over her father.

"It's all right, Papa. She's gone now."

Tolstoy did not turn. "I can't work now, Vladimir Petrovich. Come again tomorrow."

Kholkov bowed. "I'm sorry to have caused you such distress."

"It wasn't you, dear friend." The count turned toward the doctor.

"Till tomorrow," said the doctor. "Then, dear friend,

we'll settle everything." The doctor bent over the count and kissed each cheek. Tolstoy returned the embrace gratefully. The doctor departed quietly.

When the door had closed, Tolstoy beckoned his daughter. "Pull up a chair, Sashenka, and talk to me."

Sasha went to the desk to get a chair and noticed her mother's photograph prominently displayed there. The terrible scene she had just witnessed had thrust her into a turbulent muddle of emotions. "Her photograph!" she wailed, plaintively. "There, in the place of honor! And ours gone, put away? How could you, Father?"

"She carried on so—it makes no difference."

Sasha knew that for the sake of her father's health, she should try control herself, but she was too exhausted. "I never asked you to have your picture taken with me, never in my life, or bragged about my love. It was not I who put my picture on your wall. It was you. When I saw my image there, in a place of honor in your study—"

"But my feelings for you have not changed."

"And for the whim of an unhappy woman, you take it down and don't dare replace it for fear of her raving."

"I can bear no more." Tolstoy began to weep.

Sasha fell upon her knees next to the leather couch. "Don't weep, Father, don't weep. I am worse than her, much, much worse. Here, here, I kiss your hands. It doesn't matter, not a little bit. Whatever pleases you."

"I was wrong to take down your photograph and dear Vladimir Petrovich's. They're in the top drawer. Replace them this instant. Please. Enough of this catering to a madwoman. Now, now, immediately."

Sasha ran over to the desk and pulled out the photographs which she put up. "All right, all right, there, now, back on the wall, just as they were—Vladimir Petrovich and Sasha, your faithful ones, watching over you. Now, you must try to sleep; it's been an exhausting day. I'll sit here with you." Sasha tucked the cover around her father.

"Cover yourself, daughter, it's cold. But please don't leave me."

"Don't worry, I'll sit here with you." She kissed him on the forehead.

"At night, I am attacked by such horrible imaginings—you have no idea. A terrible secret burden. Poor Vladimir Petrovich badgers me to tell him, and I can't bring myself to speak. I haven't even written of it in my diary."

"You don't have to tell me."

"But I want to tell you, dear Sashenka, only you, and no one else."

"Not a word to anyone."

With his eyes staring fearfully about the room, the count recounted his tale. "It began more than thirty years ago—there had already been so many deaths—my brother Nicholas, Sonya's father, cousin Elizabeth—and more to come. I had just finished *War and Peace*, and in my exhaustion and exuberance and joy, I began to think that I might suddenly be stabbed in the back and everything I loved would be gone—just like that, at the height of my career.

Stabbed in the back! By some vagrant, for no reason! Imagine such a fear. A ridiculous fantasy, no?" Tolstoy rose up as if to get off the couch, but Sasha prevailed upon him to remain lying down. He put his hands over his eyes. "At that crazy moment of fear, I came across the notice of an extremely attractive estate for sale in the Penza Gubernia, and so I set off by train to Moscow and then to Nizhny-Novgorod, and then farther by coach. You know me, action before everything."

"An estate sale? How bizarre!"

"You're too reasonable to understand such madness. I said to myself, 'How could a man about to buy a great estate and double or triple his holdings be endangered? The Lord would not allow some stranger to strike a man dead if he were launched on such serious business.' " The count began to laugh and, uneasily, Sasha joined in. "You see why I hesitate to tell you my tales—you have to be crazy yourself to understand." Now the count rose in spite of his daughter's protests. With his blanket wrapped around him, he began to pace. "In the coach, I was full of the most heady calculations of profit and wealth, but as darkness fell, I became aware of the strange shape of the unfamiliar countryside—the ragged trees, the ominous rivers, the distant hills—five hundred miles away from everything I knew and loved.

"Longing for a cheery fire and some companionship, I bade the coachman stop at the next town, Arzamas. But it was very late when we arrived, and no one was about except the innkeeper.

"I slept only an hour or so before something awoke me—a chill of some sort—-a presence. The candles had gone out. I lighted one and looked around." The count paused and looked around the dark room as if he had been transported back to that provincial inn. "I was struck that the room was perfectly square and that all the doors and the woodwork were painted a dark red, the color of dried blood. 'Where am I?' I asked myself. 'Where am I going? What am I running away from?' With every question my terror grew."

Tolstoy stopped and stood looking out at the shuttered window as if he could see a great distance. "I paced, smoked, prayed to God, and my terror only grew stronger. 'What do I fear?' I asked myself."

He moved to the mirror and gazed into it. As he talked, he pulled the blanket around his head as if it were a cowl. "And then there, in that square room, I distinctly heard a voice reply: 'You fear me. My name is Death. I am here.'"

The count turned and stared directly into Sasha's eyes. "My whole being ached with the need to live, the right to live, and at that same moment, Death gnawed at my being, Death's voice echoed in my ear. The squareness of the room terrified me: I was trapped in an odd, square coffin. I was in agony, but I felt dry and cold and mean. There was not one drop of goodness in me. Only a hard, calm anger against myself and at the Being who had created me—an anger against . . . against God."

The count stumbled across the room and collapsed back onto the couch again, his head in his hands. Sasha arranged his bedclothes, put his limbs into a comfortable position, and began to massage his brow. She spoke softly, gently. "But so much has happened since then." Her voice trembled. She could not believe she had heard such words from her noble and powerful father. "You have lived such a full life, created, loved, prayed, and loved God—"

"The horror of Arzamas has remained, Sasha, here," he pounded his chest, "lurking, waiting—and the deaths have multiplied: brothers, aunts, three children, three and finally, Vanichka, our hope."

"And your anger against God?"

Tolstoy dropped his head. "That has remained. And God's anger against me."

"But your philosophy, your religion, all that you have taught us—"

"No more confessions tonight, daughter. I must sleep." The count shut his eyes and instantly fell fast asleep. Sasha stared down at him, stunned by his revelation. She put her hands together and began to pray to God, then she stopped, confused. Stealthily, she removed her mother's photograph from the wall and put it away in the desk. Then she took up a folded blanket from a chest in the corner and sank down in the chair next to the bed, covering

herself. "Is there no true belief?" she murmured. She put
out the lamp and in a minute was snoring.

A few minutes later, the door opened and the countess entered the room, carrying a candle. She wore her
nightdress, her hair braided for sleep. She spoke to herself.
"What a nightmare! There is a will, I know it. Or something worse. A denunciation dictated by our enemies.
Oh, what a terrible dream!" Seeing her daughter by the
couch, she stopped. The blanket had slipped off the young
woman. "Sasha, asleep here? She'll catch cold." She drew
the blanket up over Sasha and tucked it around her. She
bent and kissed Sasha's forehead. Then she began to go
through Tolstoy's desk, searching for the will. In the top
drawer, she discovered her photograph. "My picture here?"

She lifted the candle to the wall. "Kholkov's picture in
the place of honor. Horrors!" She reached into the drawer
and pulled out the revolver. First, she aimed it at her own
forehead, then at Tolstoy, and then at the photograph of
Kholkov. She pulled the trigger. A shot rang out as the
revolver jumped in her hand.

Tolstoy and Sasha started up.

"An attack!" shouted the count. "An attack! Call out the
guards!"

"What is it? Papa! What happened? Maman! Where
did you find that gun?" Sasha rushed to her mother and
wrested the gun from her. The countess tore Kholkov's
shattered photo from the wall. In spite of the broken glass,
she attempted to rip out the photograph, shouting, "Peder-

ast! Traitor! I'll tear you and burn you and exorcise you for good from this house."

"Oh my God!" cried the count. He fainted.

The countess rushed to the bed and knelt. "Lyovchka! Lyovchka! Have you replaced your wife with interlopers? Destroy the will, I beg of you. End these secrets."

"Mother! You'll kill him! Come away this minute."

The countess would not budge. "Extinguish your hatred of me, Lyovchka, your wife. At thirty-five, you, an experienced libertine, married a pure, unblemished seventeen-year-old child. In the carriage after the wedding, before we had yet arrived at the first post station, you tried to force yourself on me—"

Sasha bent over her father. "Look what you've done! He's dying."

The countess lost her voice. She stared at her daughter, her mouth open. She leaned over and listened to her husband's heart. She touched his lips with hers. Then she raised her hands in prayer. "Oh Lord! Please, not this time. Save him and I will be good and not bother him again. Please, God!"

"A wet cloth, please, Mother."

The countess ran to the nightstand and returned with a wet cloth.

"It's all right, he's resting quietly, at last. But you torture him, Maman, and torture him—"

Sasha sank back on the chair, exhausted. The countess

knelt next to her. "Forgive me, daughter. I have wronged him and I wrong you."

"What do you want?"

"Never in my life, even in my youth, have I experienced such jealousy. How can your father give all of his love to this Kholkov?"

"Enough, enough."

"I've begun to dream of them together—the two of them wrapping their arms and legs around—"

"Nastiness!"

"You saw them embracing that day—kneeling on the floor together—'hijinks,' they called it."

"Must you remember every absurd event in this household? It's your twisted imagination that tortures you, Mother."

"And who sits by his bedside when he's ill? Hour upon hour into the night? Who knits his caps and sweaters and makes pillows for his head? And his food—those infernal vegetables and soups and medicines. Who? Who? Who?"

Sasha stroked her mother's head. "Poor, dear, troubled Mother. I am so ashamed of my bitterness."

The countess looked up at her daughter and seized her by the shoulders. "Tell me, Sasha, do you ever tell lies?"

"I try not to."

"Truthfully now. Is there a will?"

Sasha hesitated. She drew in a deep breath. "I consider it monstrous to speak of wills, as if he were about to die."

The countess stared into her daughter's eyes. "It's unlike you to play the hypocrite in this manner."

"Such bare self-interest is unbecoming in a countess."

"Money? Bah! I don't care for material goods. Your father has deprived me of his affection and his confidence. Pain, I know the pain of rejection, here in my belly, in the joints of my fingers and knees and toes— pain, pain, pain."

"If you love Father so much, you would quietly submit to his wishes."

"Then there is a will."

"You must part with Father now, as the doctors advised, or you both will become truly ill. If you don't, he'll run away."

"If he does, I'll print a death letter in the papers about all that he has done to me, how he has used me, and committed filthy acts with his handsome young disciple, and then I'll poison myself and disgrace him all over Russia, all over the world."

"No one would believe the word of Tolstoy's wife over the word of Tolstoy himself. Now, come up to your room. You must sleep, too." Sasha helped her mother up and moved her toward the door. "You are as frail as Papa these days."

As she went, the countess declared, "Without Tolstoy's wife there would be no Tolstoy."

As soon as the door closed, Tolstoy, who had been feigning sleep, rose and began to dress.

When Sasha returned she found him fully clothed,

with his overcoat laid out on the bed and boots standing alongside. "Father, have you gone mad, too? Dressed at this time of night?"

"At last. I have reached sanity. Tonight. I will be free. I am leaving this house. Please sit down and copy this letter to your mother."

"But Father, perhaps—"

"Sit!"

Sasha sat and took up her dictation pad. Tolstoy paced around the room dictating: "My dearest wife, my position in my own house has become unbearable. I can no longer live in these conditions of luxury, and I am doing what old men of my age commonly do: leaving the worldly life to spend my last days in peace and solitude. Do not follow. Your coming to me would only hurt your position and my own and would not alter my decision. I thank you for your faithful years of life with me and beg you to forgive me for any wrong I have done you, as I forgive you with all my soul for any wrong you may have done me. Farewell. Put your faith and trust in God."

Two weeks later at the Astopovo railroad station, the count lay deathly sick in the poor apartment of the stationmaster. A small coal fire burned in a tiny stove, barely heating the room. Sasha sat next to her father, who spoke in a small, hoarse voice. "How am I, Sasha?" He coughed.

"Not good. I should never have left your side. The

minute I turned away to minister to Maman, you slipped off on that accursed bicycle, through mud and snow. How absurd of you to think that contraption could last more than a few minutes. You could at least have taken a horse, or a buggy. Thank God we found you, walking, wet and shivering like a beggar on the road, so far from anywhere, and carried you to safety."

"At least we're together."

"In a godforsaken railroad station, miles from home. What a foolish flight!"

"Tell your sisters and brothers that I would have called for them—but that would have hurt Maman."

"She'll be furious when she finds Doctor Kholkov here."

"Well, he has devoted his life to our cause—and he is a doctor."

"Enough, Papa, you must rest."

Tolstoy slept. Almost immediately, he began to mutter. "Run, run, away—as fast as we can. They're after us." He woke with a start. "Sasha! Write this!" Sasha took up her pad. "God alone exists truly. Man is his expression in matter, time, and space. God is not love, but the more love there is in the world, the more man expresses God, and the more truly man exists." Immediately, he fell into an exhausted sleep. A new fit of coughing woke him.

"Do you feel bad, Papa?"

"And Maman, how is Maman? I've injured her . . . Why do you not answer?"

Sasha, overwhelmed, ran from the room and out

onto the porch. Before her stretched a bleak scene: a tiny, provincial station already powdered with the early snow of winter, several passenger cars and freight cars pulled off into sidings, tracks stretching off across a broad, empty white plain. A host of news reporters and photographers and sightseers huddled around the station house, gazing across the tracks at the apartment. Doctor Kholkov emerged from the station and walked across the tracks to the stationmaster's house. He climbed onto the porch.

"Still in his right senses?"

"So weak! Barely able to talk."

"You must keep your mother from him."

"It's unnatural."

The doctor nodded across the tracks to the several passenger cars on the far siding. "To think that she's chased him here in a private train."

"He keeps asking about her."

"In terror, lest she pounce."

"She's nursed him in every illness."

"What a joyous reunion he and I had!"

"He fears that he has wronged her with his flight. He's an old man who doesn't know what to think."

"How we wept together and gazed at one another for such a long time! My coming calmed him immensely, I think."

"I don't know what to do about Mother."

"Yesterday, he said definitively that a meeting with your mother would be fatal."

"He said that? Or did you prompt him?"

"I'll show you the note."

"Look, look at that crowd of reporters and cameramen, waiting, like vultures."

"From all over the world. I must go over and continue my talk with them. Your father commanded that we give a statement."

"You just do what you want, Vladimir Petrovich, and then you declare that Father commanded it. I don't believe a word."

"Think what you like. I have the notes to prove everything."

"Damn your notes! You make them up."

"You won't damn them when your mother challenges his will."

"Don't you dare talk of his death."

"She will stand condemned in the court of the world."

"I don't want to prosecute my mother. I simply want to protect my father, to save his life."

"Remain strong, or your father and his works will be lost!"

"What a burden! Me, the sole heir! My brothers will feel betrayed."

"He's put his trust in you." The doctor moved to embrace Sasha, but she pulled away. He shrugged, skipped down the porch stairs, and went running over the rail lines to the station.

Sasha reentered the stationmaster's apartment.

After the count's flight from Yasnaya Polyana, the countess had become calm and reasonable. She worried only about her husband's health. When she heard of his illness at the Astopovo Station, she commandeered an entire train, carrying with her as many of her children as she could gather. Once they arrived, the older Tolstoy siblings pretended that they were astounded that Sasha insisted on keeping her mother from her father's side, claiming that the doctors forbade her presence. Secretly, they agreed that their mother might well do their father more harm than good. They attempted to keep her occupied until their father's health improved. She argued against them. She claimed that it was all a plot by Doctor Kholkov, and that only she could care properly for her husband.

Toward evening, she escaped her children's solicitude. In a heavy fur coat, stealthily she stepped down from the passenger car of her private train. She moved across the tracks toward the stationmaster's apartment. She carried a small, embroidered pillow. She mounted the apartment's porch steps and knocked boldly upon the door. The shades of the window were drawn aside slightly, and Sasha peered out. The countess waited a moment and knocked again. Only when she knocked a third time did the door open and Sasha step out, closing the door behind her. She remained before the door, blocking her mother's entrance.

"How is he, Sashenka?"

"Holding his own."

"Well, aren't you going to kiss me?"

Sasha leaned over and gave her mother a peremptory kiss on the forehead.

"He needs my care, daughter."

"He has the best doctors in all of Russia."

"They know nothing of what he needs. Let me in."

The countess reached for the door handle, but her daughter restrained her. "The doctors forbid it."

"You mean Doctor Kholkov forbids it."

"You know a scene would be fatal to him. For the moment, he doesn't want to see you."

"Not see his wife? But he sees that man, and you. Step aside, daughter! I don't want to wrestle with you in front of the whole world."

"The doctors feel that normal activities will keep him wanting to live."

"Has he remembered me?"

"He's deathly afraid that you will create a scene."

"Then he speaks of me with hatred?"

"With kindness and pity, rather."

"He should have thought of that before he ran off."

"He wants to die with dignity, simply, like an ordinary common man."

The countess laughed. "You call this simplicity? Six doctors, dozens of his fanatical followers, the entire station under siege by reporters from around the world, summoned by his command. An ordinary man can manage to die in his wife's arms, surrounded by his children and grandchildren. But not your father: he wants the entire world on his doorstep."

"Father did not choose to have all this fuss. If you had let him go away quietly years ago—"

"He had his feet and legs; he even had horses and carriages. In truth, he never wanted to leave me—no matter how much he threatened. He needed my care—my love— my body."

"He stayed because he was afraid that you would go mad if he left. I have to go back in."

"I've come all this way to be with my sick husband, and my own daughter bars the door."

"Not with pleasure. I've been instructed—"

"Let me in!"

Once more, the countess tried to thrust her way through the door, but Sasha barred the way, holding onto the door frame. "Don't make a spectacle, Mother."

"You would fight against your own mother? In front of reporters?"

"Whatever it takes to keep you from killing him."

The countess lost her vigor. Her shoulders sagged. She seemed to shrink. "Then my enemies have won." She turned away from her daughter.

Sasha wailed. "Sooner or later everything falls on my shoulders, on my head. Why?"

"Because you seek it. You brothers and sisters won't forgive you."

"I'll take the consequences," said Sasha, opening the door to go in. The countess turned back and handed her the small pillow she had carried from her train.

"At least give him his favorite pillow."

"I promise."

"You realize that along these very tracks, Anna Karenina took her life. 'Forgive me everything, God!' she said."

"In a novel."

"God, forgive us all!"

Sasha entered the stationmaster's apartment and shut the door. The countess walked along the porch to the window through which she could see into the room where her husband lay. She remained peering in.

Inside, the count spoke to his daughter. "Have you seen your mother?"

"She sent your favorite pillow." Sasha placed the pillow behind her father's head.

He sighed. "Is she eating?"

"She looks in good health."

"What about the muzhiks? How do the muzhiks die?"

"Like you, Papa, like all men."

"'Seek! Keep seeking! I am very tired. Do not torment me anymore."

"Rest, Papa, rest."

"Much has fallen on dear Sonya," he murmured as Sasha arranged the pillows and the bedcovers. "I advise you to remember that there are many people on earth beside Leo Nikolayevich, and you are all taking care of only him."

"Rest, please."

"Ah, what a bother! Let me go away somewhere . . . where nobody can find me . . . Leave me alone! Clear out! Clear out! I can hardly breathe."

"Papa."

"So this is the end! And it's nothing . . . The truth . . . I care a great deal . . . How they . . ." The count started up, emitted a strange rattling sound from deep within him, and then fell back, dead. Sasha cried out and laid her head on her father's breast.

"Dear Papa." She lay there for some time. Then she whispered into his ear, "At the end, did you believe?"

Slowly, she rose and went to the door. Opening it, she stood gazing up into the sky, wringing her hands. When the countess saw her daughter, she knew her husband had died. She slumped and would have fallen had she not supported herself against the building. She struggled toward her daughter. "Sasha? What is it Sasha? Is he . . . can I . . . ?"

When Sasha didn't answer her, Countess Sonya rushed in through the door. She knelt by her husband's side. "Forgive me, Lyovchka, forgive me." She took her husband's hand and then, alarmed, leaned over him, listening. "Lyovchka! Lyovchka! OOOOOooooooooooo!" She wailed the cry of mourning. After a few moments, she recovered. She closed her husband's eyes, straightened his bedclothes, and positioned his hands upon his breast. Sasha entered. She picked up a chair and carried it to her mother, helping her to sit upon it. Sasha gazed down at her father, then she slipped to her knees at her mother's side, sobbing.

Countess Sonya stroked her daughter's head and spoke gently. "I asked his forgiveness. He may have heard. No, no, you kept me away so long. It was too late . . . he did not reply."

"You should have been here with him."

"What cruelty!"

"Forgive me, Mother. I've committed a terrible sin."

"He knows the feel of my hands. I could have comforted him . . . Oh Lyovchka, my love, who has betrayed us?"

"I have. The fault is mine."

"Nonsense. That is your pride talking."

Kholkov entered, bent over to examine Tolstoy professionally, and then fell to his knees at the head of the bed, sobbing. "Master! Master!"

The countess leaned over and patted the doctor's shoulder. "He loved you dearly, Vladimir Petrovich."

Kholkov turned, thinking it was Sasha who had comforted him. "What shall I do, Alexandra Lvovna?"

"Damn you, damn you," muttered Sasha.

Kholkov regarded her with surprise. "What shall I do?"

The countess spoke firmly. "You'll carry on his preaching."

"But he'll write no more, speak no more."

The countess smiled. "Oh, he's written and spoken more than enough to fill several of your lifetimes."

Sasha waved a fist at the doctor. "No more secrets. No more spying and taking notes."

Kholkov rose slowly and began to pace, sobbing now and then into his handkerchief and returning to the bed to gaze down upon Tolstoy. "Oh, oh, I'm so unhappy."

The countess shook her head. "But you don't really know why, do you?"

"What?"

The countess spoke in a firm voice. "Your master was bound to die. We all do. But how do the three of us live out our lives, Vladimir Petrovich? We who have devoted ourselves to serving that man, our god. Now he is gone. What is left?"

Sasha hugged her mother. "Leave all that behind, Mother."

"Each of us, we ask ourselves: And I? Have I no importance?"

"Must you talk like this, here?"

"Here, above all, and now. Once we leave this place, there will be nothing to bring us together again—except our memories. And certain questions we'll ask ourselves for the rest of our lives: Do not I deserve some recognition? A role in life independent of that master whom I have served so loyally?"

"Maman, there's no need—"

"And so we will dress ourselves up in our finery, and strut about, and carry on, basking in his reflected light, all the while knowing in our heart of hearts, that we are simply ordinary human beings who serve and serve and serve, while he—he—"

"Mother, you mustn't grow too emotional. It's bad for your heart."

"My heart is perfectly strong."

The doctor stood before the countess like a chastened schoolboy, his proud head hanging now abjectly. "I cannot bear to think of what you just said, Sonya Andreyevna."

"Introspection was never your strong point, Vladimir Petrovich."

The doctor turned to Sasha. "And you, Alexandra Lvovna, will I have the honor of your aid—"

"I never want to see you again, Doctor Kholkov. You have accomplished all that you sought."

"But I thought that perhaps you would want to help—"

"Now that Papa is dead, you have no more need for me."

"But—"

"I'm not very interested in literature, doctor, or religious thought. Since my father no longer needs me, I'll return to my horses and my dogs."

The doctor put out both his hands, pleading with the young woman. "Oh, my. I never thought—Alexandra Lvovna, there is still time for us to—"

"I can't stand the sight of you, Doctor Kholkov."

"And what shall I do, now that he is gone?"

The countess gestured to the door. "You could inform the rest of the family, and the world."

Kholkov struck his forehead. "Oh, my God, the world is waiting to hear the news."

The countess spoke out in a clear voice. "And you, Doctor Vladimir Petrovich Kholkov, are Tolstoy's spokesman."

It was as if the countess had bestowed a medal of merit upon her husband's disciple. He came to attention and saluted her and her daughter. "Well, then, I'll take my leave for a moment, ladies."

Kholkov, his energy returned, darted out the door and moved with long, military strides toward the station and the waiting crowd.

The countess leaned over her daughter. "So, my shrewd muzhik, you're done with this man?"

"Not so shrewd, Maman. I feel as if I had just been thrown from a runaway horse."

The countess put her arms around her daughter and comforted her. "The pain will keep you from getting lonely."

"And you, Maman? You sound so calm."

"What could move me now?"

"It's strange, almost as if Papa's death instantly brought back your sanity."

"I have nothing more to fear."

Sasha took her mother's hand and stroked it gently. They remained silent for some time. Finally, Sasha asked, "Are you thinking of Father?"

"What else has ever been in my mind? It torments me that I didn't get along with him better."

"It's done now."

"Just remember, Sasha, I wanted only to be Tolstoy's wife."

Lenin and Martov, 1897

The Sphinx
of Kiev

INTRODUCTION

Where I grew up in Lithuania, my gang of bright Jewish
friends always hung out with the Russian kids. They were
the children of the petty bureaucrats who ruled the land
after the partition of Greater Poland and Lithuania among
the Germans, the Austrians, and the Russians. The brightest among us read Marx and Engels and Kropotkin and
Herzen. We considered ourselves revolutionaries of one
sort or another. We read Gogol, too, and Chernychevski,
and were just beginning to read Dostoevsky and Tolstoy
when I set out for America. Most of my friends revered the
Narodnaya Volya, the People's Will, and they were always
trooping off to live with the peasants in imitation of their
heroes. I went with them a few times, but our presence
always seemed to make the peasant families uncomfortable and I soon dropped out.

Two of my closest buddies, Katya Platonova and

Nacham Kurianski, labeled themselves Nihilists. They
talked of the necessity of annihilating everything, including themselves, and starting out all over again. I could
never understand how anything can start from nothing,
and we argued over this day and night. Somehow, Katya
and Nacham figured they would rise from their own
ashes and be there for the New Beginning. They both
died young in an ill-fated assassination attempt. I decided
to seek my New Beginning in America, where I peddled
textiles through the great forests and small villages of
northern Michigan. I invested wisely in the enterprises of
the robber barons who crisscrossed America with railroad
tracks, built steel mills, and dug coal mines. With my
modest savings, I managed to bring every last soul of my
family from Kovno and Pren and Keidani and Baltromans
to the inglorious but prosperous streets of Detroit. Having accomplished all I set out to do in the New World, I
returned to the Old World, which I had missed mightily.
I cannot reveal why I returned, but one day in my travels
I found myself in the beautiful, clean, and properly admin-
istered little city of Geneva on the shores of Lac Leman.

As I was not traveling first class, I found it convenient
to lodge in one of the poorer sections of the city, among
Russian political émigrés. To my delight, in this squalid
neighborhood I discovered some of my boyhood chums,
grown up now into men and women, full-fledged recognized revolutionaries, with police records and time spent
in jail. Some even proudly sported frostbite scars and miss-

ing fingers and toes from years spent in Siberian forests working off their hot-headed political crimes. What bliss it was to find myself among wild-eyed, generous-hearted, and politically entranced Russians and Jews again, screaming their bloody heads off night and day, pounding tables, swilling strong tea, swigging vodka, and threatening and embracing one another at almost the same moment.

Several days after my arrival, I was having tea at a table at the entrance of my hotel—more a hovel than a hotel— when a young giant in disreputable clothing appeared and questioned the waiter in impeccable French about the address of Nikolai Ulyanov, known as Lenin. The waiter, a rather doltish, good-natured Russian, stared in astonishment at the young man, looked around suspiciously, turned his back, and entered the hotel. I suspected that he didn't know French, although I'd wager he understood the name Lenin judging by his ashen-faced recoil at its mention.

The giant approached my table and continued in French to ask after Lenin. I knew of Lenin from his writing and the history of his revolutionary polemics, but had not yet met him, nor did I know where he lived in Geneva. I said as much and asked why he sought Lenin. "I can't say," he replied with a great sigh, gazing at me wearily with intelligent clear blue eyes. "I've been asking all over this town and no one will answer, although I suspect they know." He looked as if he were about to fall into a dead faint. In spite of his soiled and ragged old coat, galoshes

tied together with twine, and absurd torn hat, I found
the young giant very attractive. Golden curls framed a
well-shaped head with high cheekbones and a square,
determined chin. In spite of his fatigue, he held himself
straight, poised on the balls of his feet. His wide shoulders
and slim waist suggested an athlete.

"Sit down," I said in Russian, "and have some tea with
me. You look as if you've walked all the way from Russia."
He regarded me warily and cast a yearning eye at the
pitcher of tea and the plate of biscuits on the table. I tilted
the chair next to me invitingly. "Please, I'm harmless. A
stranger in town myself—born in Pren, outside of Kovno,
and a world traveler. After you refresh yourself a bit, I can
ask my friends here how to find your man. You're in no
condition to meet anyone now."

"It's essential that I see the starets as soon as possible."

I was struck by his use of that term *starets*: the head
man of a village, the boss. I assured him that a few minutes, a biscuit, a cup of tea, and a glass of vodka would not
delay the Revolution. He laughed at that and crumpled
into a chair. I called out for the waiter, who immediately
shambled out of the hotel. I suspected that he had been
lurking just inside the door watching us. I ordered a full
breakfast for the youngster and a bottle of vodka. The
boy raised his hand and confessed that he had only a few
kopeks left from his journey. I replied that nothing could
please me more than to aid an exhausted, starving young
Russian in his quest for a better world.

He stared at me quizzically and then accepted my hospitality. "You seem to understand."

"Understanding is perhaps my only talent."

After ravenously devouring a plate of creamed herring and a loaf of brown bread with cheese and downing several glasses of vodka along with a pitcher of tea, he began to talk freely as only a young Russian boy full of ideals can talk. Yes, yes, he had come to worship at the feet of the great Lenin, who was the only man who could lead a true revolution in Mother Russia. He spoke of the Revolution as if it had a capital letter—an ideal full of justice and beauty. "I got fed up with the compromisers, the 'softs,' and joined Lenin's 'hards.' " He spoke excellent Russian, just as he initially had addressed me in flawless French. He was obviously wellborn and highly educated. He told me of his student years, during which he imbibed revolutionary ideas from reading Feuerbach, Fourier, Herzen, Kropotkin, and Chernychevski. He revered the Narodniks, youthful worshippers of peasants and laborers. Out of shame for the good fortune of his birth, he went to work in the factories of his town, where he was recruited by a faction of the "hard" revolutionaries, who followed the leadership of Lenin. "I have been a worker, and I understand Russia's need." He held out his calloused hands to demonstrate his credibility and revealed his revolutionary name, Kolossov.

I excused myself and went into the hotel, where I cornered the manager, demanding to know Lenin's address.

As I had already tipped everyone liberally to procure a minimum of accommodation and now held out a further inducement, the manager provided me with Lenin's address and directions, but begged me not to reveal my source. He seemed to fear Lenin and would not even say Lenin's name directly. Outside, the young man embraced me with great emotion and promised that he would repay me in every way once he had accomplished his mission, settled in, and received some money from home.

This accidental meeting was the beginning of an interest I took in this crucial moment in the history of the Russian Revolution. The tale of Kolossov's love affair and eventual disillusion with Lenin revealed to me the way "personal matters" shape the works of humankind. When historians talk about the evolution of the Soviet government in the twentieth century, they hearken back to the underlying causes of unrest in tsarist Russia. They talk of geographical, economic, and social factors. They even argue that the imperial nation's character and the basic organization of its bureaucracy hardly changed under the rule of Soviet socialism, although the personnel certainly were of a different stamp. While this may be true, it is all too complex for a simple, straightforward mentality like mine, which can only encompass individuals. In my mind, Lenin's character was paramount in shaping the infernal destiny of that vast nation. Between 1903 and 1905, the years of this tale, the personal quirks of this lone man—his weaknesses and his strengths—began to alter the course

of the Russian Revolution and subsequent Soviet history.
Lenin's major tool for seizing power was his "hard" political faction of the Russian Social Democratic Worker's
Party. Due to a temporary victory at the Second Congress
of that party, that faction became known as the majority,
Bolshevik in Russian. The Bolshevik Party was shaped
entirely by Lenin's harsh and inflexible character. It came
into being first in 1903, precisely when Kolossov and I first
met in Geneva. Lenin was in the midst of preparation for
the Second Congress. Although for some years the Bolshevik Party was but a small portion of the movement and
had no formal standing, Lenin's party altered the debate
and grew like an ulcer within the revolutionary forces.
My account comes to a close when Lenin was thirty-five,
at the beginning of the first Russian Revolution—a revolution not very well known outside of scholarly circles. The
Revolution of 1905 was a revolution in the full sense of the
word. "The people" took to the streets; barricades were
thrown up; shots were fired; and the tsar yielded significant powers to a Constituent Assembly. These events were
the first important steps toward what was to become the
continuing Revolution of the Russian Empire—a revolution that apparently will persist beyond the end of the
century. I leave it for you to puzzle out why the story ends
where it ends.

In my opinion, Kolossov's story, as small and personal
as it was, cast a penetrating light on Lenin's character
and provided me with an entry into the complex conflicts

within the revolutionary forces that eventually shaped Russia's future. In the years leading to the Revolution of 1917 and even later in Paris, Berlin, and London, I kept in touch with Kolossov and with colleagues of Martov, whom I greatly respected. From these sources, I learned the details of the personal relationships that played such an important part in the history of that time—especially the conflict between Lenin and Martov. Oh, I might add, that long after those two complex and interesting men broke up their friendship, their love for one another continued. In fact, it is reported that on his very death bed, Lenin managed to cough up these words, "Alas, they say that poor Martov is dying too."

Geneva, June 3, 1903

Kolossov strode through the streets of Geneva, his spirits revived by the kindness of the old Lithuanian Jew. He had not met much civility on this, his first voyage to a foreign land. Often, on the long, difficult journey from Kiev, he had been tempted to abandon his quest for the legendary Lenin. The inhabitants of this tiny land in the midst of mountains and lakes were a cold, suspicious lot and appeared to hate Russians—even one who spoke better French than they. At least in Russia, Kolossov had been accepted by his fellow workers and was able to participate in their struggle against the tsarist regime. When he mentioned Lenin to the Russian émigrés of Geneva, they turned their back on him. But he had been entrusted with important documents for Lenin, and he was a man of his word. What luck, he thought, this morning to have met a world traveler familiar with the revolutionary classics, a man who understood his quest for a just world and spoke excellent French and classic Russian.

The young man began to whistle happily in appreciation now for the consummate craft that had fashioned the buildings and gardens of this immaculate city. His whistle trailed off when he made a turn into a poor warren of streets where he would find the leader of his cause. By the time he located the sorry structure in which Lenin lodged, his optimism and courage had fled. The apartments in the building that appeared to be his destination were not numbered. He trembled as he timidly raised his fist to knock on the ground-floor door. There was no response. He knocked again, a little harder. Finally, exasperated, he slammed his fist against the door so fiercely that the wall shook. A woman's voice called out in French from behind the door, "Who knocks?"

"Is this Number 37, madame?"

"*Madame*? There are no *madames* here."

"I'm seeking Lenin, Nikolai Ulyanov."

There was no response. Kolossov pounded furiously on the door. He heard a chain rattling and then the door was opened a crack. A bony, sallow woman peered out at him. "State your business," she said in Russian.

"I'm from Kiev and I must talk to the starets."

"Is that all you have to say?"

"What else should I . . ." Kolossov pounded his forehead with the palm of his hand. "Oh yes, the password: 'To the streets when it is time.' "

A gleaming smile appeared on the woman's face. She slammed the door with great force and opened it almost immediately having released the chain. She leaped at the young man, who hadn't time to retreat. She seized his arm and with great strength dragged him into a small, bare room, where a bald man knelt in the corner oiling a bicycle that hung from the ceiling. Kolossov was immediately impressed by the delicacy and reverence with which the man handled the vehicle.

"He's come, at last," announced the woman.

The man continued his task without looking around.

"Starets?" questioned the young man.

The man did not cease his oiling and wiping, making sure that every drip from the oil can landed in a cookie tin on the floor below the bicycle.

The woman nudged the young man: "Go ahead, say it again."

"Say what?"

"The password."

" 'To the streets when it is time.' "

"Ah!" exclaimed the bicycle oiler, rising. Kolossov started back in surprise; the man was very short, almost a dwarf. The man grabbed at the young man's coat, pulling it open. Kolossov tugged back, ashamed at showing his disreputable trousers, but the man prevailed. He tore open the lining, from which he extracted an envelope. He held the envelope in the air triumphantly.

"Here, here, give it, give it," shouted the woman gleefully. She took the envelope and extracted several blank sheets. Carefully, she sprinkled the sheets with powder and held them over the stove, watching the letters slowly appear. She carried the sheets to the desk, where she opened a drawer, slid back a hidden panel, and extracted a thin black book. Laboriously, she set about to decode the message.

Undoubtedly, the woman was Krupskaya, Lenin's wife, thought Kolossov disconsolately, and the small, bald man in the immaculate worn suit and vest, his collar and cuffs frayed, was Lenin, the starets of his revolutionary faction, the "hards." As Kolossov tried to tuck the torn lining back into the coat's armpit, he became aware of Lenin's intense examination of him from head to foot, as if he were some sort of exotic foreign object.

Krupskaya stood and handed Lenin the letter. "Terrible news! Your family—"

"Remove his coat!" Lenin commanded, taking the decoded letter and beginning to read it.

Krupskaya took hold of Kolossov's coat and tried to tug it off, but Kolossov pulled away from her, tearing one of the shoulders. "I'm still cold," he explained.

"Nonsense, you're sweating."

Without looking up from the letter, Lenin called out, "Off with the coat, and those galoshes, too!"

"No one wears galoshes here in Geneva," explained Krupskaya. "They make you conspicuous."

"Is that really Starets, the 'Old Man'?" asked Kolossov, in a whisper.

"None other. Why do you ask?"

"They said I was to report to the Old Man, but—but I always thought that somehow he'd be . . ."

"He'd be what?"

"I don't know, taller, bigger. I mean, we're speaking of Lenin!"

"You'll find him plenty big."

While Lenin read, Kolossov wandered around at the couple's rented room, bare of any ornament. Everything was arranged severely and functionally against the walls: a desk, chairs, two drop-leaf benches. The furniture looked as if it had been obtained at an industrial salvage yard. The most prominent feature of the room was the gleaming bicycle. A wood stove used for cooking and heat stood in the middle of the room. On a raised sleeping loft stood the narrow bed, a nightstand with a bowl and pitcher for washing, a chamber pot under the bed, and a battered bureau. A framed photograph of a young man in a school uniform rested on top of the bureau.

As Lenin read, he murmured, his voice without emotion. "My sister taken, my brothers exiled."

"It's a tragedy!" said Krupskaya.

"Nothing lost. The authorities begin to fear us."

"But your sister, Volodya—"

"No one crucial was taken."

"—your brothers? What will your mama do?" Krupskaya clasped her hands to her breast.

"Put down a reminder to send Mama as much money as we can spare—she will have to prepare packages for them: books and writing materials. At least we'll get first-hand news now of the exiles in Siberia. And buy that suitcase today."

Krupskaya wrote in her pad. "I'll buy the suitcase," she replied to her husband, "if the price is right."

"Buy it!"

"Those centimes we save will go to your mother now."

"And a large supply of medicine for Ilya's gout—a year's maybe, if it will keep. Have the pharmacist bill us—bully him—we've always paid promptly in the past."

Kolossov gawked. Here was the Old Man in a bitter struggle with his wife over the price of a suitcase. He had never met up with such queer creatures before.

Lenin interrupted the visitor's reverie with a poke to his chest. The small man stood toe to toe with the young man and stared directly up into his eyes. "Why do you keep that ridiculous coat on?"

Stunned by the concentrated power emanating from his small black-suited host, Kolossov mumbled, "It suits me so." He clutched the coat more firmly around himself.

"It says here that you are one of us: the 'hards.'" The more Lenin spoke, the more he grew in Kolossov's perception, until he seemed to fill the room with his presence. "I follow you, Old Man."

"Do you understand the current situation?"

"We heard there was trouble, rebellion by the 'softs.'"

"Nonsense. Everything is in hand. You were questioned by our man in Kiev?"

"I was." Kolossov stood at attention and pronounced his catechism: "Centralism! Organization! Discipline!"

"And your comrades?"

"Many are for compromise—they want to wait for our country to catch up. I want to act. I want to make the Revolution." In his enthusiasm, the young man stumbled over the torn lining of his coat.

Lenin smiled, steadied him by the arm, and began to walk him back and forth. Krupskaya watched the two intently to see exactly how Lenin felt about the visitor. "You are my man then. It is of extreme importance that our principles dominate the Congress."

Krupskaya spoke out, waving her pad. "The letter, Vladimir, you didn't dictate the letter that has to go out today."

"Interruptions, interruptions."

"If I don't catch the post—"

Ignoring his wife's plea, Lenin continued to pace with the young man. "An athlete, aren't you? A weight lifter?"

"A little of this and that."

"But you're the one they spoke of, the man who could lift over three hundred pounds? A remarkable feat."

"An exaggeration. The most I've ever lifted at arm's

length is two hundred and thirty—a little more than circus athletes, but no record."

"Vladimir!" Krupskaya spoke out. "The letter."

"Then surely you can get twice that off the ground?"

"If we miss today's post . . ."

The young man, embarrassed by the couple's conflict, smiled at Krupskaya and then at Lenin. "Please don't let me interrupt. I'll come back later." He moved toward the door.

Lenin gestured for him to stay and turned in a fury at his wife. "I'll dictate the confounded letter before the post. In the meantime, I suggest that you get the medicine from the pharmacist next door; it has to go out today too. And buy that suitcase."

Krupskaya rose with exaggerated dignity, gathered her shopping bag and purse, and stalked to the door.

"Please, madame," the young man waved his hand in a conciliatory gesture, "I didn't mean to—"

"*Madame* again?" said Krupskaya, glancing significantly at her husband. "He '*madames*' me like a bourgeois."

Lenin lowered his head and barked, "Not essential."

Krupskaya snorted and thrust herself outside, shutting the door firmly behind her.

Lenin turned toward Kolossov. "Now where were we?"

"Weight lifting. I was crazy about the sport until our group began reading Marx. What a revelation! Recently, I've been reading everything I can find on theories of knowledge." Breathless with excitement, the young man rushed on, "I think I've made some discoveries, which I would like to discuss—if that's possible."

"Is weight lifting difficult to learn?"

Crestfallen at Lenin's response, Kolossov replied, "One begins with fundamental exercises, like any discipline—philosophy, for example."

"Show me!" Lenin said eagerly. Then he frowned. "But I have no weights."

"Marx's sociology and his economics need a much more adequate theory of knowledge than materialism can provide. I dream of—"

At last the visitor's ideas had caught Lenin's attention. "What's this? You're not a materialist?"

"I wouldn't put it like that. I'm searching. I've been reading Avenarius and Mach—"

Lenin's cordial manner disappeared. His thumbs hooked under his armpits and he hopped at the young man. "It's a grievous error to attempt to correct Marx."

"But it's not a matter of correcting."

"Forget it before you damage your brain."

Kolossov blushed angrily at the reprimand. He lowered his head and sulked. Lenin turned away and began to search the room. His eye lit upon a broom. Grabbing it up, he charged toward Kolossov, who backed away in trepidation, thinking he was about to be beaten.

"Young man, could we use a broom?"

"For what?"

"The fundamental exercises of weight lifting."

Kolossov stared at Lenin as if he were mad.

At that moment, Krupskaya returned, brandishing the package of medicine, which she began to prepare for the post. Lenin marched over to his wife, his hands in the air. "Where is the suitcase?"

"It's still in the shop," she replied in a low voice without looking up from her postal preparations.

"Today, you will buy that suitcase." Lenin waved a threatening finger at his wife.

"He wants too much money."

"Buy it! Three centimes more or less—"

"—means a meal or no meal. Hotels in London are expensive, especially when they see a Russian coming."

At that moment, there was a knock on the door. Krupskaya put her hand to her mouth. "Oh goodness, that must be Martov! The invitation was for this morning. In the excitement, I . . ." She moved hesitantly toward the door.

Lenin turned on his heel and ordered Kolossov to depart. "But you must return tomorrow morning at this time. We still have important business to transact. And don't talk to the man at the door."

Krupskaya opened the door. On the threshold stood a slouching, angular man in a crumpled suit and thick, smudged steel-rimmed glasses. His soft beard and mustache framed a long, well-shaped kindly face, which beamed with smiling interest at Kolossov. The young man, anxious to follow Lenin's orders, brushed by the man, almost knocking him off the steps, and strode up the street.

Martov laughed as he entered Lenin's apartment. He greeted Krupskaya warmly and turned toward Lenin. "Who on earth—or what on earth—was that?"

"It's of no interest," said Lenin. "Tea for our guest," he said to his wife. Krupskaya rushed over to the stove.

Julius Tsederbaum, known as Martov, was Lenin's closest comrade in the Russian Social Democratic Workers Party. He and Lenin had founded the Party newspaper, *Iskra*. He was one of the brightest, gentlest, and most attractive members of the Party. Even in appearance, Martov was lovable. His collar was always undone. Ashes dropped from a cigarette perpetually held between his thumb and his forefinger and cupped in his palm, Russian fashion. Behind the glasses, his large brown eyes gleamed out at the world affectionately, and his sensitive mouth, almost completely hidden by his beard, smiled warmly as if he were welcoming everyone into his heart, no matter how mistaken a person might be in his ideas or his actions.

This morning, his smile was even warmer than usual. He knew that Krupskaya's invitation to tea had been more of a summons from his dearest friend than a social gesture. Generally, revolutionaries considered invitations or teas to be bourgeois conventions and avoided them. One just dropped in, or met in cafés. However, this invitation was no accidental reversion to past customs. Lenin had an agenda. Lenin always had an agenda.

An impossible man! Martov thought, as he waited for his tea and for Lenin's demands. What contradictions this friend of his embodied: sensitive, passionate, obsessive, autocratic, solipsistic, selfless. Martov pondered the absurd question that had been nagging him in recent days: Could such a man—surprisingly small, with a balloon forehead, fierce Mongolian eyes, and imperious gestures—embody the impersonal forces of history?

The tea was weak, as always. Martov sighed as he sipped. He loved good, strong Russian tea. The vodka was sparse, a few drops splashed in a dirty little glass, and not renewed. The few sardines Krupskaya served were almost gone to mold. Martov lamented the miserly existence Lenin and Krupskaya led and then hastened to excuse it, reminding himself that they devoted all their resources to the needs of their political allies and to Lenin's family in Russia.

It was Lenin's favorite ploy to remain silent, keeping his adversary on edge. And so Martov rattled on about local gossip; he wandered about the room, smoking, sipping tea, pausing to look at newspapers and books, and dropping ashes everywhere. Krupskaya scowled and followed him with a broom, sweeping up and refilling his teacup. Lenin sat in a tense, compressed posture, his face closed and inscrutable as it always appeared when he was about to explode. Finally, tired of waiting for Lenin's outburst, Martov confronted him with what he suspected to be the reason for his host's displeasure: for two weeks, without discussing the matter, Martov had been circulating his own version of the Party program for the all-important 'Second Congress of the Russian Social Democratic Workers Party. After all, his disagreement with Lenin wasn't simply a matter of an article in *Iskra*. At the Second Congress, they planned to take a great step forward toward the Revolution that would bring justice and harmony to their beloved Mother Russia. Martov admitted frankly that he had done so secretly, because he knew Lenin would have raised a great fuss about it. "It's no more than a working draft," Martov said, "that's all. You're welcome to comment."

This set Lenin off. He planted himself in front of Martov, called him a hypocritical simpleton, and accused him of skulking around behind his back, invading his proper role as tactician. "I thought we agreed on the function of the Party," he shouted, thrusting his domed forehead at his guest as if he were going to butt him in the chest. In argument, Lenin's entire body became a projectile aimed at his opponent. It was a tactic he had learned as a child to make up for his size. If he could dominate physically by sheer, compact energy, then he would easily triumph in debate.

But Martov knew his attacker too well. He smiled, the very picture of sweet reasonableness, and held his ground against the projectile. Lenin hated this gentle style of Martov, just as Martov disliked Lenin's bombast. Of course, they agreed on the essentials of a revolutionary party system, but they differed greatly upon very important details. Today, Martov was not prepared to allow his friend to bully him.

Lenin sulked. As tough as he appeared, even the slightest reprimand or defection by his loved ones wounded him. His family understood this, as did Krupskaya and Martov. Even though Martov knew how much Lenin hated being touched, he placed his hand on Lenin's shoulder. Martov pleaded with his friend to cease isolating himself, to come out to the coffeehouse and see for himself what a good lot their supporters were. If Lenin got to know them better, Martov suggested, he'd trust them to debate the principles about which he and Lenin disagreed. "You can't sit in your room directing the organization like a bureaucrat."

Krupskaya could no longer contain her exasperation. She thrust herself between the two friends, declaring that the Old Man had no time to waste.

Lenin turned on Krupskaya, harshly reproving her for interrupting.

Martov momentarily lost his presence of mind. "Look how you speak to your wife!" Martov scolded his friend. "Your faithful companion!"

Lenin and Krupskaya stared at him as if he were mad for daring to comment upon such personal matters.

Poor Krupskaya! thought Martov. More than once he'd
seen her bear the brunt of Lenin's displeasure. If she had
been more attractive or independent, Lenin wouldn't have
dared to use her as his whipping post. That fierce Mongol
slave master could not afford to lose his faithful, steadfast
nurse, watchdog, secretary, sentry, and mirror. Lenin had
such an absolute need for the confirmation of every one
of his moods, dicta, attitudes, affections, and hatreds that
Martov suspected he would fall apart if Krupskaya left
him or even expressed mild disagreement.

Martov sighed for the lot of that sad, accommodating
woman, and then, shrugging away the reproof in the eyes
of his host and hostess, he continued his scolding, "Well,
then, Volodya, if you resent my interference in your marriage, then look how you upbraid your close friend. Rep-
rimands. As if I were a schoolchild. We undertook *Iskra*
together—a common effort. Our newspaper: *The Spark*
out of which the revolution will grow." Then, to take the
sting out of his protest, he praised Lenin's plan to raise
Iskra's board above the Central Committee itself, calling
it a masterful chess move.

Martov's flattery had no effect. Lenin railed at him for
invading Lenin's own special province, organizational
matters, about which Martov always admitted that he
had little interest. Martov countered with the Saumann
situation, as an example of how organizational matters
sometimes make a vital difference to values. Saumann, a
despicable agent of the Party, had seduced the wife of his

best friend, Vrunski, and had then humiliated her until she committed suicide.

Lenin replied simply that Saumann was their best agent.

Martov knew he ought not to pursue the Saumann affair, but he could not let it go. He tried to appeal to Lenin's finer nature. "You're a man of great compassion, Volodya—who should know better than I? The way you have cared for me during my illnesses—your constant maternal chiding about my terrible habits."

"Why talk of such matters now? The Saumann business has no relevance to our work."

"It has the greatest relevance. The woman was with child."

"I feel sorry for her, her child, her husband, even her lover—for everyone in this blessed world. But it remains a personal matter."

"It's wrong, Volodya, wrong. If we ignore blatant injustices within our own ranks, how can we—"

"You waste our energies tilting at windmills when there is a castle in clear view inhabited by a dragon."

"That's no excuse for us to act like dragons."

"You lack focus, Julius."

"The woman, our comrade, killed herself—" By now, Martov had worked himself into such a state that he spilled his tea across some papers on the table and then upset an ashtray. He apologized, calling himself a clumsy brute.

Krupskaya leaped toward the table and tried to save the papers, but in her anxiety over Lenin's displeasure, she clumsily made the disorder worse. For a moment, Lenin surveyed the clutter with annoyance; then he firmly removed both Martov and Krupskaya from the jumble, after which he cleaned and straightened the table.

While Lenin worked, Krupskaya wagged her finger at Martov. "Julius, you make a mess of everything. Those confounded cigarettes and all of your loose talk. You're driving Lenin mad."

Martov took up one of Krupskaya's hands and pressed it between his, trying to soothe her. "Please forgive me, dear Nadya. I know how hard it is to keep a house straight. I would drive a wife crazy if she had to put up with me. Come, friends, let's go out to the café—there I can be as messy as I like."

Lenin called out, "Here, Nadya, finish with the floor, while I conduct our guest to the door."

Krupskaya flung Martov's hands away from her and eagerly seized the broom. She began to sweep vigorously, stirring up more dust than she collected, while Lenin propelled Martov to the door.

Martov grasped both of Lenin's arms and urged him to come along to the café. "Volodya, Volodya, how we used to laugh together! What's happened?"

"There's little to laugh about these days."

Krupskaya nodded emphatically.

"For just a half hour," Martov pleaded.

"Oh yes, my romantic friend," said Lenin, freeing himself of Martov's embrace, "how I would love to be a youth again and talk all night about the glorious future."

"Nadya needs a break."

"She's not interested in recreation."

"Only because of you. I don't like to meddle, Volodya—"

"You like nothing better."

"—but you're very harsh with her. Women need—"

"Personal needs—that's all you think about these days. What does the Revolution need, Julius?"

"I don't require lessons on the Revolution."

"Nor do I on my husbandly duties."

"You're right, I overstepped myself. But I love you, Volodya. You're too tense. You never relax anymore."

"Julius," Lenin held a finger stiffly in the air before Martov's nose, "an organization needs continuous guidance."

"And the 'Old Man' enjoys guiding?"

"Enjoy? An unfamiliar word."

"Alas."

Lenin gazed at Martov, who could see the focus of his friend's mind shift. Martov's host allowed a full minute to pass, keeping him imprisoned at the door. Martov had experienced this maneuver many times. Finally, Lenin spoke, his voice mild. "And you still insist upon being *Iskra*'s official delegate to the Congress?"

"I do."

"Even though I could do the job better. After all, *Iskra* supplants the Central Committee."

"Precisely because you would do the job too well, Volodya."

"And if I should ask you to yield the appointment?"

"I wish I could."

Lenin struggled with his pride and at last, to Martov's surprise, he humbled himself. "I ask you, Julius: yield the appointment. Please."

Martov had to summon up all of his courage to reply. "No."

Lenin flinched. His narrow eyes opened to their fullest, as if he had just been slapped, worse than slapped. "Julius?"

"No, no, no." To bolster himself, Martov found his voice take on an uncharacteristic sharpness. "For once I must take precedence. And you know why." He grasped Lenin with a convulsive hug, kissed him on both cheeks, moved him aside, and departed quickly, closing the door behind himself. One more moment with Lenin and he knew he would have conceded.

On the very night Martov refused to yield his appointment as *Iskra*'s official delegate to the Second Congress, Lenin was assailed by a peculiar hallucination. The stress of the coming Congress and the painful struggle with Martov had left him particularly vulnerable. He found himself unable to sleep. Shivering and sweating, he wrapped a blanket around himself and got out of bed. He leaned over the bureau, staring at the photograph of his brother that stood there.

Lenin had the habit of carrying on his thoughts aloud as monologues, addresses, debates. He spoke in this way to his wife all day long, but also, late at night, he harangued absent operatives, imaginary audiences, and even loved ones in Russia. Oddly enough, he communicated most often with his brother, Alexander, who had been executed by the tsar. Krupskaya, an extremely jealous woman, took great pride in Lenin's monologues to her, but she found this habit extremely annoying when it came to his family, especially to his dead brother, whom she considered her most dangerous rival. When she cleaned, she treated his brother's photograph rather roughly. Long ago, she had broken the glass; the poor frame would not last much longer.

On the sleepless night after Martov's visit for tea, Lenin eloquently addressed his brother's photograph, expressing the anger he felt at Martov's obstinate disagreement about the function of the Party and his insistence upon representing *Iskra*. Lenin stepped down from the loft and began to pace about the room, indignantly excoriating his close friend. When he paused to catch his breath, he became aware of a curious, deep whirring and moaning sound behind him—in part mechanical, in part human. The sound filled him with such horror that he could hardly force himself to turn and face whatever produced it.

There before him, encompassing the rickety stove in his frugal little room, stood a carousel topped by a many-sided chandelier. From the spokes of the chandelier, slender filaments hung down, each one attached to a man, a woman, a child. As the chandelier whirred and turned, the creatures below, moaning in pain, were swept around in a grand circle, jumbled together and thrown apart in all sorts of accidental and purposive arrangements. Above this sad multitude of ghostly creatures, the panels of the chandelier were etched with stern renderings of scenes: battles, treaties, trials, assassinations, the occupations and labors of man, breech births, stillbirths, ordinary births, deaths by disease, by violence, by accident, lovemaking in all positions, courtship, moneylending, and invention.

Lenin understood at once that "History" itself had invaded his room to confront him. At that moment in the middle of the night, the embodiment of human events in time appeared not as a metaphor, but a very real, oppressive edifice. Lenin's knees shook, his body turned cold, he could barely keep from crying out. He was certain he had gone mad. He tried to reassure himself with thoughts of mirages, Bishop Berkeley's philosophy, and memories of his studies in platonic idealism and realism. He reassured himself that this absurdity was only a brutal daydream brought on by exhaustion and Martov's bullheadedness.

Still, he could not reconcile himself to the anomaly represented by this carousel. Even in his exhausted state, he found it appalling that history should appear in the guise of a mechanism with a circular and endlessly repetitive movement. He knew very well that history moved in a dialectical spiral toward revolution, the grand climactic finale to which he devoted all of his efforts. History was not circular, it was not repetitive, not endless, and yet, here it was before him, this illusion of his own mind's making: a carousel. In horror, he understood that deep within he harbored tormented doubts about the most basic tenet of his creed.

Among the multitude of creatures the carousel dragged along, one figure in particular stood out. He was illuminated by a dim, ethereal light that obscured his features: a slender young man in an old-fashioned ruffled shirt and tight trousers. As he passed by, Lenin addressed the apparition. "This bicycle—" lectured Lenin, pointing to his bicycle, hanging in the corner of the room, "this bicycle operates upon an extremely simple principle involving the vector of applied force. Once force has been imparted to the foot pedal . . ." His voice faded when the bright figure in the ruffled shirt detached himself from the turning carousel, leaned against the wall, and languidly examined the room. Lenin clapped imperiously, speaking like a teacher in a classroom. "Pay attention, here! This is a lesson that must be learned early in life!" The young man, an amused smile on his face, cupped his hand to his ear comically as Lenin pointed to the parts of the bicycle. "Once force has been imparted to the foot pedal, it travels in a totally consistent way from the pedal to the arm, to the ratchet, to the chain, to the back ratchet, to the wheel, to the ground, thus impelling the entire vehicle and the rider through the frame forward in a line determined by the angle of the front wheel. It does not move in endless circles. Understood?"

The young man snapped to mock attention and saluted. "Understood."

"Now I ask you: Is there any confidence between the chain and the back ratchet?"

"None."

"Is there friendship between the back wheel and the frame?"

The young man's grin widened. "An absurd proposition."

"Must we banish the pedal for its immoral behavior? Do the parts vote democratically before they drive the vehicle forward?"

The young man laughed aloud and Lenin started, recognizing the laughter. It was the laughter of his older brother, the young man in the photograph on his bureau, executed at the age of twenty-one for attempting to assassinate Tsar Alexander III. Lenin had been seventeen at the time. Lenin had talked to the photograph of his brother many times over the years, but this was the first time his brother had ever appeared before him, the first time he had ever answered back.

Lenin cried out, "Sascha!

"Volodya!" the ghost replied. They regarded one another with affection. "So you have become a bicycle professor?"

"Not the professor you were—with your bomb in a hollowed-out book."

Mockingly, Sascha crossed his hands over his breast. He cast his voice in an affected manner as if making a public statement. "There is no finer death than death for one's country's sake; such a death holds no terror for sincere, honest men."

"A fine speech you made in court! Full of candor and goodwill. All Russia was impressed."

Sascha's ghost acknowledged his brother's praise with a nod and continued the speech he had made in court. "I had but one aim: to help the unfortunate Russian people. I take complete moral and intellectual responsibility for my act."

"Did you ever understand your act?" Lenin asked.

Sascha's voice dropped to a conversational level. "I was much younger than you are now, Volodya. I worried that my comrades might think I was an egotist—trying to take all the blame for our attempt on the tsar's life."

"Everyone thought you were a decent, honest boy. But they killed you all the same. And your liberal intellectual friends wouldn't answer the door to Mama—the mother of a regicide."

"Not quite a regicide—not by a long shot."

"You couldn't even blow yourself up."

Sascha laughed again, his boyish face filled with delight. "Well, it was my first bomb."

Lenin regarded his older brother sternly. "Spontaneous acts accomplish nothing."

"That may be, but our nonviolence did little enough, except to get us beaten and arrested. So why not change tactics? It seemed logical at the time."

"We've learned much since then—some of us, that is. Discipline's what's needed, and I'll teach it to our dreamy democrats."

"Well, good luck, 'schoolmaster of the bicycle.' Think of me sometimes."

"If I could stop thinking about you, I would."

Lenin stared at his brother and the carousel as both faded into the dark shadows of the room. He moved forward, holding his arms out, his fingers spread, as if he could embrace the apparition. When his hands encountered the cold, damp wall, he shuddered. "I must be mad, arguing with a ghost, lecturing my poor dead brother as if he were a young student today."

Then he sighed and almost sobbed, when he thought how closely his brother and his friend Julius resembled one another: twins, with their simple goodness, their belief in others, and a fatal attraction to democratic principles.

"Alas," he turned and growled toward the bed, where
Krupskaya lay, pretending to be asleep, "Revolution takes
a new sort of man—underline *new* three times. *A new man.*
If the revolutionary movement is a hydra with too many
heads, what of Russia itself?" He paused and then sighed.
"Centralism, organization, discipline—what a way to live!
Could my brother have lived that way? Of course not.
Even after those filthy liberals betrayed him and Mama,
my brother was willing to forgive. The high ideals of 'the
ancient ones' in the Party and of Martov, now." Lenin
stared around the room and called out in a soft, hoarse
voice, "Sascha!" He could barely utter the name. "What
have you done to me? You were the favorite, everyone's
favorite. Mine, too. How could you have been such a fool?
A bomb in a book. How angry I was with you. It overturned my life. For a brother, I was traded a revolution."

June 4, 1903, early morning

While Lenin sweated, lamented the defection of his dearest friend, and anguished over the apparition of his lost
brother, two of his henchman spent the night carousing.
They were the very two involved in the crucial Saumann
affair over which Lenin and Martov seriously differed
in their first major confrontation. Saumann was accused
by his best friend Vrunski of seducing Vrunski's wife,
ridiculing her in public, and causing her suicide. At Lenin's
insistence, on the principle that private matters should not

interfere with Party matters, the Party Disciplinary Committee took no action. Both Saumann and Vrunski lived at Lepeschinsky's decaying hotel, where a number of revolutionary exiles had found shelter. Vrunski worked there.

Martov at first found it difficult to understand why Lenin had chosen such men as his close associates. They were not educated; they lacked breeding. In other words, they possessed few virtues save loyalty to whomever they considered the strongest leader. As the years passed and the struggle within the Party sharpened, Martov began to understand the logic of such followers. In truth, it was a sort of Marxist logic. These men were indeed men of the people. According to Martov, they possessed all of the vices of the people, but, alas, little of the goodness so remarkable among the Russian peasant and laboring classes. These followers, whom Lenin himself called "mean, brutish, shrewd, and dull fools," were the sort of men who willingly followed the harsh, inflexible paranoiac leadership of Lenin.

That evening, Saumann had inveigled his estranged friend Vrunski into a night of heavy drinking. They ended up in Geneva's central park, next to the lake, where Saumann passed out, slipping from a park bench onto the ground. Orderly flower beds stretched in all directions, colors separated judiciously by generations of unimaginative Swiss gardeners. Vrunski, a fat, bearlike young man of twenty-six, stared stupidly down at the wiry little figure of his betrayer. He nudged him with his foot. Saumann turned over and took a fetal position. The faint light of the muggy, overcast dawn reached Lac Leman from behind the high stern mountains; the dark waters took on a ghostly gray light; the distant shores began to glow.

There was an emblematic irony to the apparition of these two petty, disorderly men playing out their destiny in a beautiful, rationally planned and tended garden against such an awesome natural background. Who could have guessed that the massive order of tsarist Russia would soon be threatened by such men?

Vrunski peered warily around, afraid now that the police would discover and arrest him and Saumann. He held a half-filled bottle of schnapps in his immense hand. He stared at it, raised it up to the light, tilted it to see how full it was, sighed, and took a swig. Once more, he nudged Saumann's recumbent figure with his foot. Saumann did not move. Vrunski poured a few drops of liquor on his friend's head. Saumann passed his hand over his face, licked the liquid, and continued to sleep. Exasperated, Vrunski kicked Saumann, who groaned and curled even more tightly into his fetal knot.

Vrunski rose and strode away. At the park entrance, he stopped, turned, and stared back at his former friend lying on the path. He continued forward and was about to set off toward the hotel, when, on the promenade along the lake, he saw a policeman strolling along. In alarm, he ran back to Saumann and with a single movement hoisted the limp body to his shoulders as if it were a sack of flour.

Bearing his burden and the half-filled bottle, he marched out of the side exit of the park. Carrying Saumann, he made his way stealthily through the narrow cobbled streets of the poorest quarter of Geneva.

When Vrunski approached the seedy hotel-restaurant with the name "Lepeschinsky" scrawled on a placard in the front window, Saumann, still curled around Vrunski's neck and shoulders, began to talk. "There, you see, we're still friends." His voice was quite clear and pleasant, as if they were taking a stroll together.

Vrunski stopped. "We're not friends." He made no move to put Saumann down.

Saumann settled himself more comfortably around Vrunski's shoulders. "Then why're you carrying me home, old buddy?"

"Because I have to go to work."

"You could've left me—we still had a half bottle left."

"If they found you out there, you'd have been arrested."

"Then we're friends, because friends take care of friends—they don't let them get arrested no matter how they feel about them—it's the dialectic."

Vrunski dropped Saumann on the stairs of the hotel-restaurant with a thump and stood over him, his face set, enclosed, angry. "We're both Social Democrats and that's where it ends."

Saumann had landed heavily, in an awkward position, his leg bent, his head half on the step. He made no attempt to get up. Instead, he stretched, spread his legs and arms and looked appealingly up at Vrunski. Vrunski stepped over him and entered the hotel. In a few moments, he came out wearing a black apron and carrying a broom. He began to sweep the steps, barely avoiding the figure of Saumann, who lifted one leg to accommodate the broom.

"Here, my good man, brush my trousers while you're at it." Vrunski swept under Saumann's leg, and then jabbed Saumann's bottom with the broom. "Gently, gently. You know, you wouldn't have to stoop to this ridiculous drudgery if you joined Lenin's faction."

"I don't understand Lenin's faction; I don't even understand *Iskra*'s position. I just know that when I went to them for satisfaction, your Lenin refused me."

"There, see, you want to talk things over, like a good boy, and be friends again."

"Fuck you!" Vrunski stepped over the inert form of Saumann and swept the walk in front of the hotel.

Saumann arranged himself quite elegantly on the steps, his head propped up with one arm, as if he were on a divan. "Stubborn mule. After the Revolution they're going to make you head janitor, waiter, and bottle boy of all of Russia as a reward for your valuable services to the cause in exile."

Vrunski ignored Saumann. He went inside the hotel and brought out a table and two chairs, which he set up carefully. Saumann sighed. "And I broke my ass to get Lenin to have you appointed a delegate to the Congress."

Vrunski stopped his work suddenly and turned. Saumann began to whistle. Vrunski walked slowly toward Saumann and stood over him. "A delegate?"

"Comrade Vrunski, delegate-at-large to the Second Congress of the Revolutionary Socialist Democratic Workers Party—in London, England—all expenses paid by the Party. Sounds sweet, don't it? Too bad you prefer carrying tables and chairs around the streets of Geneva."

Vrunski reached down, picked Saumann up, shook him roughly, and sat him in a chair, as if he were a doll. Saumann did not resist. Once seated, he took out a crumpled cigarette, carefully straightened it, and lit it, with elaborate genteel gestures, as if he were on stage.

Vrunski stood over him, sputtering in rage. "How much of your shit do you think I can take?"

"It ain't shit, my good friend."

"Torment good old Vrunski, that's all you know how to do, since we were kids. You shit on me, and shit on me, and then we're friends—just like that. But after Elisabeta . . ." he began to sputter, "I swore that was the end. She was my wife, you bastard, my wife. You killed her." Tears poured down Vrunski's cheeks.

Saumann threw his arms in the air, pretended to grasp onto an imaginary railing, and rose acrobatically. Woozy, he swayed and gradually came to rest with his fingers extended over the table top. "We went over all that—a thousand times—just last night, in fact. It was your wife's fault as much as it was mine, and yours too: if you hadn't been such a good-hearted, trusting bastard of a husband, why your wife and your best and only friend would not have sinned."

"You drove her crazy." Vrunski's sobs subsided.

"I committed adultery. She committed adultery. In any case, she was born crazy and you know it. Everyone in town knew it from the day she was born."

"I don't know anything."

"I told you not to marry her. Your mother told you not to marry her. Even Father Makon told you she was unstable."

"You wanted her for yourself."

"I didn't want her—that was the problem."

"Damn your lying tongue."

"Anyway, if that's all it takes to break up a profound, life-long friendship, then I made a mistake about you. I'll just go tell the Old Man to withdraw his request for your credentials." Saumann began to mount the steps of the hotel, when Vrunski grabbed him by the jacket and threw him back in the chair.

"You know damn well that I want to be a delegate more than anything else in the world. If this turns out to be a joke, I'll kill you."

Saumann raised his right hand, palm down and curling as if it were grasping a head. "On my poor, dear mother's head, I swear."

Vrunski stared intently at the hand for a full minute. "I liked your mother," he sighed. "She was mean, but, you could always trust that she meant what she said." He sank down in the other chair. "Even so, I'd make a lousy delegate. I don't really understand things well enough. You and Lenin and the rest always spouting off about *Iskra*—*Iskra* policy, *Iskra* party, *Iskra* power. And what is *Iskra*, anyway? A newspaper. How can a newspaper lead the Revolution?"

"Do you believe in Lenin?"

"I did until—"

"That's inessential, private." As he spoke these words, Saumann's voice imitated Lenin's intonation. "We're talking revolution. Do you believe in Lenin?"

"More than the others. He's a true worker. He does his job and no shit. But if we're supposed to be materialists, how can a newspaper—?"

"For Christ's sake, since when did you become the theoretician? Lenin does the job, you say? Then let Lenin do the thinking."

"I should do my own thinking."

"You just got done telling me you don't know how to think. Your mother told you that for years. Even Father Makon told you that in school. And you still want to be a delegate?"

"It's my dream."

"Can you think better than Lenin?"

"Stupid question."

"Okay. Let's shake on it." Saumann put out his hand.

Vrunski ignored Saumann's hand. He scratched his

head, muttering to himself. "Lenin refused to let the board reprimand this bastard for what he did to my wife—to me, to our unborn child. Fucking bastard killed my child, too." He began to cry once more.

"Personal affairs! Personal! This is the Revolution."

"I don't know what I think."

"Let Lenin think!"

"Well, he couldn't think any worse than me."

"Then it's settled. *Iskra* is the spark that will start the Revolution, and it will be Lenin's hand that strikes the spark."

"And the kindling?"

"It isn't going to be us, old buddy, not if you stick with me." Saumann rose and clapped Vrunski the back. Then he grabbed Vrunski's hand and tried to get him to rise.

Vrunski wouldn't budge. He remained seated, head down, brooding. "I don't know, I really don't know."

Saumann began to knead Vrunski's shoulders as if he were a masseur. "You don't have to know anything, old buddy. The Old Man will do our knowing for us."

Strangely enough, Saumann really cared for Vrunski; he counted on his companionship. They were linked by a common childhood, by Saumann's crime, by Saumann's need to rule someone while he himself was ordered and commanded and whipped and admonished and beaten. Even the unprincipled Saumann craved the nourishment of love and loyalty. In this way, somehow the friendship between the sly Saumann and his good-natured friend

Vrunski echoed aspects of the relationship between Lenin and Martov. Not that Martov was the least bit dumb. He knew very well what Lenin was up to, and yet, like Vrunski, he allowed himself to be manipulated because of a deep-seated need to give and to receive love. If Martov had been able to carry out his resistance to Lenin at this early stage, the Revolution might have taken a very different course.

Inside his house early that morning, Lenin exercised vigorously without pausing: toe touches, push-ups, and sit-ups. He had recovered completely from his troubled night thoughts.

Krupskaya, still in bed, groaned. Her body and head ached from lack of sleep. She had spent most of the night tending to her husband after Martov's surprising rebellion. She forced herself out of bed, washed, and slipped on a gray, nondescript dress that hung limply down to her ankles. She brushed her hair without looking into a mirror—she never used a mirror for anything save decoding. For jewelry, she wore only a plain gold wedding band. She put water on the stove and moved around the room, arranging papers and books. Then she set the table for breakfast. As she worked, she groaned and sighed, pining for those lost hours of sleep.

"Do you think the young man will come on time?" asked Lenin. In his disappointment with Martov, he had ended his troubled night by placing undue importance upon Kolossov—almost as if Kolossov had come as a replacement for his dearest and oldest comrade, who had defected. Krupskaya, dreading the return of this new rival, now tried to ease her husband out of this ridiculous hope.

"I wouldn't expect too much of this lad. People have a way of disappointing you."

"He's an athlete. And I trust athletes more than I do intellectuals."

"He didn't seem very interested in athletics."

"He's a giant—he lifted three hundred pounds."

"He said two hundred thirty."

At his wife's resistance, Lenin leaped up and mounted the loft. There he began to talk to the photograph of his brother. "It's queer, Sascha, but I can feel myself losing my ability—my ability to trust people. I can feel it leaking out. It's a terrible way to live. And my wife doesn't help."

Krupskaya quailed at this unusual admission. She called out, "History has granted you, Lenin, the vision, the role of leader."

Lenin dismissed her words with a wave and continued his monologue with his dead brother. "God, I hope this new man turns out to be decent. I'm fed up with the others: mean, brutish, shrewd, and dull. All the good men have too many scruples for politics." He stared accusingly at his brother. "You and Martov, what a pair! If you romantics only knew how much I need some comradeship in the battle."

Krupskaya stared at him, her face momentarily convulsed in grief. She shuffled up onto the loft to confront him. "And me? Am I not your comrade?" She put a hand out as if to remind him through her touch what they were to one another. He shrank away from her. She put her fingers to her mouth and bit the tips of her fingers for having dared to touch him. Then she shrugged, sighed, and spoke under her breath to her late brother-in-law's image. "Ahh, what's the use. He never hears."

Lenin's sensitivity to physical contact was well known. His followers found it just another sign of his power: a separate, sacrosanct presence with whom one must not be familiar. His enemies speculated upon his sexual life with Krupskaya, some even going so far as to guess they never made love. Krupskaya knew of this gossip and longed to announce the intimate nature of her marriage. Beneath his armor, she wanted to declare, Lenin was a caring man; he never neglected his husbandly duties. Of course, they did not touch one another in public—it would have been unseemly—but they caressed and comforted one another in the night. Last night, after seeing History's apparition, her husband had been insatiable. And yet today, he was longing for this unproven young comrade as if she did not exist. Krupskaya secretly hoped that Kolossov would forget his appointment.

She was sorely disappointed when, sharply at nine, the young man appeared. He had shed his torn coat and galoshes, but his ragged laborer's clothing still bore the marks of a Russian immigrant. He bowed to her, at which she cringed and wagged her finger. "No *madames*, if you please," she said, turning her back. He marched over to Lenin and stood at attention before him. "At your command, comrade."

Lenin strode to the corner and picked up a broom. He returned to Kolossov and handed it to him. "You said you could demonstrate weight lifting to me with a broom."

Kolossov stared down at the broom. "That was why you ordered me to return?"

"It's of the utmost importance."

Kolossov regarded his starets thoughtfully. He grinned. It made sense that such a small man should take athletics so passionately. "Of course, a broom will do very well." He twirled the broom gaily and bowed before Lenin, who returned the bow. "Now, watch closely! First you take the bar with two hands, like this. You lift it rapidly to the chest." Kolossov lifted the broom to his chest as if it were a barbell and then proceeded to demonstrate as he talked. "And then, in a second movement, pushing with your hands, legs, back, and entire body, you raise it until your arms are locked overhead. This movement is called the 'clean and jerk,' or the 'shoulder throw with two hands.' "

Lenin took the broom and imitated the exercise with a stately style, quickly and elegantly, flourishing the broom with joy. He handed the broom back to Kolossov as if he were a courtier handing over his sword.

"Not bad. Now here's another lift, in which the bar is not thrown, but lifted slowly in one motion from the chest to the locked-arm position overhead. I think it's a much more difficult exercise than the first because you get no help at all from the legs." Kolossov demonstrated.

Lenin took the broom and went through the motion, jerking the broom.

"You'd never get the weight up like that. The exercise demands an extreme tension of biceps, triceps, shoulder, and chest muscles. To make it easier, you can bend your body slowly backward in an arch, and remember, the legs must be apart for the most support. If they are together, you'd get no lift at all."

Once more, Lenin tried to imitate Kolossov's motion.

"No, no. You are not allowed to use the legs." Kolossov grinned, clearly enjoying his role as master.

Lenin tried again.

"Arch the back next time, and remember—a single concentrated motion."

Lenin paused for some time to think out his move. He then performed the maneuver. As he slowly lifted the broom, Krupskaya giggled.

Lenin dropped the broom to his side and stared at his wife. "Don't be foolish, Nadya. This is something of the highest importance." He turned his back on his wife, handing Kolossov the broom. "Well, my athlete, was that better?"

Frowning, Krupskaya busied herself making up the bed.

"Not bad for a novice," said Kolossov. "Before we continue to the third exercise, comrade, I would like you to look at this object." He held up the broom. "What is it?"

"A broom."

"And yet for the last few minutes we've agreed to a linguistic convention that transforms the broom into a barbell." He laughed, quite delighted with his clever analogy. He had not given up his quest for a serious philosophical discussion.

Lenin would have none of it. "The broom remains a broom. The Revolution needs high-jumpers now, not thinkers."

"And yet if you asked me how to sweep, it's unlikely that I would show you with a barbell."

"The third exercise, please."

Krupskaya smiled to herself at her husband's chiding tone.

"I'll let you off now, Old Man, but one day we must talk. I have a contribution to make to the theory of our Party."

Krupskaya snorted. Lenin frowned. "Your body will be more essential to the future than your brain."

Somewhat glum again, Kolossov continued his instruction on the final exercise, the snatch. Once more, Lenin concentrated deeply when he received the broom. Then, with panache, he executed a perfect snatch.

"Bravo. Now all three in a row, twice."

Lenin performed all three exercises twice.

"Good! Perfect! Superb! An excellent student." Kolossov clapped Lenin on the back.

Annoyed by the familiarity, Lenin drew away. With a cold voice, he complimented the visitor. "It takes an excellent master to make an excellent student," he paused, "and an unquestioning follower to make a good Party member."

Krupskaya noisily brought out a pad and pointed to it. "That letter to Kharkov must go out today at least."

Lenin came up behind her. "What time is it, Nadya?" He spoke in a gentle voice.

"Fifteen minutes before the post."

"Shall we do the letter then?" Having turned his anger toward the young man, he was willing to talk soothingly to his wife.

"If you're through with your athletics."

"I hope I'll never be through with them." Lenin began to pace around the room, dictating. "To Levin in Kharkov. Comrade and all that: we must make sure of the Congress. First, the Bund must yield its autonomy to the Party—if not, we'll oust them." He mounted the raised sleeping loft and continued dictating as he changed into a suit. His movements were crisp, precise. "Second, complete support of *Iskra* program, and none other. Be prepared to divide the orthodox from the unorthodox on matters of principle."

He descended, marched over to his wife and stood in front of her for inspection. She noticed a button missing, brought out a needle and thread, and began to sew it back on, clumsily. Impatient, Lenin grabbed the button, needle, and thread. He waved his wife back to her pad, removed his coat, and tore away her bumbling attempt at repair. Continuing to dictate, he sewed on his button. Now and then, Krupskaya looked up from her writing, regarding her husband's quick gestures with envy and admiration.

Kolossov, standing motionless against a wall, watched and listened in astonishment. It was as if he were not present in the room.

"Third, and most important: *Iskra* dominance. Subordinate even the Central Committee to *Iskra*, the central organ—after which, as much centralization as possible. Underline *centralization* three times."

Lenin finished sewing with a flourish, bit off the thread, put on his coat, and began to pace again. Krupskaya followed his steps, her pad in hand, waiting for him to continue his dictation. As he paced, he corrected his wife's housekeeping. He swept, he dusted, he straightened. When the room was finally acceptable, he stopped, turned, and exclaimed: "How I long for the Congress!"

"This time, we'll shape it correctly," she replied.

"Where was I?"

Krupskaya read from her pad: "'After which, as much centralization'—underline three times—'as possible.'"

"It is of the utmost importance to decide point three, and to flush out all opponents upon this basic question."

"Once we have separated on a serious issue, we can get a clear picture of the entire Congress. I confide in you, comrade, that the organizing committee is very much in doubt. Unless you push your own people onto as many local committees as possible, by any means necessary, we will find ourselves faced with a do-nothing, runaway Congress. There will be arrests; make sure it is our opponents who are taken."

This last sentence shocked Kolossov. "Arrests?"

Lenin waved for him to be silent and continued his dictation. "Guard yourselves and your people more closely than the apple of your eye. The majority must be ours. This is most important! Be in this bolder, more impudent, and more ingenious, and in the rest, quieter and more careful. 'Wise as serpents, and gentle as doves.' All yours, the Old Man. That's all, Nadya. Code that and get it out immediately."

While Krupskaya went about her encoding task, Lenin turned back to Kolossov. "Comrade Kolossov, if you keep your infernal questions and theories to yourself, you may make an excellent delegate to the Congress."

"But I was not elected by the Kiev group."

"There will be absentees. The police have been, fortunately, selective in their latest crackdown. For some strange reason, our opponents in the Party find themselves lacking in candidates."

"I can't believe that you—"

"You will be an extraordinary delegate-at-large."

"To use the police on our own comrades? The elected representatives?"

"There are many sorts of comrades. Do you accept?"

"It's flattering, of course—" The young man was torn between his shock at Lenin's tactics against his allies in the Revolution and his desire for Lenin's approval.

"Don't be insipid. This has nothing to do with you personally."

"It's a big responsibility."

"In return for your excellent instruction in weight lifting, I will instruct you in politics. First of all, you must buy acceptable clothes. You are much too conspicuous."

"But I have a wife and infant at home. They need money."

Lenin hooked his thumbs under his vest, stepped back with an elaborate, ironic bow, and then leapt forward, hop, hop, nose to nose with the young man, opening his fingers wide, like fins or wings. "Private matters! Private! You are about to be a delegate to the Second Congress of the Russian Social Democratic Workers Party. Don't talk of your family. There is the Bund to worry about, and the weak, soft ones, Axelrod and Zasulitch; there is the organizing committee to discredit, Martov to watch like a hawk, Plekhanov to guide, and the Economists to force out."

"Axelrod, Zasulitch, Martov, Plekhanov: your comrades on the board of *Iskra*?"

"Do you want to make a revolution?"

"I'm with you, Old Man!"

"Then prepare for the Congress. Here are twenty francs. There's a suitcase for sale in the window of the leather store at the head of the street. Go buy it for as little as you can, and bring it back immediately. Then buy yourself a decent suit of clothes with what's left."

At this instruction, Krupskaya dropped a bundle of silverware she had been laying around the table. She stared balefully across the room at Kolossov. Then, in a voice of command, she added to her husband's orders: "And stop all your bowing and 'madaming' or you'll never be a revolutionary."

PART TWO

London, August 10, 1903

he Second Congress of the Revolutionary
Socialist Democratic Labor Party convened on
August 10, 1903, in a London flour warehouse converted
into a meeting hall for the purpose of this event. In a short
time, Kolossov had become essential to Lenin, almost an
adopted son. Like a son, he revered "the Old Man" and,
simultaneously, viewed him critically, surprised and dismayed by his failings.

Kolossov began his party career with little patience for
the practical business of politics. There seemed something
trivial and demeaning about the constant manipulation
involved in the voting process: the barter and trade of
loyalty, the loosening of moral positions, the collecting
and payment of past debts, many of which were incurred
under criminal circumstances. To Kolossov, ordinary business, the buying and selling of goods for cash, appeared to

be an infinitely more honest and moral occupation than politics. Entranced as he was by Lenin's masterful plan for the Second Congress, he took exception to Lenin's attitude toward his dear friend Martov. Kolossov knew that a belief in the morality of friendship violated Lenin's revolutionary rule. Friendship was "personal" and must be ignored as extraneous to the dialectic of history. This was a lesson that, unfortunately, Kolossov could never quite digest.

The amenities at the flour warehouse were few: a pump outside with a spigot for cold water and three hastily constructed outhouses in the field surrounding the building. Inside the structure, red bunting covered every possible protuberance, while the outside of the warehouse had been left bare for fear the authorities might interfere. The English possessed little sympathy for these noisy foreigners.

The Congress opened with the singing of "The Internationale." Many of the delegates wept, for this Congress was the culmination of a lifetime of struggle. When the singing ended, a general emotional hubbub ensued. The gavel sounded, and Plekhanov, the grand old man of the movement, came to the podium, greeted with thunderous applause. He stood there above the crowd, a distinguished gray-haired gentleman in a fine suit; he would have been admitted without question to the most exclusive clubs of the city of London. Only after several attempts did he finally manage to make himself heard.

"Comrades! I hereby open the Second Congress of the

Revolutionary Socialist Democratic Labor Party. In spite
of the many disruptions, differences, and disagreements
among us, I wish to believe that at least some of us are
fated for a long time yet to fight under the red banner,
shoulder to shoulder, with new, young, and ever more
numerous fighters. The state of things is so favorable for
our party that we can all exclaim the words of the humanist knight Don Quixote: 'It is wonderful to be alive at such
a time.' "

The hall erupted in cheers. Kolossov was beside
himself in ecstasy over this invocation of the "humanist knight" and the unanimity of emotion that gripped
the hall. Alas, poor Don Quixote disappeared almost
immediately, as did any semblance of harmony. With
reluctant admiration, Kolossov watched his beloved Old
Man deliberately foment brutal dissension in the Party.
As Plekhanov launched into a long, involved history of
the Party and of revolutionary impulses in Russia, a pan-
demonium of plotting went on below the podium. At this
moment, the groundwork was being laid for three days of
resolutions and votes and caucuses that would determine
the party platform and program for the coming years. The
short, balding figure of Lenin leaped from group to group,
shouting, gesticulating, and pointing as he prepared his
forces for an assault upon the central power structure of
the Party. And Kolossov stood at Lenin's side, proud to be
his trusted aide-de-camp in his wily maneuvers.

The bearlike Vrunski and the small, wiry Saumann

followed after Lenin and Kolossov, glancing from side to side, warding off potential interruptions as if they had been appointed Lenin's bodyguards. At one point, Saumann tried to wedge himself between Lenin and his young disciple. "What's this?" asked Lenin, indignantly. He turned and confronted Saumann and pointed to Vrunski. "You two should be out canvassing our people. Get moving!"

"But, Old Man—" Vrunski began to protest. Saumann, saluting Lenin, drew his friend away, out into the lobby of the hall.

As Kolossov watched the two retreat, he shivered, for he recognized that his intimacy with Lenin had put him at risk with Lenin's other allies.

Kolossov had reason to worry. Saumann was already plotting to depose the young man from favor. He hated Kolossov's "high-toned" manners and his philosophy; worst of all, he sensed in the young man's idealism a contempt for the "practical" men with whom Lenin had surrounded himself.

Lenin's "hards" carried the first vote. Lenin waved them back to the lobby, where Krupskaya and Kolossov joined them. Lenin quizzed them. "Divide!" he said.

Saumann replied, "On a question of—principle."

"Separate!"

Kolossov replied, "On a serious issue!"

"Who shall control?" Lenin stared at Vrunski, who trembled and stuttered.

"Uh, mmmnn, *Iskra?*"

Saumann and Kolossov applauded. "Bravo! *Iskra!*"

"That's my boys."

Krupskaya cast a grim smile at her husband. "What about Martov?"

"That's my business."

"Unless we neutralize him, permanently—"

Lenin turned away from her. "Saumann, you point your rude finger at the Bund, and you, Vrunski, at the Economists. For the time being, we'll be wise as serpents—"

"I'll brain the bastards," shouted Vrunski.

"When I tell you. For the moment, gentle as—"

"Doves!" replied Vrunski. "Serpents and doves! I got it."

Krupskaya sneered. "Your doves got eaten in Brussels by the Martovites on the organizing committee."

Lenin turned on his wife. "Our soft enemies shall not win another vote. We'll be ultra-centralist in every other article. We must bind the cask with double hoops and load our weapons with double charge. It'll be victory for centralism or war with the Congress."

A bell rang, signaling the next round of votes. Lenin waved, and the five started for the doors into the hall. Lenin grabbed Kolossov's arm and held him back as the others disappeared, fanning out through the hall. "Kolossov, you've shown yourself to be a true revolutionary, and loyal to the 'hards.' I want you to delegate your vote to Kalitsky and return to Russia. Tomorrow. Papers will be ready and many messages."

Kolossov pulled up short, looking surprised. For a moment, he thought of resisting the command—he longed to be present for the total victory of Lenin's program. But Kolossov had learned when it was permissible to argue with the Starets and when it wasn't. It had been a difficult lesson for the proud young man. He had come to Geneva prepared to worship at Lenin's feet, but he hadn't expected his leader to be an even more inflexible autocrat than the tsar. He bowed now to necessity, replying to Lenin's command in a sober voice. "I'm ready, Old Man."

Lenin, aware of the young man's hesitations, now deigned to explain himself, a privilege he afforded few of his henchmen. "We have to strengthen our position at home—otherwise the 'softs' will destroy the cause."

Kolossov nodded, his face doleful. Despite Lenin's unwillingness to discuss philosophy, the Old Man had questioned him closely about his life as a laborer, his battles with the police, and his time in prison. Kolossov had been flattered by Lenin's interest. "I'll miss our talks," he said, wistfully.

Lenin shrugged. His gaze softened. "I, too, will miss you. As you can see, I'm not surrounded by educated men or brilliant conversationalists." From inside the hall came an uproar of shouts and applause. He stiffened. "But this is the moment for business. To work, before you leave for Russia."

Kolossov's mood veered from triumphant joy over Lenin's victorious maneuvers and his apparent affection to puzzlement at the sly nature of those maneuvers, and finally to an almost desperate doubt about the morality of the entire effort of his admired leader. Martov was the key to Lenin's victory. Kolossov, still at Lenin's side, watched with amazement as Lenin played upon his old friend's loyalty.

At a crucial point in the deliberations, Lenin drew Martov out into the lobby. Kolossov lurked in a corner. "History is no moral governess, Julius," Lenin spoke harshly. "If *Iskra* loses control, everything will be lost."

"I don't enjoy all this jockeying."

"But that is what a Congress is for! Opinions are expressed, tendencies revealed, groups defined, hands raised, a decision taken, a stage passed through." As he talked, Lenin's expression relaxed. He looked years younger—happy. "Forward!" Lenin exclaimed. "That's what I like. None of your wearying discussions that only end because people fall asleep." Now that the Congress had finally begun, Lenin was in his element: politics.

Martov regarded him fondly, but still could not resist chiding him. "You're the one who makes them endless with your unwillingness to compromise."

Lenin stared at Martov. His voice became harsh again. "You must never forget, Julius, that I will fight to the end for what I believe."

Martov stood back, surprised at the threat in Lenin's voice. "I've always proved my bravery."

"You and I must be in agreement about what to do

with the Bund, the *Daily Worker*, the Economists. If we don't cut off a few limbs and cauterize the wounds, the Party will bleed to death before we're able to send the news back home."

Martov paced back and forth in the empty lobby. He muttered to himself, argued, debated. Kolossov found himself silently hoping that Martov would remain firm, but Martov wavered. "Of course, there's something to be said for your narrow Party concept." He came to a stop in front of Lenin. "Volodya, I don't want us to become enemies."

Lenin would not relent. "Admit then that you were wrong about your broad membership clause!"

Martov sighed. "Oh well, what's the use, we'll always disagree on some things."

"But we do agree on *Iskra*'s central role?"

"I believe in *Iskra*. I believe in Lenin too, if he would only keep his balance."

"That's why I have my Martov."

The two clasped one another around the shoulders and, together, reentered the hall. Kolossov followed.

Now, through a series of censure votes, which Martov joined, Lenin managed to alienate the delegates representing the factions opposed to *Iskra*: the Economists, the Bund, and even the Dawn Group, led by Martov's dear friend Alexandrova.

At the same time, behind Martov's back, Lenin had appealed to Plehkanov's aristocratic temperament, persuading him to put aside, for the present, the very democratic principles Martov had fought so hard for in his draft resolution.

Plekhanov's concluding speech on this subject brought the entire proceedings to a riotous halt. "Universal suffrage," the elegant speaker intoned, "is one of our foremost demands. But let's not convert universal suffrage into a fetish. Now, for the good of the Revolution, we must give up our petty local concerns. While we believe in the rule of law as the fundamental principle of democracy, at this moment we must act under the fundamental principle of revolution: The health of the Revolution is the supreme law. Therefore it would be a crime to hesitate if the safety of the Revolution demands a temporary limitation of one or another of the democratic principles." At Lenin's prodding, Plekhanov had left his "humanist knight" standing by the roadside.

A wild tumult erupted in the hall: booing, whistling, stamping of feet, coupled with a few scattered cheers. Furious arguments broke out in the hall.

"Depose him!"

"Let the truth be heard!"

"Revolutionary tsars!"

"Anarchists!"

The voices of Saumann and Vrunski rose above the others. "Throw out the Bund! Down with Economism!"

Martov, realizing his collusion had made such a travesty possible, plunged into the lobby, his glasses askew, his hair wild, his coat buttoned wrong. Lenin joined him, a broad cat-like smile resting lightly on his lips. "We're doing it, Julius, you and I." Kolossov stood a few yards away, watching.

"My God, Volodya, you've made me denounce a life-long friend, a loyal comrade."

"It was either that or fifty more years of ooze and muck."

"The siege is over, I declare it."

"This is no time to go soft, Julius."

"Volodya! We've expelled the Dawn Group, we've censured Alexandrova, we've stacked the Congress, and we're ramming our program down everyone's throat. Isn't that enough for you?"

"Is any sacrifice enough for the Revolution?"

"It's time to bring everyone back into the fold, or we'll destroy unity forever. Call off your thugs."

"We have the votes. The Grand Dame, the Jewish needle-threaders, and the professors will either bow down or get out."

"That's obscene!"

"It's plain Russian language—the words of our people. We're not in a popularity contest. You wanted to be *Iskra*'s delegate? Well, there's a price."

"I made no such bargain." Martov stalked back into the hall.

Kolossov felt happy, exalted even at Lenin's victory, but at that moment he sympathized greatly with Martov.

Still, he dared not argue with his leader, the father of the Revolution. He was totally committed to Lenin's party, no matter how much he rued Lenin's tactics.

"Young man!" Lenin's harsh voice called Kolossov to attention. "This is no time to stand around with your mouth wide open. Inside to the battle!"

Kolossov ran through the doors. Lenin followed more slowly and then stopped as the door closed, shutting off the noise of the hall. Although, in Kolossov's eyes, Lenin appeared to be totally in command of these events at the Congress, Lenin was by no means at peace with himself. At the very moment he grasped triumph in his hands, to his shocked surprise, he heard behind him, in the empty lobby of the flour warehouse, the peculiar whirring and moaning sound that had been haunting his sleepless nights since Martov's defection. Slowly, he turned to see the dreaded carousel, sweeping its massive burden around and around in its relentless a circle. Never before had the apparition appeared in daylight and never when he was in the midst of battle. Yet there it was, in the lobby, undermining the very notion of the dialectic, with its eternally circular movement.

A plaintive voice called out. "Papa Lenin! Father of the Revolution! And where are your own children, Volodya?"

There, in the midst of the horde being swept along, Lenin made out the figure of his brother, Sascha, who called: "Where are my nieces and nephews?"

Lenin paced alongside his brother, speaking half to

himself and half to the young man. "My own children? None, Sascha. We chose not to."

"What does that mean?"

"We never tried."

"It would be ironic if you were one of those so-called 'barren' couples."

Lenin winced. "Perhaps we are simply afraid."

"Instead you want to make all the Russian people your children. Another Little Father, perhaps, like the tsar?"

"No one else is willing to take the responsibility, Sascha. The Russian people are brutal, prey to superstitions, hatred, lust—they are lazy. And yet their souls—their dreams are pure."

"Ahh, my dear Volodya. Why are you so afraid of the personal? the private?" Sascha shook his head sadly. "And why attack your friends? Don't you have enough other enemies, Volodya? The tsar, the nobles, the industrialists, the landowners, the kulaks, the generals, the governors, and all the petty bureaucratic bullies who enslave our people."

"First, we must destroy the enemies within. A man must act. He must decide that he will not stand for one single moment more of suffering on this earth. And he must arm himself—even against his brothers." Lenin sighed. "What a task!" He knotted his fists over his stomach, clenched his jaw, and shut his eyes. With his utmost strength, he willed the carousel back to its resting place within the recesses of his mind. The time had come to purge the Party of his closest associates and his dearest friend.

Lenin opened his eyes. He peered at the empty lobby. "Goodbye, Sascha." He looked sharply at the entrance to the hall. "And goodbye, Julius." Taking a deep breath, he marched into the hall.

As the speeches and votes succeeded one another in rapid succession, Lenin once more heard the whirring and the moaning sound and felt the immense weight of History's contraption directly overhead, almost as if it had seized the entire Congress in its network of filaments. With the force of his spirit, he commanded himself and his colleagues out of the incessant, repetitive cycle of that carousel, willed them toward a higher and higher plane tending toward their common goal.

First, he prodded Martov to offer a motion that the Bund give up all its autonomy to the Party. Not satisfied, he pushed his friend once more to move that the Bund dissolve its entire hierarchy in favor of the Central Committee so that there would be no confusion of loyalty.

When Martov offered his motion to dissolve the Bund, Kolossov was standing next to Paul Axelrod, an older man, in his early fifties, one of the so-called "ancients," a life-long revolutionary, and, currently, a member of the board of *Iskra*. Axelrod had the gnarled, tanned face of someone who has spent his life outdoors. His hands were large and calloused from hard labor. He was a man of simple tastes and a very clear mind—one of the most truly intelligent among the revolutionaries. He knew at once the effect of Martov's motion, and he shouted out. "My God, Julius, you're cutting your own throat."

Lenin drowned out Axelrod's protest by making a motion for the dissolution of the *Daily Worker*. Plekhanov railroaded the vote to completion.

"Much too fast," Axelrod cried, his voice echoing in the vast dusty hall. "For Christ's sake, give the delegates time to think."

Vrunski stepped in front of the older man, shouting out a motion to abolish all foreign organizations except *Iskra*.

Saumann seconded all the motions as they came up. Plekhanov called for voice votes, declaring each motion passed without bothering to count. The hall erupted in a massive commotion. Delegates raised their fists, wrestled, challenged, and struck one another.

Finally, Axelrod leaped to the podium, elbowing Plekhanov aside. "Out, out, everyone walk out!" he shouted. "Follow the Bund, the Economists, the *Daily Worker* out the door. The Congress has been seized by a Robespierre who will execute us all if we refuse to join him. Quick, out now. We can no longer participate in this farce. Revolutionary unity is at an end."

Axelrod jumped down from the podium and led half the delegates out the door. Plekhanov climbed back to the podium. Lenin joined him. Martov stood directly below, pleading for a restoration of sanity and order. Lenin's eyes gleamed, tiny points of light. He had seized control of the carousel, and was directing it upward, sweeping them all toward a new plateau on the journey to the heights of revolution.

Lenin spoke. "Therefore, we have all accepted in principle the subordination of the Central Committee to the board of the central organ, *Iskra*."

Martov objected.

Lenin pointed down at him. "The entire former board of *Iskra* has been dismissed by the Congress as inadequate to deal with the new realities. Plekhanov, Martov, and Lenin have been nominated as the new troika to run *Iskra*."

Saumann seconded the nominations.

Martov objected again, pounding the base of the podium to get Lenin's attention. "Such wording implies a censure of true comrades."

Plekhanov called for a vote. The remaining delegates shouted, "Aye."

"All opposed."

Martov alone called out, "Opposed." The rest of the opposition had walked out with Axelrod.

"The motion carries."

"A foul, a foul, Volodya." Martov appealed to his friend on the podium. "You agreed to the co-optation of the old board."

Lenin peered down from the podium. "Is there a question from the floor?"

Saumann turned to the other delegates. "Martov knew, he agreed."

Vrunski backed his friend up. "Martov was willing."

Martov shouted, his voice hoarse. "Volodya, I refuse to serve on such a board."

Saumann laughed and pointed at Martov. "The 'soft' Martov protested, but here is his agreement." Saumann waved a sheet of paper in the air as if it were an agreement. "Here is the proof. He traded a Central Committee of 'softs,' the heads of his old comrades."

Vrunski called out. "Martov traded the 'ancient ones' for his own rise to power."

"A forgery," cried Martov. "We are beset by robbers, liars, and thugs. Defend yourselves."

Vrunski replied. "I was there when Martov supported the reduction of the board."

"Calumny!" shouted Martov.

Lenin pounded the podium. "A triumph for the majority, the Bolsheviks. Let he who wishes to serve the Revolution serve with us. The others will get what they deserve."

"Volodya!" Martov's voice cracked. "You've dishonored the finest veterans of the Revolution! You've betrayed your old associates! This sort of brutality will destroy the Revolution. I beg, I plead."

Saumann pointed to Martov. "In the place of a period, put a tear in the minutes."

"The rag is sopping with tears." Vrunski playfully wiped his eyes.

Saumann raised his hand. "I nominate Noskov, Krzhanovksy, and Lengnik to the Central Committee."

Vrunski seconded the motion.

Saumann exhorted the delegates. "Vote, vote the Leninists in, the Bolsheviks, the 'hards,' the centralists.

Lenin smiled. "The motion carries. The Bolsheviks have spoken. Next, the Revolution!"

"My God," said Martov, stumbling from the hall. "What have I done? What has Lenin done? My friend! My comrade. My brother."

Kolossov watched these proceedings in a state of confusion. Tears of joy and sorrow mixed on his cheeks. "We won," he murmured, "but at what price?"

PART THREE

Geneva, February 10, 1904

Six months after the Second Congress, the political situation among the émigrés had altered radically. Lenin's Bolsheviks, named for the Russian word for *majority*, had become a minority. Lenin was on the defensive. A master tactician, he continued to call his "hard" group the Bolsheviks to distinguish them from Martov's Mensheviks, the "soft" minority, who had walked out of the Second Congress. But the Bolsheviks would not become a majority again until they seized the Revolution by force in 1917 and eliminated all opposition.

Lenin confessed to his dead brother that he felt isolated and alone since he had broken with Martov. With bitterness, he complained about the type of men with whom he had surrounded himself. Only young Kolossov remained to remind him of Martov. Back in Russia, the young man had distinguished himself during a general strike in Kiev and would soon be returning to Geneva, where a man of his intelligence was sorely needed in the battle against the Mensheviks. Lenin sighed and confided softly, "You know, Sascha, that young man reminds me of you: sincere, passionate, humble, and noble-hearted. He is very much like Martov was in his youth."

On the day of Kolossov's arrival back in Geneva, he sat in Lenin's flat, being entertained by Krupskaya as he waited for the Old Man. The young man had grown thin and stooped during his months in Russia. The skin of his face hung in pasty, gray folds. Exhausted and sickly, he greedily spooned up the soup Krupskaya thrust upon him. She circled him like an inquisitive mother, refilling his plate, and then dusting and arranging the apartment, her eyes never leaving him.

Kolossov sighed. "Twelve years, fifteen! When will it come?"

"Eat your borscht while it is hot. History moves in its own time. You don't look so good."

"I fasted again in prison, like a fool. The very night I got out, Krassikov showed up and ordered me back here. He wouldn't say why."

"Don't worry. The Old Man will explain everything."

"My son is very ill. I'm worried."

"The Revolution comes first."

"'The Revolution, the Revolution. My wife isn't strong—she needs me, and yet she ordered me to come, too."

"A good comrade."

"This business is hard on women. You remember that girl, Katya, our angel? I told you about her—how she believed in socialism! Well, she—"

Krupskaya took little interest in Kolossov's family or his friend Katya. "Hard as life is, it's been an enormous privilege to live with Lenin." She began to cut up vegetables for dinner.

Kolossov sighed. "I can think of nothing else but my son, my wife, and the angel Katya. Their eyes torment me night and day."

"Just eat your soup, boy!" said Krupskaya. "We must forget personal matters."

Kolossov frowned. He was tormented over his hurried return to Geneva and longed to talk about it. "Admit, at least, that our Starets is a devil to live with. All that impatience!"

Krupskaya waved a carrot at Kolossov. "He's dictated every one of his pamphlets to me. I was the first human being to hear 'What Is to Be Done?' "

"Always in such an infernal hurry."

"He's impatient for the Revolution, I'll tell you that. It burns within him."

"It burns within all of us."

"But not as fiercely." Krupskaya hummed a bit and talked to her vegetables, her mood lightening as she worked. "Sometimes he's very patient, too. None of you see him as he really is."

"How is that?" asked Kolossov, distracted somewhat from his sorrow by this unexpected warmth in his hostess. "How is he, really?"

"Oh, nothing." Krupskaya busied herself about the room again, cleaning and straightening, humming and smiling. Krupskaya's tender feelings had been inspired by the sudden appearance of the handsome and mannerly young man, who acted so bravely for the cause in Russia. She had been brought up, after all, as the daughter of a nobleman, albeit a minor one.

"How is Lenin patient?" prompted Kolossov.

"Ways."

Kolossov had never seen Krupskaya in such a gay mood. Indeed, for the first time he found himself attracted by her womanly qualities. Intrigued, he got up and moved toward his hostess. "Women and their mysteries." He moved with her, step by step, as she worked. "I'll follow you until you tell us about Lenin's patience."

She turned, her hands on her hips, and confronted him. She appeared younger to him, almost coquettish. "Do you really want to know? Truly?"

"Of course I do."

"Well, when he . . ." She hesitated, blushed, put her head down and then, mastering herself, continued. " . . . when he wants to learn something, a language say, then it's down to work with a pile of books and 'Do Not Disturb' for as long as it takes—three weeks, sometimes."

Kolossov waved his finger. "That's not what you started to say."

"But that's what I'm telling you."

He marveled at the change in Krupskaya. She looked radiant. Kolossov stared at her, and then his gaze faltered and fixed itself, beyond her, through the window, as he thought again of his wife and his son and his comrade Katya. "Well, I wish he'd been feeling patient when he sent for me." He began to pace up and down the room. "Three days? One day? Would it have made such a difference? The Revolution will take fifteen or twenty years, if it ever comes."

"Don't blaspheme."

"How can you live with it day and night? And nothing else in life."

"We manage," she muttered, somewhat crestfallen at his reversion to his family and friend. She retreated to the stove, where she placed the vegetables in a pot of water over the fire and added seasoning.

Kolossov followed. "Nevertheless, admit that it's a hard life."

"And the workers? The peasants? This is luxury."

"They say you were the daughter of a count," said Kolossov.

Krupskaya preened mockingly. "Noble blood, can't you tell? Ha! Luckily my father lost his estate and his position early in my life. He was in the judicial courts for years."

"A crime?"

"They say he danced the mazurka with the wrong sort of people. They said all sorts of things. Public funds, private pleasures. A fine count! I began giving lessons when I was eleven—but still I was privileged and comfortable, compared with others."

"A hard life for a young girl with spirit," sympathized Kolossov. "Lessons at eleven—a servant."

"There's nothing wrong with being a servant," Krupskaya replied tartly.

Kolossov began to pace again. "Oh, how I miss my wife, my son. Did you ever wear perfume?"

The question startled Krupskaya, who asked, "Perfume?" as if she had misheard.

"It's strange," said Kolossov, "but I love the smell of perfume. I think all women should wear perfume."

"Animal smells!"

"There's something irresistible about a woman with perfume. You should try it."

"Soap after a hard day's work is good enough for me."

"Women should have something more, something to make up for their hard life." The young man warmed to his subject. "A mystery. When I smell perfume, the world is transformed."

"You're talking nonsense."

"The workers in my circle knew about this craziness of mine, and they chipped in and bought me a bottle."

"Whoever heard of such a thing? Workers buying

perfume for a revolutionary." Krupskaya appeared both scandalized and thrilled.

"That was before I met my wife. I kept it in my room. It helped with the loneliness."

"Your wife wears perfume?"

"Of course. She's a woman. I miss her terribly, and my son. They'll be coming here soon—if all is well."

"Perfume is a subject I wouldn't bring up with the Old Man, if I were you."

"I think I'll buy you a bottle."

Krupskaya replied in a faint voice. "You wouldn't."

"To surprise him."

"You'd better not."

Kolossov reached into his pocket and pretended to bring out something in his cupped hands. "In fact, I brought a little bottle here with me to combat the loneliness. I think I'll give you a spray." He advanced slowly.

She retreated. "Now, you go away. Go 'way, now."

"I'm going to get you. I'm going to spray you with decadent bourgeois scent."

Krupskaya ran around the table, followed by the young man. His hostess, he knew, was enjoying the game, an event which he imagined did not occur often. Just then, the door opened and Lenin appeared behind Krupskaya. Kolossov saw him and whistled.

Krupskaya, unaware of her husband's entrance, continued the game with a cry of outraged delight. "Stop it, you foolish young man, do you hear!"

Lenin slammed the door. "I could hear you down the street." He waved a greeting to Kolossov. "Welcome, comrade! And you, Nadya, what's all this chattering about, anyway?"

Krupskaya sighed, her hands on her reddening cheeks. "Oh my!"

"Well?"

"We were talking about you."

"About me? What about me?"

Krupskaya spoke to the floor. "Only that you were both an impatient man and a very patient man."

"A subject of no importance."

"Patient in laying plans and impatient for the glorious day of the Revolution."

"Better not to talk about me at all." Lenin stared fixedly at his wife to make his point, and then turned to Kolossov, who was examining the bicycle, now battered with dents and scratches. "Well, weight lifter, you've been busy since we last saw you."

"What happened to your bike?"

Lenin held up some leaflets. "I've been out collecting garbage. Look here, comrade, at the sniveling inanities of the precious tit-sucking old men of our party."

"Starets had an accident," said Krupskaya.

"Minor."

"A serious accident."

"Of no importance, except that it occurred at the worst possible time—on the day of the Foreign League meeting, when Martov managed to turn Plekhanov against me. Our fickle George is prey to any flattery."

"He was almost killed by a streetcar," said Krupskaya.

Lenin took Kolossov's arm and deliberately turned away from Krupskaya. He handed Kolossov a leaflet. "Look at what that scoundrel Axelrod calls me: 'a Jacobin, a utopian theocrat!'"

Krupskaya followed the two men around the room. "It isn't just!"

"It is just!" said Lenin without looking at his wife. "I am a Jacobin! Aren't I, Kolossov?"

Krupskaya turned away and retreated to the bed loft.

"I suppose you are a Jacobin," said Kolossov, "if the others represent the forces of moderation."

"I will show them Robespierre, weight lifter." He pointed out another article. "Oh yes, my athlete, Robespierre himself. And here is what Martov, my friend and comrade, has to say about Lenin. Here, read it."

While Kolossov read, Lenin stood back, glancing at the raised loft where Krupskaya sat upon the bed, her head down, brooding over his reprimand.

"Nadya? Come see how Martov mocks everything we have battled for together.

Krupskaya remained stubbornly seated on the bed.

Kolossov, aware of the marital discord, spoke up. "I brought letters. Nadezhda was kind enough to—"

Krupskaya rushed down into the main room and snatched up the letters from the desk. "Here, here.

I decoded them the second he came. But I wasn't sure you would want me to—"

Lenin patted Krupskaya's arm. "It's all right, all right. I was upset. I shouldn't have spoken so harshly." He read through the letters, pacing briskly back and forth. "Too soon, too soon. No one is ready. Everywhere I am checked by Martov. Where has the righteous warrior, my Julius, gone?" He confronted Kolossov. "Do you know what he said at the Foreign League?"

Kolossov shook his head. Lenin continued, imitating Martov's voice. " 'My honor has been impugned by this Robespierre Lenin who is sinking into the swamp of a personal war against his own comrades.' Imagine, a man who writes pamphlets like these has the hypocritical gall to accuse me of personal wars."

Krupskaya vigorously stirred the vegetables in the pot. "Martov's a woman!" she said. "All of them are soft women."

"You were right, Nadya," Lenin smiled, "from the beginning. I shouldn't have written them that conciliatory letter after the Congress. I was the victor. We were the majority. I should have shown no quarter."

"You thought you could win them back."

"They smelled my weakness, and so the dogs turned. *Iskra* without Lenin, can you imagine that?"

Kolossov stamped his foot. "A disgrace."

"The gentle Martov, the loving Martov, he turned them all." Lenin walked to the bicycle and touched its damaged parts tenderly. "If I hadn't been delayed—if I hadn't skidded on that damned track. He turned Plekhanov back upon himself—and the two of them opened their arms wide and embraced the past."

Kolossov murmured. "His brother is the police commissioner of Morschansk."

"What?"

"The town I grew up in—Plekhanov's brother is the police commissioner there."

Lenin brightened suddenly. "Ahh. Now, there is something useful, young man, something that will certainly help our war against the Martovites." Lenin sat down at his desk.

Kolossov approached with some well-folded thin sheets of paper and handed them to Lenin. "While I was in prison, I finished my article on a true revolutionary theory of knowledge. I wonder if you would read it?"

"Show it to Plekhanov—he is our philosopher."

"But he has betrayed you with Martov—he co-opted all the 'ancient ones' to *Iskra*'s board. Plekhanov's a traitor."

Lenin stood and poked Kolossov in the chest. "Never say that again. He has momentarily fallen away, and he'll return through the door that we will leave open. He's our greatest theoretician, he'll give you good criticism, won't he, Nadya?"

Kolossov looked bewildered. "But you said: 'War with the Martovites.'"

"There has been no schism—nor will there be one."

Lenin put his arm over Kolossov's shoulder and began to walk him back and forth. "We'll bring the generals back to their senses."

Kolossov marveled to see the instant changes in Lenin's tone. The thunder of the Old Man's anger was followed immediately by the warm sun of his irresistible charm.

"We?" responded Kolossov. "Yes, we must. I'll do whatever you say."

"Keep your eyes on the people—they must be ready."

Kolossov sighed. "I don't understand the people. They suffer and bear their suffering and worship their false masters. An enigma. I've worked with them, spoken to thousands, and still I don't understand them."

"We've heard of your exploits, young man. Nadya," he gestured grandly toward Kolossov, "you see here a man who announced a general strike to three thousand workers."

"Twenty-five hundred, if that many. The strike was already on."

"What luck! Once I spoke to ten people at a market. I don't even know if my voice would carry in such a crowd. What was it like?"

"I hardly know." The tall young man gazed out of the filthy window. He spoke almost dreamily. "I was so keyed up. The blood rushed through my body like a river. My head rang like a bell. How they shouted! But there was more terror in their silence."

"They heard your message."

"I don't even remember what I said."

"They heard. We've had reports."

"We weren't prepared. The police split us up like sheep, and then herded us off. Too few were willing to fight. The committee was surprised that the workers struck at all."

"But you fought."

Krupskaya echoed her husband. "You fought."

"The police didn't even ask us to disperse. They were like machines. They came at us with batons—you couldn't even see their faces."

"How high did they hold their batons?"

"How high? Different heights I guess." He prodded, lashed, and poked with an imaginary baton. Lenin observed his motions carefully. "One caught me across the side of my head finally—he was screaming, 'Student scum!' And then it was prison." Kolossov massaged the side of his head tenderly.

"And no one fought back except you?"

"A few threw stones, some ripped up fence stakes, two or three burned trash cans—we threw up flimsy barricades. But we had no plan. It was over too soon."

"A few fight back now, but many will fight soon."

"We were such children. We had no idea they would rise up. We'd been haranguing the workers for years, and they laughed at us, beat us up, hassled us, and then, like a Sphinx suddenly endowed with will, they rose up as one animal and marched into the teeth of the cossacks."

"You were there, Kolossov, when the Sphinx moved. And I sit here in this shopkeeper's clinic of Geneva, suffocated by the smoke of my weak-willed comrades' cigarettes, deafened by their continual gossip, bored to death by their democratic pieties."

"But then, Old Man, without apparent reason, the people went back to their homes and jobs and we were left alone on the streets. I thought the dawn of true socialism had come, and all because a few workers stood up with me against the foe. Poor Katya's eyes shone like suns that morning. Ahh, Katya." Kolossov gasped and walked to the window, staring out. "I had forgotten. So soon. Our Katya is dead. She lay on the snow at the border for two nights, coughing her life away." He went to the window and pressed his cheek against the dirty, cracked glass.

"How many then do you think you need?"

"What?" Kolossov did not turn.

"How many workers to make the Revolution?"

"More than three or ten or twelve thousand."

"Wrong." Lenin took the young man's arm and gently turned him. "It will take only a handful—if they truly believe—concentrated in the central industries of the nation. It will come in our lifetime, if we believe."

Lenin mounted the loft and stood next to the bed as if he were on a platform in front of thousands. Krupskaya and Kolossov stood before him—his audience. Even as he stood, mesmerized, the young man marveled at the scene:

here was the leader of a minor faction of a thoroughly disorganized revolutionary movement, speaking as if he were about to become the leader of all of Russia.

"It will take only a handful to forge a strong true ring of pure metal and put it through the nose of the Sphinx and lead it to a clean, high meadow. Only a handful to construct a large, clean house for that Sphinx, where it can live and love, beget itself, sing, and be happy."

Kolossov chimed in. "A clean, high meadow and a large, clean house."

Lenin continued. "A strong, true ring of pure organization and ideology: that is our task. We have no time for dreams of the future. Now, our task is victory. Victory is the only true orthodoxy." He stepped off the loft and embraced Kolossov. "It's war, my boy. The Sphinx must not be led astray. I need strong men, strong allies. You've proven yourself in one sort of battle—now I have a new mission for you."

"At last," sighed Krupskaya, "war with the Mensheviks."

"No, no, my dear Nadyushka. We're not going to break with 'the Mensheviks, but we must let them feel our power." He paced back and forth, dragging Kolossov with him. "Next week, there will be a meeting of the attachés for the Foreign League, and you will appear with a report from the homeland. You, Kolossov, will talk especially about the exploitation of the milkers by middlemen like Axelrod, who once was a worker, but had become a bureaucrat."

"Why Axelrod, Volodya?" asked Krupskaya. "Martov is the true enemy."

"I'm not yet ready to declare war upon my closest colleague and the best revolutionary we know. Martov will be our man again."

Krupskaya retreated again up onto the bedroom loft, shaking her head.

Lenin turned to Kolossov. "Where were we?"

"The milkmen."

"Yes, Axelrod represented the dairy people back home. He'll defend them, and then Kolossov will deliver his oration--—an attack upon the breast-feeding democrats who suck the udders of the Revolution dry. Kolossov will recount how the dairy people will be the first to run from the police and give in to the liberal bourgeois ladies. You will especially attack old weak men of the party who have given up Revolution for their democratic creameries. Finally, you will demand that these old men be put out to pasture with their cows."

"Me attack Axelrod? Well, now." Kolossov paced up and down, raising his fist in the air and then tucking it into his pocket. He stopped near the stove and struck a pose. "Down with the tit-suckers!" He blushed, so ashamed was he of his pride at being chosen by Lenin for this task. He would find it very difficult to attack a fine old warrior like Axelrod. And yet, and yet, the Old Man trusted him for this task. "Down with the tit-suckers!"

Lenin applauded. "That's the way, my boy. And I want a full report upon Plekhanov's police commissioner brother and his noble family."

"But you said I should never—"

"There may come a time when a certain Mr. Nilov writes a long letter to *Iskra* about noble traitors."

"First Axelrod, and then—my God—Plekhanov."

"Names, young man, just names."

Geneva, February 17, 1904

Just over a week after Kolossov's arrival back in Geneva, he sat in Axelrod's bare little hotel room with its cracked, curtainless window. To his acute embarrassment, the young man was being served tea from a dented samovar by that powerful, gnarled, aging revolutionary. The narrow room was furnished with a single bed, a chair, a table, a radiator, a bureau, and crates full of books. Kolossov, in his bathrobe, sat on Axelrod's bed, clasping his arms about his knees, as if he were protecting himself. Kolossov's underclothes were spread over the Axelrod's radiator, the back of the chair, and the desk. Axelrod moved about the room as if he were out of doors. He seldom sat; instead, he squatted wherever there was something to be done. He treated Kolossov tenderly, as if he were an invalid or a child—cutting cheese, filling the his guest's tea again and again, and turning the laundry so that it dried on both sides.

Kolossov kept excusing himself: "I hate to impose. I really had no intention—"

"How else will you dry your underwear?"

"But the first week my radiator worked."

"An old trick by Lepeschinsky," explained Axelrod, "on newcomers. He gives you enough hope so that you'll wait patiently when the heat stops."

"You have heat here."

"One has to work one's way up the ladder. Some never get a heated room."

"When you knocked at my door, Comrade Pavel," said Kolossov, "I thought you had come to pay me back for my public attack. I thought I'd had it—I'm pretty weak these days."

Axelrod laughed. "I haven't beaten anyone up in years."

"Why did you knock in the first place?" asked Kolossov.

"Are you afraid I'm plotting to overthrow your hero?"

"I don't know why I told you about my wet underwear. It's strange. How stupid to wash it and then to have no heat to dry it with! For some reason, I knew you would understand."

"Because I'm the common sort—I understand underwear. Now, eat more cheese, young man, and drink the tea while it's hot. If they didn't make decent cheese, this country would be a total loss. Their animals live better than our people, but, by God, it takes a martyr to live here. A true Russian peasant would have gone mad years ago." Axelrod paced, pausing to check the laundry. "Tell me about our country. I've been gone too long. Do they still live the same? Still swine—drunken and cursing, and battling one another, complaining and fawning and grumbling and working like horses? Aiee, I've been too long in this gray land."

"The barns in Switzerland are better than our houses," replied Kolossov. "We slept in a Swiss barn the first night over the border, and when I woke up I thought I was in the reception hall of my uncle's manor—except for Katya coughing her guts out."

"Craftsmen, all of them. Prudent craftsmen! More cheese, boy?" Axelrod thrust a chunk of cheese at the young man. "Drink your tea! They'll prudent me to death. They move like their clocks—no wasted effort, no madness. Was it a cold winter?"

"My tears froze."

"How I remember that feeling."

"At the Sumurumu Bridge, the blackbirds went mad—attacking people who passed over, swooping down, aiming for the eyes—the only moving wet thing in the landscape: the eyes."

Axelrod paused at the frosted window and gazed out as if he could see his beloved landscape. "Those Russian blackbirds! They'd take the sausage out of your hand before you could get it to your mouth."

"It's the worst winter they've had in a century. I received a letter—my son's very ill—my wife hasn't even enough wood."

"Oh, how I miss it. They don't know what cold is in this mediocre country."

"We're strangers here. They still stare at me on the street."

"It'll get better for you here once you get used to it, which is worse, because you begin to forget where you come from. Even the police here lack imagination—they work only on one side. Who is Katya?"

Kolossov stared at his host. "You heard me when I said—?"

"Coughing her guts out in the barn, was she? And your son sick?"

"Personal problems, I guess."

"Ah. The voice of the Old Man."

"I have my own voice," replied Kolossov, irritably.

"Don't mind me—an old meddler. We 'softs,' we're all meddlers."

Kolossov looked as if he were going to cry. "Katya was a saint. When she spoke to us of life after the Revolution, her eyes shone so that there were times when we thought ourselves already in paradise. She found paradise, all right, lying in the frozen waste on her bare legs, waiting for the cops to pass, without a whine or word or cough. And all the while, the disease was devouring the tissues of her lungs."

"She should have stayed home," said Axelrod.

"She died trying to come here to find out why her heroes were struggling among themselves."

"It's what we do best," said Axelrod.

"God knows!"

"You caught on soon enough."

"I didn't enjoy attacking you."

"Come on, boy, you loved sticking it to the old fart." Axelrod grinned and made an obscene gesture with his forearm and finger.

"Well—"

"I don't hold it against you. You were following orders."

Kolossov stood up. "I acted out of my own conviction. I'm a 'hard.'"

"Lenin's bullshit. We're all drowning in it, and I'm pleased that it was out of conviction that you called me names and asked for my retirement. That's wonderful. It soothes my soul."

"I didn't enjoy it. I hold you in deep respect—for the past, that is. But this war began before I arrived. Why are you all against the Old Man?"

"The Old Man? Starets! Our own Little Father, eh? Tsar Lenin."

"At least he'll make the Revolution and not just talk."

"Perhaps."

"His is the voice of the future."

"That's what we fear. And your Katya wouldn't find it a paradise—God bless the child. But of course God doesn't exist, so may your Katya have history's blessing."

Kolossov sat down, exhausted by his effort to appear self-sufficient. "You're all—"

"Don't argue with me today, God damn it. I'm tired of Lenin's curses. And don't worry—I'll pay you back for your attack—you and your Old Man—because I too have conviction. So shut up for a while and get your strength back. You're going to need it when I strike back."

"By God, don't think that just because I'm sick—"

"At the moment, there's no need for politics. You are mourning for Katya, the revolutionary angel; you're sick with fear for your son and your freezing wife; and I'm a forlorn, aging fool consumed in a senseless squabble with an old friend and dying of homesickness."

Kolossov sighed. "You're right. I'll shut up. You're being damned kind."

Axelrod shrugged off the compliment as if anyone would do the same. He sighed and now spoke longingly of home. "When someone was ill in our village, the peasants used to say, 'Either he'll get better or he'll die.' That comforted them more than prayer, but I never understood it until life beat the shit out of me."

Kolossov stared down into his tea. "I left them cold, without much food, no money, and I came here. Why do we do things like this? Was I right to come?"

A gentle knock sounded on the door. Axelrod opened it and Martov, in great disarray, entered. Newspapers stuffed the pockets of his large coat.

Axelrod pounded Martov on the back. "Welcome, Julius."

"The papers." He pulled the newspapers out of his

pockets helter-skelter and for the first time noticed
Kolossov and the underclothes strewn about the room.
"Have you begun taking in laundry, Paul?" In the warm
room, his glasses steamed up and every few minutes he
had to wipe them off.

"You know Kolossov, Julius?"

"Of course," he stared, nearsightedly at the young man.
"How could I forget such a masterfully scornful opponent?" Martov put out his hand toward Kolossov. "Good to
see you, boy. Are you still as 'hard' as ever?"

Kolossov rose and reluctantly allowed his hand to be
shaken. "Harder, if anything."

"Good!"

Kolossov, suspecting an ambush, sneered at his host.
"I suppose this is all a coincidence?"

Axelrod shook his head. "I told you I was out to sub-
vert your cause. But you'll have to wait while I read a little
of home." He grabbed the papers and hungrily began to
leaf through them, muttering and chuckling. Kolossov sat
down, depressed. He wanted to walk out of the room with
dignity, but he could hardly leave while his underwear
remained half-dry.

Martov poured himself some tea, lit a cigarette, and
examined Kolossov curiously. "You've lost a lot of weight
since the battle of the Second Congress. I hear you've spoken and fought bravely at home—and been to jail."

"Don't you consider me an enemy?"

"I don't consider anyone my enemy."

"But the way you write about the Old—about Lenin."

Martov shrugged and turned to Axelrod. "Well, Paul, what have you found?"

"Beautiful, beautiful," Axelrod chuckled, "even the worst drivel is beautiful in our language. The wife of the governor of Bratsk has given a luncheon—beautiful."

"Your tea is improving."

"Really? You like it? I found a new blend that comes a bit closer to our village slop."

Martov sniffed, sipped, and rolled the liquid around in his mouth as if it were wine. "Hmmmn, yes, quite good, with just enough of that Slav bitterness, you know, just enough."

"You hear, boy? High praise from our local connoisseur. Hey, why so glum? Julius had no idea you were here. And I knocked on your door only because I longed for the smell of Russia. Just a whiff, you know, but you had already washed it off you and your underwear."

"It isn't that." Kolossov's voice had a mournful moan to it.

Axelrod explained to Martov. "Our boy here lost a friend coming across the border, a young girl, dead of consumption, and he left a sick child to come join our squabbles. I think he's beginning to doubt the existence of God, perhaps even of history."

Martov put his hand on Kolossov's shoulder. "I'm sorry." Kolossov, his head in his hands, drew away. Martov shrugged. "I'll leave, Paul. The young man doesn't trust us."

Kolossov protested. "No, no, don't go. I'm just being sentimental—personal." Once more, he could hardly contain his tears. The two older men turned away while he collected himself. After some time, to their surprise he suddenly burst forth with a torrent of words. "I have something I want to ask you—both of you. I have this idea, this theory —that—and who knows when I'll see you again. I was a student in philosophy—a dabbler, but not bad at it. I was just beginning to develop some ideas about Marxism. I even put something down on paper before my last arrest. They beat me badly the second time, and what with my fast, and solitary—I hung onto those ideas."

Axelrod pounded his fist in his hand. "A true Russian student. They beat him, and he has ideas."

"It's silly, I know, but every time I thought of my wife, my boy, or my friends, it was unbearable—and so the ideas became more and more important."

"Don't mock him, Paul," said Martov, his face mirroring Kolossov's pain. "He acted well."

"I don't deny it," said Axelrod.

Kolossov plunged ahead. "The night I got out, my son had a high fever, my wife looked wasted, my friends were scared, and I was ordered here. Then Katya died one day into Switzerland—and so I still have these ideas. Do you understand?"

"More and more Russian," sighed Axelrod, gazing at the young man.

"And I think I'm correct, but the Old—I've been told

to take my ideas to Plekhanov, himself, and it scares me. I wondered if—whether you two would hear them and advise me?"

"Of course," said Martov. He swept Kolossov's laundry from the chair and sat, leaning toward the youngster. "Talk! We love ideas, don't we, Paul?"

"Not much." Axelrod picked up the laundry, folded it, and stacked it neatly at the foot of the bed. "I've become tired of ideas. But go ahead, anyway."

"Marxism, to be a truly total conception of the world, needs a theory of knowledge equal to its brilliant theory of politics and economics." As he spoke these words, Kolossov's entire being seemed infused with energy and delight. It was as if he had stepped into the mind of the world and found nourishing substance there. "Materialism is simply inadequate to do all these jobs."

Axelrod squatted and rolled his eyes. "Oh, my!"

Martov shook his head sadly. "You're not a materialist?"

"What's needed is a critical purification of the fundamental concepts we use all the time."

Martov echoed Axelrod. "Oh, my!"

The young man stared intently into each of their faces. "Do you understand?"

Martov sat up. "Maybe it would be better if I read your article first."

"I've given it to a neighbor, but I'll have it back next week."

"Good. Next week, then. And we'll talk philosophy."

Martov walked to the door, put his hand on the handle, then hesitated and turned back. "We'll talk, young man, but I fear that you've embarked on a dangerous and misguided attempt. Though I'll withhold judgment, you should know my prejudices."

Kolossov stood. "I'm sure I can convince you."

Martov spoke seriously now, out of conviction. "Our current theory has worked out quite well—it has held up during many battles—and I'm not sure that changes now would be beneficial to our cause. Even ideas must pass the muster of practice."

"My theory is based on that which every man knows—the given of the mind."

Martov opened the door. "I'll listen. Have hope for your son." He stepped out of the room and turned back. "Oh, and I wouldn't approach Lenin again with your philosophy. He won't understand. *Au revoir*, Paul."

Kolossov stepped to the door. "Thank you, sir. And you should know that Lenin still has a very special feeling for you."

Martov's face stiffened. For the first time, he looked severe. "I think I know that subject better than you."

Kolossov blushed. "He's not the monster you all think he is."

Martov looked at Axelrod. "There are no monsters, are there, Paul, just human beings—all too human. Good day."

He shut the door firmly behind him.

Kolossov turned to Axelrod and asked if he had offended Martov.

"Probably."

Kolossov slumped on the bed. "The workers starve, they're arrested, whipped, killed, and you sit here fighting against the Old Man."

"Your Old Man knows nothing about the workers. He's never really worked a day in his life."

"What difference—?"

Axelrod took hold of one of Kolossov's hands and held it up. He ran his fingers over the rough skin of the palm. "You see these calluses? They earn you the right to scold at me. Don't ever lose them."

"I'm not—"

"You're right, about us, of course. We sit here Lenining each other to death. It's Lenin this and Lenin that—you'd think he was the tsar. It's all Lenin and no revolution." Axelrod did a mock Lenin bow, thumbs in his armpits, and hopped forward twice.

Kolossov laughed at the imitation in spite of himself. He imitated Lenin's voice. "The majority has voted— you're being insubordinate."

"And have the people voted?"

"Alas, given the chance, they'd vote for the tsar."

"Heresy! Heresy. Drum the youngster out of the 'hards.'"

"I don't understand the people."

"How could you? You're not one of them, nor is your

Lenin. A rare worker, indeed! He sent his wife to the factories with questionnaires! He dressed that woman up in worker's garb and sent her to the factory gates while he toiled—in the library. Oh, well, he's not a bad man."

"Our people speak more of him than of any of you."

"A first-rate organizer; a masterful publicist."

"He's become the image of their dream."

"This time their father will be truly a *little* father."

"He's given the young hope."

Axelrod did not immediately respond. He gathered up the laundry and helped Kolossov on with his clothes. As he did so, he began to speak. "Either you people—the intelligentsia, the children of comfort—despise the workers or you kiss their fucking asses. No one treats them like human beings. They make you all uncomfortable because your noses have never been rubbed in it. You don't know what hatred is, or anger—twenty-five years, fifty years of rage." His voice grew louder; his face turned red. "Oh, the people will rise and turn human; their children will read, and everyone will be free. All men will be brothers. But not with your cadres, your organization, your central organs. All that's a nightmare." He paced about the room, staring at the walls as if he were about to break through them. "An axe—God, what I wouldn't do to have one axe and a pile of frozen wood, my tears icing my cheeks, the blackbirds diving, and the rage of my youth again. Done, done with this bickering, this complaining, this 'Lenining' me to death."

Kolossov rose, alarmed. Axelrod eased him back onto the bed and handed him some more cheese. "Eat the rest of the cheese, child. You're still weak."

Geneva, May 3, 1904

All spring, Lenin and his Bolsheviks struggled to regain their momentum in the revolutionary movement. It was a grueling time and Lenin suffered. More and more, he leaned on young Kolossov, who became the object of envy not only of Krupskaya but also of his henchman, Saumann. One bright May day, Lenin and Kolossov strolled on the quay by the lake. A light breeze ruffled the blue waters. Sunlight glittered off the waves. In the distance, the great white peaks of the Alps rose. Lenin looked exhausted, his eyelids swollen, his face pale. Every few paces, he paused to breathe deeply. For the last few months, it had taken a tremendous effort to control his rage against his old comrades: Martov, Axelrod, and the rest of the Mensheviks.

Kolossov suggested that they stop for a coffee at an outdoor café just across the street. Lenin hesitated. Just then, Saumann and Vrunski came along.

Saumann called out a cheery greeting. "Comrades!"

"A fortunate meeting," said Lenin sourly.

"What's up, Old Man?" asked Saumann.

Lenin invited Saumann and Vrunski to join him and the young man for a drink. They agreed readily.

As they sat down, Kolossov smiled. "What would our enemies say? The prudent Lenin and his comrades in a café at midday."

Lenin laughed. "Let's show them that we too know how to enjoy life. The war has not yet begun in earnest. Anyway, I'm tired."

Vrunski went in to get the drinks.

Saumann punched Kolossov's arm. "How's the philosophy game, weight lifter?"

"You win a few and lose a few. Knifed any liberals lately?"

Lenin glanced sharply at the young man. "Kolossov!"

Kolossov looked abashed. "Sorry."

"I want to relax, young man," Lenin said, sighing. "You once began a tale to me about Plekhanov's brother. A district police chief, wasn't he?"

Vrunski returned, passed out the drinks and sat down.

Saumann pounded Kolossov on the back. "Our philosopher here is going to tell us a tale."

Kolossov bowed and began. "About Grigori Valentinovich Plekhanov, Morschansk district police chief."

Saumann sneered. "Now there's a tidbit we can use."

Vrunski laughed. "Wonderful, Kolossov. You're an asset to the 'hards.'"

Lenin leaned forward. "Tell us the details—I want to hear stories today."

Kolossov took in a deep breath and spread his arms. "Well, now, this is the tale of the illustrious district chief and a lowly student. It all took place in the Morschansk Public Garden, on a Sunday spring evening long ago. Oh, how the air smelled of lilacs! The citizens of the town walked up and down the majestic central pathway of plane trees in the park. The scent of lilacs was joined by the divine odors of roast chicken and piroshki, all of which danced about our nostrils to the tunes of the military wind ensemble sitting stiff and martial in the band shell, playing waltzes. I sat down on a bench and who should sit next to me but Chief Plekhanov, whom I knew because he came often to our house to play whist with my father."

Saumann nudged Vrunski and counterfeited a look of horror. "Your father played cards with the chief of police?"

Lenin rapped the table impatiently. "Quiet."

Kolossov moved his chair closer to Lenin's. He continued, as if for the Old Man's benefit alone. "Together, we gazed across the path at the statue of Empress Catherine, founder of our town, and for some reason I said: 'Grigori Valentinovitch, if there is a revolution, someone will overturn the statue of the empress.'"

Saumann muttered: "Grigori Valentinovitch, eh? Pretty familiar."

Kolossov ignored the interruption. "The police chief turned and stared at me, a child, a student, as if I were a madman whom he had never seen before. 'What a stupid thing to say!' I replied, 'During the French Revolution, our history professor told us that they profaned even the tombs of kings.' The police chief then turned purple and stated, 'There can never be revolution in Russia. We are not in France.'"

Everyone except Saumann laughed.

Vrunski thumped on the table. "'We are not in France.'"

Saumann snarled: "We'll stand the empress on her head and bugger her."

"But that can never happen in Russia," chortled Vrunski.

Lenin looked quite pleased. "The brother of our great theoretician is the police chief of Morschansk?"

"A very distinguished family," affirmed Kolossov.

"Your father's chum," prompted Saumann.

"Our brothers' lives!" exclaimed Lenin, with a sigh. "How they betray us. Brother Sascha! Dear, dear Sascha! How tired I've become. And we are still in Geneva."

Kolossov sighed. "I weep when I remember the odors of lilac, roast chicken, and piroshki."

Saumann, a sly smile on his lips, leaned back on two legs of his chair. "Well, now, listen to the country squire, bragging about his father's noble whist games, moaning over his lost properties, lilacs, and piroshki, while bands of assassins play waltzes."

Kolossov would have liked to overturn Saumann's chair, but he restrained himself, knowing Lenin's dislike of dissension in the ranks. Under the table, he saw Saumann's foot move over and prod at Vrunski's leg. Vrunski, looking a bit ashamed, leaned toward Lenin, saying, "Dangerous talk, isn't it, Old Man?"

Saumann rose. "A true revolutionary should never abandon himself to sentimental memories." As he talked, he imitated one of Lenin's bows and three of his backward hops. "After these concerts, masters still strike their peasant slaves with birch rods."

Vrunski followed his friend's lead. "You begin with memories, and then you long for your old property, your title, eh?"

Kolossov glared at the two of them. "I broke with my family three years ago and have never once regretted the choice—but the beauty of our land—"

Saumann interrupted. "If you keep on like this, you'll soon buy back the few souls you need to work your land while you lie in your hammock reading German philosophy!"

Kolossov stood up in a stiff military posture and advanced toward Saumann, but Lenin leaped between the two men and thrust Kolossov back into his chair. He turned and confronted Saumann and Vrunski, his thumbs under his armpits. For a moment, he recovered his former energy. His eyes blazed. As he spoke, he hopped at them, emphasizing each sentence. "Comrades, you astonish me. You would burn all of Russian literature—Turgenev, Tolstoy, Aksakov—because it was written by landowners? I find this sort of attitude an echo of simplistic populism. We Marxists, thank God, have been delivered from such reasoning. All the culture from the past grew on a base of slavery. History decreed it so." By now, he had backed his two henchmen around the table. "And you attack this poor boy because he longs for the beauties of his native land. You say that because he smells flowers, he will exploit the people. Ha! It is you who are strange and odd and unorthodox, comrades. You do not understand history."

Saumann and Vrunski tried to escape the onslaught, but Lenin kept jumping in their way, herding them back toward the table. "Deign to pay attention, comrades. I also grew up in the house of a landowner. In a sense, I too was the son of a country gentleman—and I have not forgotten the smell of plane trees, or of flowers and piroshki. So punish me, punish Lenin!"

Saumann put out his hands, pleading, palms upward. "Sorry, master, sorry, comrade. I misunderstood history. Stupid of me."

Lenin stood nose to nose with Saumann. "You admit then you have been a trifle severe toward memories?"

"Hasty of me, Old Man."

"And you, Vrunski?"

"I'll go over there right now and try to remember the beautiful flowers of my childhood." He took his chair and moved away from the table, banishing himself from the others. He appeared to be thinking very hard. "The trees and . . . but there were no gardens where I grew up. The trees, then." He sat forlorn, his chin in his hands.

Kolossov felt sorry for the poor man, whom he knew was simply a good-hearted fellow manipulated by Saumann. The young man turned and embraced Lenin, who drew back at the familiarity. "Thank you, Vladimir Ilyich, thank you for defending our great literature. I would hate to part with those memories."

Exhausted, Lenin crumpled into a chair. No one spoke. Vrunski and Saumann sat with their heads down, dejected and demoralized by their leader's tongue-lashing. Lenin put out his hands toward them. "Forgive me, comrades, for taking my rage out on you. The 'soft' Mensheviks have us in retreat. One step forward, two steps back." He shook his head. "Vrunski! Cheer up! It's time to hear one of your lovely songs. Sing for the Bolsheviks. The 'hards' are out of sorts temporarily, but on the verge of a comeback."

Vrunski looked up, not quite trusting this change of tone. He began to sing softly, but as the verses followed, he sang with more emotion, rising from his chair.

> The heat became stifling and I opened the window;
> I fell on my knees before it,
> And the night sent the springtime to me
> In a fresh breeze, embalmed with lilacs.
> From afar I heard the song of the nightingale,
> I heard it and it filled me with great sadness . . .

As the song progressed, Lenin became more and more moved, so much so that when Vrunski finished the song, he seemed startled that it was over and urged the singer to sing the last verse again.

Vrunski, emboldened, dragged his chair back to the table and began to sing:

The heat became stifling and I opened the window;
I fell on my knees before it,
And the night sent the springtime to me
In a fresh breeze, embalmed with lilacs.

Vrunski finished and fell to his knees dramatically. Everyone laughed to see that crude, round bear overcome with romantic emotion.

"Hey," shouted Lenin, his spirits revived, "let him alone. He sang well. Our hearts have been touched. Music is good for us. I'd like to hear Beethoven's 'Apassionata' every day. It is marvelous, superhuman music. When I hear it—perhaps it is naive of me—I always feel great pride at the accomplishments of human beings."

Kolossov shouted. "Hurrah for Beethoven! Hurrah for Vrunski!"

"Our superhuman musician!" Saumann nodded benignly toward his friend.

Lenin shook his head sadly. "But I can't listen to music too often. It affects your nerves, makes you want to say stupid, nice things and stroke the heads of people who can create such beauty while living in this vile hell." Lenin raised his hand gently toward Vrunski and stroked the air. "These days you mustn't stroke anyone's head—you might get your hand bitten off. You have to hit them on the head without mercy, eh?" Lenin slashed his hand toward Vrunski and clapped it onto the table, frightening Vrunski.

Kolossov leaned toward Lenin. "Vladimir Ilyich, you once spoke of your days on the Volga in a beautiful way. Tell us about that river now."

Lenin looked around the table. He shrugged violently. "Talk, talk, talk. We are backing up at a tremendous rate, and I sit here chattering like a monkey. I must stop the retreat, recover the reins, organize our forces."

"Hurrah!" said Saumann, nudging Vrunski with his elbow. "Then we'll finally break with the Martovite Menshviks!

"No! No!" Lenin reacted violently. "No secession yet! Remember little fox, don't go into the water before you find the ford."

Vrunski spoke slowly, glancing at Saumann to make certain he was on the right track. "Every day they undermine the Revolution more."

Saumann nodded. "They're plotting against you all the time, Old Man!"

Lenin rubbed his eyes. "I wish I knew what they were up to today."

Saumann grinned across the table at Kolossov. "Maybe you could help us, Weight Lifter?"

"What?" Kolossov looked up in surprise.

"Oh," said Saumann, innocently, "I thought you were a great friend of Axelrod's."

Lenin looked sharply at Saumann. "What's that?"

Vrunski blinked his eyes. "Didn't I see Kolossov coming out of Lepeschinsky's the other day with Axelrod and Martov?"

Kolossov turned to Lenin. "I haven't seen Martov in months."

Lenin stared at him. "Axelrod? Martov? When did you see Martov? Where?"

"Months ago. An unimportant matter."

"Really?" asked Saumann. "I heard you were quite chummy with Axelrod."

Kolossov stared back at his wiry tormentor. "Is this a trial?"

Saumann smiled. "Everyone knows he got you the room next to his at the hotel—a damned good room. You could help us a lot if you told us what they were up to. The Old Man just said he'd love to know."

Kolossov's face turned red. "I don't agree with Axelrod's politics, if that's what you're hinting at."

Lenin scowled at Kolossov. "Chummy with our enemies, Kolossov? Explain yourself."

"I'm not chummy. Axelrod was very good to me when I was sick, just after my return from Russia. He was kind, even though I attacked him. He let me dry my things in his room—that's all."

Lenin pounded the table. "Fool!"

"But you yourself said that the time was not ripe for a break. The man came to my room and offered—"

"A poor student learns half a lesson by heart. You've read the tripe he prints about me?"

"He respects you, though."

"The man's a master at seduction   they all are. He can break your back with his sweetness. You've committed a great error. He's been wooing you."

"And I haven't succumbed. I know what I believe."

"What is that?"

Kolossov stiffened and recited: "Centralism, cadre, organization, discipline!"

"And no personal feelings?"

Kolossov sighed. "That's the hardest lesson of all. Whatever his politics, Axelrod is an honest man. Now, Plekhanov's a different matter—such a snob, such airs, the lord of the manor, treating comrades like serfs. He kept me waiting for three hours in his lobby, and then had the gall to criticize philosophers twice his stature without reading them. I set him right!"

Lenin's eyes widened. He sneered. "On what subject did you set him right?"

"He assumed I was a materialist."

"You're not a materialist?"

Kolossov drew himself up with dignity. "The theories of Avenarius and Mach provide a much surer basis for a theory of knowledge than any sort of materialism."

Lenin jumped up from the table. He hooked his thumbs into his armpits and hopped forward at Kolossov. "Avenarius? Mach?"

"No need to get so damned angry!"

Saumann winked at Vrunski with satisfaction. At last he had begun to drive a wedge between Lenin and the young athlete.

Kolossov wished he had followed Martov's advice and kept his mouth shut about philosophy. But now that the subject had come up, he would not back down.

Lenin stood leaning over Kolossov. "You want to correct Marx with those bourgeois birds?"

"Have you read them?"

"I know them well enough. If they're not materialists, they're not Marxists, and it's all the same to me."

"Avenarius and Mach are profound enemies of metaphysics."

Saumann and Vrunski laughed to see Kolossov squirm. Lenin turned on them. "This is no joke, fools. Leave us!"

Saumann and Vrunski leaped up and disappeared into the café. Neither Lenin nor Kolossov noticed. Lenin proceeded to give the young man a lesson in philosophy, like a schoolmaster. "Now, weight lifter, I thought we had buried this subject once and for all. Marx needs none of your bourgeois corrections." He sat upon a chair, his back straight, his small eyes boring into Kolossov.

Kolossov stared out over the lake. The light on the waves had become brassy and gray. A thin string of clouds had appeared in the west, masking the afternoon sun. A chill invaded the breeze, making him shiver. When he spoke, his voice was low and firm. "There is no such thing as a bourgeois theory of knowledge. There's only truth and falsehood."

"If you come across a corpse in the road, you don't have to touch it to know what it is. It stinks."

Kolossov flinched as if he had been struck with a ruler over his knuckles. "In class, Boulgakov used to say that truth is found in the confrontation of ideas: free, honest, open confrontation."

"Ah, you were one of Boulgakov's priests. That's more news." Lenin rose and paced up and down in front of the young man for a moment before he continued. "Social Democracy is not a seminary where you go to see ideas confront one another."

Kolossov put his head in his hands. "This is terrible, terrible. I don't want to argue with Lenin."

Lenin pointed down at Kolossov's head with his index finger, punctuating his lecture. "You have joined a militant organization of the revolutionary proletariat. There is a program, a conception, ideas we all accept."

"The theories of Avenarius and Mach will advance the Revolution."

"Freedom of discussion is a bourgeois intellectual prejudice."

Kolossov put out his hands in an exasperated plea. "Read them, please. The only idea of Boulgakov I subscribe to is that truth comes from discussion."

"Truth comes from history."

"No one denies that. The question is how to define

history. How do we know history except by the examination of the mind?"

"Ha! The filthy subjectivist monster appears. You prefer to examine the mind and not the world."

"But there is no mind without the world. It's a coordinate relationship."

"Enough learned double-talk. I don't intend to go back to school until the Revolution is over."

Kolossov slipped to his knee in front of Lenin. "Please, Old Man, for my sake, suspend your judgment until you read these authors. I plead with you. I need your judgment."

Lenin stared down at the young man. "Well, in that case—"

"I promise I'll listen to what you have to say."

"—I'll read your authors."

"All I ask is your patience in reading and talking to a young follower."

Lenin's voice did not soften. "Drop your books by my house," he commanded, "and you will get my opinion in two weeks. Now leave me!" He turned away as if the sight of the young man sickened him.

Kolossov stood and backed away, almost bowing. He strode down the street. At the corner, he looked back and saw that Lenin had sunk down at the table, his high forehead resting on his hand. Beyond the empty roadway and deserted quay, harsh winds whipped the dull and threatening lake waters. Over and over again, Kolossov condemned himself for not following Martov's advice. He knew very well that for Lenin philosophy was a practical matter: Marxist materialism, as Lenin used it, worked; it was useless to argue. What he had yet to learn was the limit of Lenin's tolerance.

Geneva, September 19, 1904

Although Kolossov dropped books by Avenarius and Mach off at Lenin's apartment, Lenin refused to see him. Then the young man received news of his son's death. Immediately he tried to get Party permission, the papers, and the funds to return to Russia to care for his wife. The Bolsheviks refused to honor his request, while the other Party factions saw him as Lenin's man and were content to leave him in limbo.

Again and again, Kolossov attempted to approach the Old Man. Lenin would not grant him an interview. Every time the Old Man heard the young man's name, he exploded into one of his tirades, hopping like a fierce bird, his thumbs tucked under his armpits. He was like a father whose son has betrayed him and all of his beliefs. If Lenin had been Jewish, he would have recited the prayer for the dead over him. Saumann's poison had done its work.

One day, in great desperation, Kolossov approached the door to Lenin's miserable room, determined to swear his loyalty to the Bolsheviks and to plead for an opportunity to work for the cause in Russia. He would not, he cautioned himself, mention his son or his wife. No personal matters, no personal matters, and no philosophy he repeated grimly to himself as he knocked on the door.

Krupskaya opened the door. When she saw Kolossov, she began to close the door. "He's not in," she screamed.

"He is in," said Kolossov, jamming his foot through the door.

"He's busy."

"Please, Nadezhda Konstantinovna, when I arrived in Geneva the second time, you were so cordial and kind and sweet—like a mother, no, like a sister and now you treat me like scum."

"He's not in."

"I'm still his man. I always have been."

"I'll report you called."

"I have very little time. My son died—a month ago— my wife hasn't much stamina. I must—" Kolossov clapped his hand to his mouth. "Forget my personal problems. I want to go home to fight—in Russia! Fight for the Bolsheviks, for the Old Man."

"We were sorry to hear of your bereavement." Krupskaya's voice was cold, matter-of-fact. "Lenin asked me to convey our sympathies. Please don't create a disturbance."

"I'm doing nothing here in Geneva. The Old Man must see me, he must hear my plea."

"He has no time for pleas."

"I could tear this door from the wall."

"He's busy organizing loyal comrades."

"Let me talk to him, for God's sake. I have to return to the real revolution. This is a farce here in Geneva. The Minister Plehve has been assassinated, the Japanese are besieging Port Arthur, strikes are spreading throughout Russia, and here we are like little children scolding one another."

Inside, Lenin thrust Krupskaya aside and confronted Kolossov. "Stop this infernal disturbance."

"Only if you listen to me."

Lenin stared stonily at the intruder. "Come in then, but make it brief."

As the young man entered, Krupskaya retired to the loft.

Kolossov pleaded. "Please, Old Man, I want to return to Russia. I requested a passport and money months ago."

Lenin turned his back on the young man. "Do you still belong to our group?"

"I have never left the Bolsheviks."

"Why didn't you sign the Protest of the Thirty-seven?"

"I lost my son. I went crazy for a few weeks. I couldn't read or think or anything."

Lenin fixed his gaze on Kolossov. "I wonder if the explanation is not elsewhere. As a member of the Bolsheviks you have acted in a way that is absolutely inadmissible. Everyone has known for a long time that you wanted to return to Russia."

"Of course I have. In Russia the Liberals are acting, the Socialist Revolutionaries are acting, but we, the true revolutionaries, sit here in Geneva on our behinds."

"To obtain your passport you have paid assiduous court to me, to Krassikov, and to Bontch-Brouevitch."

"I've seen no one since my son died."

"Then how has it come to my attention that you've been running to our enemies, willing to make any sort of oath or declaration of loyalty to obtain what you need? According to my information, you've played a disgusting double game."

"That's a slander."

"First, you cottoned up to Axelrod."

"That was last winter, long before any of this came up. I explained all that."

"Do you deny that you've been whispering sweet nothings into Martov's ear—like 'Give me a little passport, darling Martov, and a bit of cash, and I'll quit that hard Lenin.'?"

"Lies, lies. Who told you these lies?"

"My little finger."

"It was that brute Saumann, wasn't it?"

"Deny that you've been talking to Martov."

Kolossov paced about the room in great strides. "Of course I've talked to Martov—last winter in Axelrod's room and several times after—the same Martov who was your closest colleague, whom you called the one true man in the movement. Is that such a shameful duplicitous act? We spoke neither of the Party, nor passports, nor money."

"The weather, perhaps?"

"Philosophy, and my son." The young man came to a

halt before Lenin, clasping his hands together with all of his might until his knuckles turned white. "Both of which have become—for some mad reason—entwined."

"All of which obviously supersedes the Revolution. Listen closely, Herr Professor. I know Martov, and I know that he hasn't much interest in philosophical questions."

"He, at least, was willing to take me seriously."

"What exactly did they charge you for a passport and money? No one enters the charming company of Axelrod or Martov without a litany against Lenin."

"None of you understands philosophy. Mach, Avenarius, Berkeley don't deny the existence of walls." Kolossov turned and slammed his fist against the wall, cracking the plaster. "I know this wall exists—I've been kept out by it for weeks. We're not speaking of the world, but of the process of knowing—underline *process* three times—*process*. I would only like to give to Marxism a theory of knowledge equal to its theory of history."

"You and your philosophers believe that only subjective sensation exists. The man who would build his philosophy solely on sensations is a maniac who should be locked up."

"Enough maniacs, enough locking up, please. I don't deny the existence of my dead son, but I only know him through these arms, these eyes, this heart that beat next to his when his blood leapt through his veins and warmed his cheeks. Avenarius and Mach are against solipsism—"

Lenin tucked his thumbs under his armpits and bent

toward Kolossov. "Herr Professor speaks, but none of your fancy bourgeois language can cover up the fact that the external material world exists independent of your Avenarian Machian asses."

"Process—not the world!"

"We'll bury your asses of reaction in their own shit holes."

"Each individual is the central element of a system of cognitive relationships that—"

Lenin threw his arms in the air and called out. "Nadezhda!"

Krupskaya strode forward. Kolossov continued, "—relates him to the environment and other individuals."

"Nadya, the interview is at an end. Send this child away."

Krupskaya took hold of Kolossov's arm. The young man fended her off, shouting. "The 'me' and the 'not me' are coordinates. There can be no subject without an object. But man can never free himself from himself."

Lenin laughed harshly. "I congratulate you, weight lifter."

Krupskaya pushed at Kolossov. "Leave our house immediately, fool! You're upsetting the Old Man."

Wild now, his eyes turned up at the ceiling, Kolossov went on as if he had no idea where he was. "When we say an object exists, we mean it enters our field of sensory perceptions, nothing more."

Lenin hopped backward three times. "The shit hole of

idealism! Tell me, Herr Professor, when our earthly globe was but a mass in fusion, where was perceiving man?"

"How do you know that the world existed before man?"

Krupskaya stood between the two men, her hands on her hips. She addressed Kolossov. "Were these the reactionary theories you taught the workers of Kiev—along with your perfumed women?"

"How does he know the world existed? How? How?"

Lenin turned his back and leafed through papers on the table. He trembled with anger. "I want the daily correspondence."

Kolossov darted around Krupskaya and bent toward Lenin, hissing in his ear. "Perhaps an angel came to you in the middle of the night, Old Man, or a devilish spirit? No. You learned about the world before man because a scientist, a knowing subject, discovered it through a combination of research and hypothesis. This earth in fusion of which you speak with such certainty is only a hypothesis that may well be replaced some day."

Lenin thrust his forehead in Kolossov's face. "Then Marxism is only a hypothesis?"

Kolossov did not yield. "The greatest hypothesis ever advanced about the process of history."

"And may be disproved in the future?"

"Because of its broad and inclusive nature, it will more probably be added to, clarified, sharpened, but never proved or disproved."

Lenin clasped his hands together as if he were preparing to strangle the young man. "There is only one process suitable for such revisionists as you and your holy philosophers."

"Please don't make yourself vulnerable to our enemies by espousing weak philosophy."

"How could I, when you envelop me in the thick fog of your big words? Start talking to your Kiev worker about *subject, object, process, perception* and he'll just scratch his head. A worker eats a sausage and earns five kopeks a day and knows very well that his boss steals and that the sausage tastes good. But you bourgeois philosophers turn everything around with your theories so that the boss could very well be his benefactor and the sausage nothing but chopped leather."

"Since you reduce philosophy to chopped leather, there is nothing more to be said."

"Then we'll consider the philosophy lesson at a close."

Lenin marched to the door and opened it, gesturing for Kolossov to go.

Kolossov stood very still, attempting to control the tears of frustration that kept welling up in his eyes. "I came to Geneva against my will this time because the Central Committee ordered it. It was the Party, not the Bolsheviks or Mensheviks who paid my passage. Now I must leave this madhouse of polemics and return."

"You're a free man."

"But you control the purse strings overseas."

"It is obvious that the Bolsheviks made a bad investment in you."

"I am no one's property. I remain my own man, a servant of the Revolution and not the slave of any one of your stinking investments."

"Go to your true friends, then, for support."

"And yet you bankroll Saumann, who defiles his fellow comrade and spends his money drinking swill in whorehouses."

"You'll do worse than drink up our money. You'll lie down with those Menshevik whores and piss the money away watering down a strong Marxism."

"All villainy, then, is allowed a man who agrees completely with you. Everyone else is slandered and ignored."

"This is no institute for noble young ladies. Marx was a master of scorn—that is how we deal with our enemies."

"And you're a master of slander."

"Thank you. Everyone who moves an inch from Marxism is my enemy."

"Discussion, then, is impossible."

"At last, perception dawns in your dim brain. And don't expect our help in returning to Russia." Lenin mounted the bed loft and pulled the screen behind him.

Kolossov took hold of the door to the room as if to rip it from its hinges. Instead, he pounded his head upon it. "And yet this man fights for a righteous cause."

Tears streaming down his cheeks, he marched down the streets of Geneva, devastated by the knowledge that his beloved Old Man had embarked upon a destructive course of action that would end in the ruin of all that the young man held most dear.

Geneva, January 1905

A sleepless, tormented man paces about his barely furnished rented room after midnight. He wears a torn nightshirt over a sweater and trousers. The room is so chilled that a film of ice covers the water on the nightstand bowl next to the bed. His wife lies awake in bed, watching him while pretending to sleep. Her long, bony form barely disturbs the smooth shape of the stuffed coverlet. She knows that he would assail her furiously if she made the slightest attempt to comfort him—until, that is, he had exhausted his internal debate and collapsed into her arms.

The man is a Russian political émigré. His obsession is revolution in history. There are hundreds of such men in cities throughout Western Europe, men haunted with the specter of injustice in their homelands. Fervently, these men plot the overthrow of the current governments, each man convinced that his particular scheme is the only one adequate to achieve that purpose. The small, fierce inhabitant of this freezing room was born on the Volga with the name Nikolai Ulyanov, son of a minor, titled educational bureaucrat. Later, once his revolutionary career was well launched, he adopted the name Lenin, and most recently he had been dubbed, by his wife and his close henchmen, with the name Starets, meaning "Old Man" or "Boss," to indicate his position of power among them. Tonight, Lenin paces about the room, pausing frequently before his bicycle, which hangs from two chains in a corner. He examines its chain, its pedals, and its wheels. Occasionally, he picks up an oil can and presses its nozzle to one of the moving parts, and then fastidiously wipes the metal with a rag. Below the bicycle, a rectangular tin catches any small drops of oil that happens to evade his cautious hand.

"A schism, at last!" mutters Lenin. "Martov and all the little Martovites proclaim that democracy has an absolute value." At the mention of his name, Julius Martov, a slouching, angular man in a crumpled suit and thick, smudged steel-rimmed glasses, materializes in the shadows by the stove. Lenin looks up and berates him. "Martov turns his back on Lenin. He frowns and whispers insults and makes faces at his old friend. Then let it be. A split."

Martov holds out his arms to embrace his friend Lenin. "Look at you, Volodya. I've never seen you in such a mess, not even in jail. A torn nightshirt? An untrimmed beard? It's a relief to see that you, too, are human."

Lenin hastily straightens his clothes. "Just because I don't wear humanity on my sleeve." He hands an ashtray to his guest, who ignores it. "For God's sake, Julius, mind your ashes for once." Martov waves his cigarette toward the ashtray, but the ash drops to the floor.

A second dim figure, Kolossov, steps out of the shadows. "Excuse me, comrades. Russia is losing the war to the Japanese. Port Arthur has fallen. In Mogilev, Kherson, and Vitebsk, reservists are rioting in the streets. There are major disorders in Transcaucasia, in the Baltic Provinces, Finland, and the Congress of Poland."

Lenin and Martov ignore the interruption.

Martov speaks, gently. "You are destroying the Party, Volodya."

"And you, Julius, are destroying the Revolution."

"The Revolution is not Lenin."

Kolossov raises his voice, attempting to capture the attention of the two older men. "Three hundred and fifty members of the Assembly of St. Petersburg Factory Workers are meeting to protest the dismissal of their brothers Fedorov, Sergunin, Subbotin, and Ukolov from the Putilov Iron Works. The seed is sprouting. The spark is catching."

"Your tactics, Volodya," Martov waves his cigarette at Lenin, ashes flying everywhere, "will destroy years of work, the unity of the movement."

"If only I hadn't fallen in front of that damned trolley." Lenin moves toward the bicycle and runs his hand over the fender. "Ah, my beauty, you're marred now. I had the right of way, but that confounded conductor pushed ahead. If I hadn't skidded—they wanted to drag me to the hospital, but I made them bandage me there on the street. And even then I was too late to win back the majority." Shaking his head, Martov retreats. Lenin calls after him, "I bleed, Julius, just like everyone else. And I can weep, too."

"Old Man!" Kolossov pleads. "Fifty thousand workers have struck in Baku! They not only ask for shorter hours and more pay, they demand a constituent assembly and civil rights!"

Lenin points down at his bicycle, patting the fender and turning the wheel with his other hand. "You see this machine, Julius? It is perfectly organized. Organized!"

"And you, Volodya," Martov's voice is fading, "are the only one who knows how to ride: the Napoleon of bicycles."

"And you, Julius, just another aristocratic anarchist, a lover of coteries, circles, salons!"

"Please, Old Man!" Kolossov's voice cracks with emotion. "On Sunday, 600 workers from the iron works gathered at the Old Taskent and voted to strike. They've raised their demands, do you understand? They want an elected grievance committee to pass on all dismissals."

Lenin sits down on the worn bench and leans against the wall, weary.

"Old Man!" Kolossov calls out from the darkness. "On the fourth, 2,000 workers from the Franco-Russian

Shipbuilding Plant went out. On the fifth, 11,000 others joined them; on the sixth, 25,000; and on the seventh it was a general strike with 150,000 workers—while you sit here bickering. Shipyards, steel plants, textile mills, chemical plants, piano factories, chocolate factories, furniture factories, even breweries, all shut down. Father Gapon is writing his petition—he is writing it without us."

Lenin mutters to himself. "How many hard men are there in this world? Discipline is what's needed, and I'll teach it to you dreamy democrats." He stands, loops his thumbs under his armpits, bows backward one step, and commences to lecture the vacant room. "They call me a theocrat! I'll show them a pastor. I'll whip that flock's behind bloody."

Now the figure of Sascha Ulyanov emerges from the shadows behind the stove. Lenin cries out: "Sascha! Sascha! Mama had to go alone to the train to meet your body."

Sascha replies sternly. "Personal, Volodya, personal."

"I begged from door to door, but our dear friends, the liberal intellectuals, did not deign to answer. I hate them, Sascha."

"You were born out of their midst, brother, and remain tied to them even now."

"No longer. I've changed. I looked clearly into the dense suffering of our people and had a vision of that slothful monster, that enigmatic beast of a Sphinx. I know what is needed to keep it moving." Lenin lunges forward and twirls the pedal of the bicycle. "Simple clear-cut orders, rules, system, an organization that cannot be breached by personal whim—that is the only salvation of the Russian people. We shall be the schoolmasters of the Revolution, and of the state that afterward will abolish poverty, suffering, and disease."

Sascha laughs bitterly. "You sound like Father, the model petty official: bureaucracy in our blood. Bureaucracy in the blood of all the Russians, great and small."

"And how would you move the people, Sascha? With detonator caps?"

"I wouldn't move them. I did what I had to do. There are perhaps ten men in all of Russia who have the will to move people: six are industrialists, two are policemen, one is a minister, and the final one is you. One day, you will all be together in the Winter Palace, the leaders of the people—stern, unyielding, demanding, full of love for the soul of our land, and afraid. The hands of all of you will be drenched with Russian blood."

Lenin shouts toward the darkness. "You young men talk too much. I'm done with the past, done with mourning for you, Sascha. I no longer need you."

Lenin mounts the loft and turns toward the room as if he was on a platform. "One day, the Sphinx will move, the Sphinx of Kiev will heave up its ponderous belly, shake off a hundred thousand bureaucrats and landowners, take one step, crushing a million wealthy noblemen, and then will lie down and sleep for another thousand years while the shit piles up to bury it. Or worse, the Sphinx will rise up starved by centuries of fasting, and will begin to eat its way furiously, losing itself in its hunger. It will devour its own tail, its legs, its body, its organs. Blood flowing, it will eat until there remains only the furious wide mouth, the shreds of one eye, the hairs of a nostril, and then there will be nothing left of this beautiful earth or suffering humanity."

The voice of Kolossov calls out: "Wake up, Old Man! The Sphinx is moving, and you are asleep. The people' are gathering around the city of St. Petersburg for their peaceful march to beg honor from the emperor and autocrat of all the Russias, of Moscow, Kiev, Vladimir, Novgorod—the tsar of Kazan, Astrakhan, Poland, Siberia, Tauride, Chersonese, and Georgia. The leading regiments of Petersburg are proceeding to their appointed stations with brutal orders."

Lenin continues his speech. "Be true to the Sphinx, comrades, which is made up of all men who slave for the rich rulers of this rotten world."

The soft voice of Martov pleads from the darkness: "Bend, just a little, Volodya, my comrade, my friend. Yield just a part of your terrible vision."

Lenin reaches out in the direction of Martov's voice, but then shivers and drops his hand. He steps down from the loft and sighs. "I regret losing you the most, Julius. A large, warm human being, you see everything—too much. This is the wrong world for you—the wrong endeavor. Do you understand? You are my greatest threat. I will not enjoy tearing you to bits."

Kolossov announces: "Columns of men, women, children, dressed in their Sunday best, saying their prayers, singing 'Our Father' and 'Save, O Lord, Thy People' begin their solemn march toward their Little Father, carrying icons, religious standards, the Russian flag, the two-headed eagle of the Romanovs, and the portraits of their beloved rulers. The police clear the route to the fatal intersection where the tsar's crack regiments await: the Semenovsky Guards, the Horse Grenadier Guards, the Pavlovsky Guards, the Chevalier Guards, and the Preobrazhensky Guards. Old Man! Have you no words, no deeds to help our people?"

Lenin peers into the room and strives to hear. He hears nothing and sees only the stove and the bicycle. He turns to the bicycle. "I am alone now. Even the 'I' is gone. Nothing remains except for the evil loose in my country. I feel no guilt—neither toward friends, nor comrades, nor family. It has been granted to me to know how to get things done." He mounts the small sleeping loft again and unfurls a proclamation and reads:

"Traitors of the Revolution have illegally overturned the will of the majority and are in possession of the central organ. We of the Central Committee must seize the central organ by revolutionary means if necessary. The only salvation is a new Congress, its slogan: 'War with the Disorganizers.'"

Kolossov calls out: "Lenin! While you declare war on your fellow revolutionaries, Father Gapon leads the good workers of Petersburg forward, petition in hand, which reads:

Tsar of all the Russias, our Lord and Little Father. We the workers, our children, our wives, and helpless old parents have come to seek truth and protection. We are impoverished and oppressed; unbearable work is imposed upon us; we are despised and not recognized as human beings. Treated as slaves, we must bear our fate and be silent. We have suffered terrible blows and now we are pressed ever deeper into the abyss of poverty, ignorance, and slavery. Despotism and arbitrary rule throttle us and we choke. We have no more strength, O Lord. The limit of patience is here. The terrible moment has come when death is better than the continuance of these unbearable torments.

Kolossov's voice continues to cry out: "At the Narva Triumphal Arch, at Sascha Park, near the Troitsky Bridge, on Schlüsselburg Chaussee, on Vasilyevsky Island, Palace Square, Nevsky Prospect, at Police Bridge, and before the Kazan Cathedral, the confused crowd is charged with whips and sabers. The poor people of Petersburg are ordered to disperse. Shots are fired over their heads. The troops fire directly at the people."

Lenin, unhearing, continues his own proclamation: "A Congress of the majority announces the creation of a strictly revolutionary Marxist Party."

Kolossov reports: "One hundred and thirty dead, two hundred ninety-nine wounded. What is your answer, Old Man?"

"The Congress of the majority hereby formally breaks all ties with the minority."

Kolossov's mournful voice fades slowly: "The Sphinx has risen, its blood flows into the streets while its self-appointed keepers struggle with one another in a distant land."

AFTERWORD

In 1905, while Lenin fumed and sputtered denunciations against his democratically inclined revolutionary allies in exile, the Sphinx rose. As a result of spontaneous uprisings throughout Russia, on October 17, 1905, the Imperial Manifesto promised universal suffrage to elect a constitutional government under the tsar, thus providing a foundation for promised civic freedoms. This sudden collapse of the Old Regime caught the nation by surprise. The liberals and the revolutionaries had no plan for a sufficient organization to take over power. Chaos reigned. Prisons were stormed, prisoners freed, armed bands roamed the countryside, strikes paralyzed the railroads and heavy industries, and estates were burned. The intensity of the violence and the fear it evoked allowed the Old Regime to subdue the revolution.

By 1907, the tsar and the aristocracy had retaken power

without solving the problems that had shaken the nation. Seven years later, when the Old Regime came under the strain of the First World War, it crumbled. The German army advanced. In 1917, the Sphinx rose again. Once more, in Geneva Lenin paced, fumed, and denounced his allies. This time, however, the German government recognized Lenin as an invaluable ally as they confronted the tsar's armies in the east. The kaiser provided Lenin with five million marks and transportation on a sealed train to the Finland Station in Petrograd. That money, the unrelenting obsession of Nikolai Ulyanov, and the violent suppression of his socialist allies eventually propelled the Bolsheviks to power over the Liberals and the other revolutionary forces. On March 3, 1918, Russia under the Bolsheviks signed the Treaty of Brest-Litovsk, ceding much territory and exiting World War I. By armed violence, Lenin's Bolsheviks then proceeded to eliminate all other contending parties and consolidate the Soviet state. Lenin's "revolutionary vanguard," obedient to his credo of centralism, cadre, organization, and discipline, became the totalitarian rulers of the former Russian Empire.

ACKNOWLEDGMENTS

I am very grateful to Yvonne Tsang for her careful and expert design of this book. My wife, Gloria, has been my life-long editor and beloved companion. Whatever was good in the conception of this book has been improved by her wise counsel.

The photograph of Wolf Keidan at the beginning of the book comes from the Broder family archive of photos.

BIBLIOGRAPHY

Tolstoy's Wife and *The Sphinx of Kiev* are based on extensive research into historical sources. Following are the major works I consulted in writing these novellas. Some of the material on Lenin was useful also for the Tolstoy story.

Tolstoy's Wife

Edwards, Anne. *Sonya: The Life of Countess Tolstoy.* New York: Simon & Schuster, 1981.

Gorki, Maxim. *Reminiscences of Tolstoy, Chekhov, and Andreyev.* New York: Viking Press, 1966.

Tolstoy, Countess Alexandra. *The Tragedy of Tolstoy.* Translated by Elena Varneck. New Haven: Yale University Press, 1933.

———. *A Life of My Father.* Translated by Elizabeth Reynolds Hapgood. New York: Harper and Brothers, 1953.

Tolstoy, Count Ilya. *Reminiscences of Tolstoy.* Translated by George Calderon. New York: The Century Company, 1914.

Tolstoy, Countess Sophia Andreyevna, The Diary of Tolstoy's Wife, 1860–1891. Translated by Alexander Werth. London: Victor Gollancz Ltd, 1928.

———. *Countess Tolstoy's Later Diary, 1891–1897*. Translated by Alexander Werth. London: Victor Gollancz Ltd, 1929.

———. *The Final Struggle: Countess Tolstoy's Diary from 1910* (with extracts from Leo Tolstoy's diary). Translated by Aylmer Maude. Oxford University Press, 1936.

Troyat, Henri. *Tolstoy*. Translated by Nancy Amphoux. New York: Harmony Books (Doubleday), 1967.

The Sphinx of Kiev

Balabanoff, Angelica: *Impressions of Lenin*. Ann Arbor: University of Michigan Press, 1964.

———. *My Life as a Rebel*. Bloomington: Indiana University Press, 1973, by arrangement with Harper & Row, New York, 1938.

Fischer, Louis. *The Life of Lenin*. New York: Harper & Row, 1964.

Getzer, Israel. *Martov: A Political Biography of a Russian Social Democrat*. Melbourne: Melbourne University Press, 1967.

Harcave, Sidney. *The Russian Revolution of 1905*. London: Collier-Macmillan Ltd, 1970.

Lenin, V. I. *What Is to Be Done?* New York: International Publishers, 1929.

———. *Two Tactics of Social Democracy in the Democratic Revolution*. New York: International Publishers, 1935.

———. *Karl Marx*. Peking: Foreign Language Press, 1967.

Pares, Sir Bernard. *Russia, Between Reform and Revolution: Fundamentals of Russian History and Character*. New York: Schocken Books, 1962.

Possony, Stefan. *Lenin: the Compulsive Revolutionary*. Chicago: Henry Regnery Company, 1964.

Trotsky, Leon. *Lenin*. New York: Capricorn Books, 1962.

Troyat, Henri. *Daily Life in Russia Under the Last Tsar*. Translated by Malcolm Barnes. Stanford: Stanford University Press, 1979.

Ulam, Adam B. *Russia's Failed Revolutions: From the Decembrists to the Dissidents*. New York: Basic Books, 1981.

Valentinov, Nicolas. *Mes Rencontres avec Lenine*. Translated from the Russian by Yan Margarith. Paris: Plon, 1964.

BILL BRODER has published six books of fiction: *The Sacred Hoop*, Sierra Club Books; *Remember This Time*, written with his wife, Gloria Kurian Broder, Newmarket Press; *Taking Care of Cleo*, Handsel Books/Other Press; and *The Thanksgiving Trilogy*, including *Crimes of Innocence*, *Esau's Mountain*, and *What Rough Beast?*, The Ainslie Street Project. He has published one book of nonfiction: *A Prayer for the Departed*, The Ainslie Street Project. Broder has also acted as member, executive director, and artistic director of a playwrights' workshop, California On Stage, and has completed a number of full-length plays, which have received staged readings throughout the San Francisco Bay Area. Two of his plays were presented as staged readings at The Second and Third Annual California Studies Conference in Sacramento, California. His play *Abalone!* was produced in Carmel, California.

29919668R10182

Made in the USA
Charleston, SC
29 May 2014